MOST
WANTED

Books by Sasha White

PURE SEX

THE COP

LUSH

SEXY DEVIL

PRIMAL MALE

MOST WANTED

Published by Kensington Publishing Corporation

MOST WANTED

SASHA WHITE

APHRODISIA

KENSINGTON BOOKS
http://www.kensingtonbooks.com

APHRODISIA BOOKS are published by

Kensington Publishing Corp.
119 West 40th Street
New York, NY 10018

ISBN-13: 978-0-7582-2862-8
ISBN-10: 0-7582-2862-7

First Kensington Trade Paperback Printing: June 2009

10 9 8 7 6 5 4 3 2 1

Acknowledgments

Thank you to Susan Lyons for helping me get the details right. To Delilah Devlin and J.J. Massa for cheering me on. Yes, I know, I am the queen of the last-minute pressure crunch. I appreciate your helping me stick to my goals.

Thank you to Erin Suitor for always being there to read for me when I need you. Your input is important to me, and I truly appreciate it.

The ladies at Romance Divas are the best! Jax, Lisa, and Kristin, thank you for creating such a fantastic community that offers support and research help for all sorts of things (*wink*). And thanks to all the Divas of the "Secrets" section for being there any time day and night to help out a crazed writer on a deadline.

A special thank-you to Nickelback for their song "Animals," and Theory of a Deadman for their song "Bad Girlfriend." Those songs really helped me pound out a few scenes.

And last, but definitely not least, thank you to my readers for always wanting more. These stories are for you.

Contents

HIDDEN CRAVINGS

1

Heart pounding and blood heating, Lexy stared at the man leaning against the red brick of her apartment building. Unmoving in the shadows just beyond the light of the entrance, he was barely visible. Yet, as she slammed the car door and moved steadily across the dimly lit parking lot, her insides knotted with an undeniable excitement.

Devon Kaye. It wasn't really surprising her body recognized him before her brain did. After all, the man had worked her body in ways that, a year later, still lived on in her dreams.

Stifling the urge to jump on him with open arms and eager lips, Lexy kept her steps slow and even, and her expression casual. It was almost nine o'clock at night and the August night sky was still darkening, creating shadows that danced against the walls of the brick building.

When she got close, he shifted out of those shadows and she stopped in front of him. Planting her hands on her hips, she tilted her head to the side and took her time checking him out. *Delicious.*

He was six feet of lean muscle covered by scuffed biker

boots, faded denim jeans, a plain white T-shirt, and a black leather jacket. His midnight hair was mussed, his jaw unshaven, and his piercing gray eyes turbulent.

Lexy's hormones settled into a holding pattern and she spoke softly. Gently. "Hey."

"Hey."

Talking never had been their strong point. The first night they'd met, Devon had said they were two of a kind, and it was true. They'd connected almost immediately on a very physical level. Even as they stood there, silent, the hunger for Devon's touch gathered strength inside her.

Without another word Lexy turned away, unlocked the door to the building, and went in. She noticed he carried a worn duffel bag with him, but she didn't ask about it. They didn't talk in the elevator or the hallway, but as soon as the door closed and they were inside the apartment she tossed her keys on the sideboard and turned to him.

"You look like shit." It was a lie. Despite the roughness of his appearance, he looked dangerously sexy, as always.

Devon's hot gaze ran over her demure slacks and simple blouse and she wanted to cringe. She'd been on a date with a nice guy she'd met at the gym. A nice *boring* guy. The almost demure clothes had been her effort at dressing up while trying not to look like she'd been dressing up.

One side of Devon's mouth had tilted up in a crooked smile that didn't quite reach his eyes. "You look great, as always, Alexis."

Something soft fluttered in her chest at the way he said her name and she forgot all about what she was wearing. To everyone else she was street-smart and sexy Lexy Signorino, private investigator and skip tracer, unafraid to use her sex appeal to get the upper hand in any situation. But Devon had called her

Alexis from day one, and the way her full name rolled off his tongue never failed to make her feel beautiful . . . special.

As hot as her blood was running, the tension in his body and the complete blankness of his expression made it obvious the desire for an erotic fling wasn't what had brought him out of her past and onto her doorstep. Something was seriously wrong. All romantic thoughts slipped away and she smiled at him. "Why don't we go into the kitchen and you can tell me what's up?"

"Sounds good," he said, dropping his duffel bag on the floor and following her to the small kitchen area.

Devon settled himself into one of the cheap folding chairs set around the kitchen table and Lexy grabbed a couple of cold beers from the fridge. She handed one to him and twisted the cap off the other before settling across from him. As soon as her ass hit the chair Devon started talking, his words slow and precise, his voice calm. "My cousin Theresa called me this morning and asked me to come out and see her. She didn't tell me why, just said she needed me."

"And she's family, so you dropped everything and came," Lexy said with a nod.

Her own family was small. She only had one living relative, Uncle Tony, who'd raised her after her parents were killed in a home invasion when she was a kid, but her family included one other man. Jimmy D was her uncle's best friend, and she'd do anything for either of them. Family wasn't always about blood. It was about love and loyalty.

"My flight landed just after noon, and Theresa was supposed to meet me at the airport. She wasn't there." His expression was carefully blank, but his eyes were dark with worry as he stared at her. When he spoke next, his voice was tight with controlled emotion. "I've called her cell numerous times, no answer. I went by her office, figuring maybe she got held up, but they said she left for lunch and hadn't come back. No one seemed worried, but I know something has happened."

Lexy listened as Devon told her about going to his cousin's apartment where he discovered the door unlocked, but nothing was missing or out of place. He'd waited around her place for a bit, in case she'd just gone to the store or something, but deep down he'd known it was useless. While he was waiting he'd called a couple of her friends, but no one knew where she was. "And the cops won't get involved yet because she's an adult and it hasn't been long enough. They won't listen to me because they don't know me, and they think I'm just overreacting."

"Are you?" After being raised by a couple of overprotective Italian men, Lexy knew how they could overreact when it came to the safety and protection of women. Devon had never struck her as that type of macho man, but she had to ask.

He shook his head at her. "Theresa called *me* to come out and see her, not one of her brothers, or her dad. And I think she called me not just because I'm family, but because of what I do for a living."

"The body guarding?" Devon's official job title was personal security specialist. They'd met when her uncle had hired him to look after her, without her knowledge.

"Yeah. She didn't say it when she was on the phone, but she was worried about something—scared almost. If I'd been here I could've protected her, but I didn't get here in time to help her. Now I need to find her, and to do that I need someone who knows this city, who has ties to the police, and who is an investigator." His piercing gray eyes pinned Lexy to her chair. "I need *you*, Alexis."

Lexy's heart slammed against her chest and she sucked in a sharp breath. *He needs you to help him*, she scolded herself. *Not for an erotic fling.*

Shoving aside her heart and her hormones, she glanced at the wall clock. It was barely ten o'clock. She stood up and nodded at Devon. "Let's get to work then."

Lexy headed off to her bedroom to grab her laptop, but as her fingers wrapped around it she caught sight of herself in the mirror and froze. Her long blond hair hadn't changed, the shape of her body, or the clothes covering it, hadn't changed. But the look in her eyes had become as muddled as her chaotic emotions.

Devon.

Here, in my apartment.

She closed her eyes, breathed slowly and deliberately for a minute, then slammed the door on the memories trying to get hold of her. Devon had been able to get under her skin from the first moment she'd set eyes on him. They'd only spent a week together, yet she got the feeling he knew her better than anyone. The thought of spending more time with him now thrilled her . . . and scared the shit out of her.

A year had passed since she'd first met Devon. A year had passed since she'd last seen him. Only months since she'd talked to him, and days since she'd dreamed of him. But he wasn't there for *them*, he was there for his cousin. She needed to remember that.

Laptop in hand she went back to the kitchen and focused on the job at hand.

"Okay," she said, setting the laptop on the kitchen table and opening it up. As a private investigator with a sideline of skip tracing for collection agencies and bondsmen, she was used to tracking people down. The best place to start was always to compile as much intel about the subject ASAP. "Start with the basics."

Devon took a long pull from his beer then started rattling off facts. "Theresa Jane Williams. Born 1979. She's a probation officer—"

"Wait a minute." Her fingers froze over the keyboard and she stared at him. "Theresa's a probation officer and the police didn't take her not showing up for work seriously?"

Devon shook his head. "They said she didn't have any appointments scheduled for the afternoon, so she probably just took a day off."

"Well, I guess I can see that, but they should listen to what you have to say. Not only are you family, but you spoke with her just this morning."

"That's another thing. They said if I spoke to her that morning it was even more likely she was fine. Maybe we just missed each other at the airport or she stopped to have lunch with a friend or something."

"Okay, we'll deal with them later. Let's keep moving forward for now. Do you know her hobbies? Hangouts?" Wanting to chase the worry from his eyes Lexy gave him a sassy smile. "Credit card numbers would be helpful too."

Less than half an hour later Lexy was starting to go a bit stir-crazy. Devon was alternately pacing her small apartment and calling hospitals to ask about accident victims while she did her thing on the computer. She went into the voting registry and got Theresa's social insurance number, then hacked into her employment files thinking a red flag might pop up there, but no such luck. There wasn't any new activity on her credit cards or in her bank accounts, either.

"Fuck," she muttered under her breath as she closed one program and opened another. There wasn't much else she could do on the computer, and they were getting nowhere fast.

She looked up from her computer, her gaze instantly finding

Devon. He stood at the window, arms folded over his chest, staring out into the night.

Their personal history hadn't come up yet, and part of her wondered if it ever would. Devon wasn't exactly the type of guy who liked to talk about his emotions, it was one of the reasons she'd always felt such a connection to him. As if he'd always understood what she never said, as if they were always on the same wavelength.

Lexy wondered if he was as hyper-aware of her as she was of him. Just being in the same room with him had her sex juices flowing. She remembered the way he'd stroked her cheek the first night they'd met. He'd had her pinned to the wall of the back room in a bar, where he'd finger-fucked her to orgasm only to refuse to fuck her.

"Why not?" she'd asked.

He'd gently stroked a calloused finger down her hot cheek and said, "Because this is just the beginning."

As if sensing where her mind had gone Devon spun around and caught her staring at him. Heat flared between them and her body hummed its acknowledgment. *Time to play,* her hormones cried out.

Yet, she held back.

She dragged her gaze away from Devon and pretended to focus on the computer screen while her body practically screamed in frustration. Sex wasn't something she normally shied away from. She didn't hold with the whole "sex has to equal love," or even romance, thing. To Lexy's way of thinking, sex was a natural urge. Sex was a pleasure. Sex could even be considered a form of stress release or exercise.

But sex with Devon was dangerous. Dangerous because it— because *he* was so addictive.

It was hard work keeping her eyes on the computer screen with the erotic tension so thick in the air, so she shut down the search program and jumped out of her chair. "That's all we can do from here right now. Let's go. I want to check out her apartment."

He scowled. "I already did that."

"Yes," she said, striving for patience. "But you're not a woman. Not only will going over her place give me a feel for her, but I might see something you didn't."

Devon's lips pressed together and he nodded. "You're right. Let's go."

She grabbed her purse and car keys and headed for the door. As she passed Devon he picked up the duffel bag he'd dropped earlier and she hesitated. Danger had never stopped her from doing anything before, so why let it now?

Her hand on the doorknob, she turned back to him. "You can leave the bag here if you want."

Their gazes locked and sparks flew. They were definitely on the same wavelength. Devon nodded and dropped the bag, and they left without saying anything else.

It seemed talking still wasn't their strong suit, but they communicated just fine.

2

It took just over fifteen minutes to get to Theresa's apartment building and they didn't talk during the whole drive. Once Lexy realized Devon wasn't going to bring up the past, the tension eased from her shoulders and left her feeling excited that he was there, and determined to ease his worry by finding Theresa fast.

She parked in front of Theresa's apartment building, ignoring the TOW AWAY ZONE sign, and Devon used his key to let them in. The first thing Lexy did was check the door frame. "No signs of forced entry," she noted before closing the door and following him into the space.

He nodded, but didn't say anything, just went over to the answering machine and pressed play.

"An answering machine will make things easier for us than voice mail. Grab the code from the bottom of the machine and we can check the messages at any time." It would help if there *was* a message though.

Devon stood aside, tension radiating from him as Lexy did a slow walk-through of the place. It looked lived in, but not rifled or disrupted. No signs of a struggle, or a search. "You said you already went through her desk and stuff?"

"Yeah. I found her old-fashioned address book there and called a few friends whose names I recognized. Nothing."

He obviously had the right touch with more than a woman's body.

Theresa's apartment wasn't anything special on its own—neat and mostly clean, but not overly so with good, but inexpensive furniture. But beyond the bones of the apartment there was a whole hell of a lot of personality. Colorful pillows were piled high on the sofa, scented candles on the table, various plants placed sporadically throughout the space.

It looked lived in. Like someone who enjoyed life lived there. Someone who had a life beyond work.

A twinge of discomfort went through Lexy as she wondered what Devon had thought when he'd gone from Theresa's apartment to hers. Her place was similar in size and layout, but it was clean, uncluttered, and unemotional. The only personal touch in her own place was a couple of framed photos on her bedroom dresser, which few people ever saw.

Lexy shut the door on her personal issues and began to move through the apartment. She was there to do a job, to find a clue to where Theresa could be, or why she was missing in the first place. She moved carefully through the living room, to the bookshelf. Running her fingers over the book spines, she stopped when she reached a shelf full of framed photos.

Devon spoke from behind Lexy. "Her and her parents, those are her brothers and that last one is from our family reunion three years ago."

It was easy to spot Devon in the reunion picture. Even though many of the others had the same coloring and height, Devon just jumped out of the crowd, his rakish smile both daring and sexy.

Lexy pulled her gaze away and moved from the living room

to the kitchen, noting the two sets of dirty dishes in the sink, and the beer, cheese, and fruit in the fridge. No notes stuck to the fridge or left on the countertop saying she'd be right back.

After another swing through the living room she was in the bedroom.

The first thing she noticed was the unmade bed. It struck Lexy as something out of the ordinary in the organized space, almost like Theresa had been too distracted or in too much of a rush that morning to care about the small daily things.

She moved to the closet, not surprised at the limited amount of shoes there. The idea that all women were shoe whores made her laugh. A small pile of neatly folded laundry on the floor caught her eye and Lexy's brain kicked into gear. She rifled through them quickly, noting that they were indeed men's clothes.

"What?" Devon asked from the doorway as she moved swiftly across the room. She pulled the bedside drawer open and saw a notepad, a pen, and a paperback novel.

"What are you looking in there for?" Devon's voice had a little snap to it.

She nudged things around a little, ignoring Devon's question. Beneath the paperback were some scattered condoms, and three Polaroid photographs.

Each photo showed the same couple sitting at a small candle-lit dinner table. The woman was a pretty brunette with bright eyes and a ready smile. The guy had shaggy dark blond hair, and thin wire-rimmed glasses framed dark chocolate eyes. In the first photo he looked pretty geeky, but whatever Theresa had done to him before the second picture was snapped had made him genuinely smile, and it lit up his face making him pretty good looking.

She flipped the photos over and saw the name of a nearby restaurant and the date they were taken written clearly across the back.

"You didn't look in here, did you?" she asked with a glance at Devon.

He looked uncomfortable. "No, this is her private stuff, hardly stuff that would tell me what she was scared of or worried about."

Lexy gave him a small smile. "This is why you need me. I'll look at things that might make you, her cousin, uncomfortable. And as a woman, this is definitely where she'd keep some important things. Things like this." She held the photos out to Devon. "Was Theresa seeing anyone?"

"She hasn't mentioned anyone in a while," he said, studying the images before handing them back to her.

"When was her last relationship?"

"When was *your* last relationship?" he snapped.

She looked up in surprise. There was a definite undercurrent in Devon's question that she had to nip in the bud. "I don't do relationships."

Face blank he nodded. "Is that why you stopped taking my calls? It was starting to feel like a relationship?"

So much for not talking about the past.

She'd thought they were on the same wavelength, the same page. Two of a kind, he'd called them. That meant she shouldn't have to have this conversation.

Well, fuck. She pocketed the photos and closed the bedside drawer before facing Devon head-on again. "We didn't have a relationship, Devon. We had sex."

"We had more than sex."

"A fling then."

His eyes flashed and all thoughts of Theresa flew from her head. He hadn't moved, his stance hadn't changed, but the angry passion filling his gaze fanned the need that had been simmering deep inside her for too long.

Her gaze locked on his, she moved toward him. "So we spent

a few nights fucking each other's brains out, it didn't mean anything, Devon. All it meant was we were good together, and I'm not denying that. In fact, I'd love to have a few more nights just like them." She stopped when they were only inches apart. The flare of his nostrils was the only sign that her nearness was affecting him. She placed a hand on his chest. "I think you would too."

They stared at each other, Lexy's blood heating, pulsing through her veins and waking up all her nerve points. Her stomach quivered, her nipples hardened, and her pussy drooled.

"What if I want more than a few nights of fucking?"

She quickly squashed the flare of emotion that rose up in her chest and gave him a sultry smile. "That's all I'm offering, sugar."

Devon's piercing gaze roamed over her face, but he said nothing. Finally, unable to stand the tension, Lexy shrugged and brushed past him on the way to the door. "That and to help you find Theresa, of course. We're done here, let's go."

The heat of Devon's gaze burned through Lexy's clothes as she lead the way back to her car, and Lexy smiled. Devon was not as impervious to the idea of a few nights of naked playtime as he'd like her to believe.

Lexy glanced at the clock on her cell phone as they walked back to her car. The pictures were a lead, and it wasn't eleven o'clock yet. She wanted to visit the restaurant the photos were taken in and see if anyone remembered Theresa and her date. If they could find out who the guy was, she could find out where he lived and see if he knew anything about Theresa's disappearance.

Devon was silent as she started up the GTO and pulled away from Theresa's apartment. The steady purr of the big V-8 engine filled the silence she was trying so hard not to notice. It wasn't uncomfortable, but it wasn't relaxing either.

15

She was full of mixed emotions about the man next to her. No, that wasn't true. Her feelings about Devon were clear. She liked him, she trusted him. She wanted him.

It was the fact that he was right next to her in the car that had her all mixed up. The fact that he'd come to Vancouver for someone else, but not for her.

It was unfair of her to blame him for not being there for her. After all, she'd been the one to basically cut off communication between them. But knowing that didn't erase the small part of her heart that wished he'd come to town for her, and not for his cousin.

Devon's voice pulled her thoughts back to the problem at hand. "Where are we going?"

"The pictures were taken at a restaurant just up here. I want to see if anyone there recognizes the guy in them."

"You think he has something to do with this?"

She shrugged. "I don't *know* anything yet, but the more knowledge we have, the easier it will be to find her."

He didn't say anything and minutes later she found an empty space in the restaurant's small parking lot. "You can wait out here if you want," she said. "This shouldn't take long."

He didn't answer, just got out and followed her across the lot and into the building. They entered the store together and Lexy went straight to the girl at the small hostess stand.

She was in her mid-twenties, with flowing black hair, heavy black eyeliner, and piercings in her eyebrow, nose, and lip. She smiled when Lexy stopped at the counter, and Lexy realized the Goth girl was quite pretty.

"Table for two?" she asked in a soft lisp.

"Not tonight, thank you." Lexy smiled in return and held up one of the Polaroids. "For now I'm just interested in finding the person who took this photo."

The girl glanced at it for a brief second before walking away.

When she came back a young guy in dress pants, a button-down shirt, and a tie was following behind her. "I'm Jason Chevy, the photographer on weekends here at La Scalia, miss. How can I help you?"

Aware that Devon was walking around the small vestibule, checking out the couples inside the restaurant discreetly, she pulled one of the photos out of her pocket and held it up. "Did you take this picture?"

His back straightened and he glanced from her to Devon. "I believe so, yes."

"Do you remember this couple? Do you know him? Or her?"

"I remember them. He was very shy, and she wasn't. She also wasn't happy with the first picture so she made him pose for a couple more. That happens sometimes, but they were one of the few couples who insisted on paying for all three photos and keeping them all, even the not-so-great ones." He grinned crookedly. "They were obviously in love."

"What else can you remember about them?"

Her questions finally registered and he glanced from her to Devon, who was standing at the entrance to the restaurant, staring at the couples inside the dimly lit dining room. She could practically see the thoughts flashing through his mind. Cops? Spouse? Or stalker?

Sensing his cooperation fading she had a quick mental debate and decided to go with the truth. She pulled one of her cards from her pocket and held it out to the guy. "My name is Lexy Signorino and I'm a P.I. The girl is Theresa Williams, my client's cousin, and she's missing. I was hoping you could tell me something about them, anything. Are they regulars here? Do you know them? Have you seen him in here with other women? Do you know his name?"

She smiled and let her eyes trail over the photographer's

body in a subtle flirtation. "Any information you have could be helpful, and I'd really appreciate it."

"I'm sorry, Miss Signorino, I wish I could tell you they were regulars. That I knew a name or anything about them, but I don't. It's five dollars a picture, cash. Maybe they can find a credit card bill for you?"

Jason went to get the manager and Devon came to stand by her. He was still and silent as they waited and a twinge of concern went through Lexy. It was his cousin, his family that was missing, and she knew that was never easy. Before she had a chance to ask him how he was doing, Jason and the manager returned.

After explaining why they were looking for the information, Jason told them what night Theresa and her date had been there, and the manager went into the computer for them. It took less than five minutes for the manager to go through the credit receipts from that night . . . and learn that Theresa didn't pay by credit, and none of the other names on the bill jumped out at Jason, or the waitress who had worked that night.

Lexy made sure the manager and the waitress also had her card in case they remembered anything, and they left. As soon as they were settled back into the car, Devon turned his head and looked at her. "That's it?"

"No, that's not it." She faced him, working to keep her own frustration from her voice. "It was just one lead that hit a dead end. I'm not giving up, Devon."

Their gazes locked and sensual awareness flared between them. Lexy's heart thumped in her chest and her hands twitched with the need to touch. She lifted a hand and cupped Devon's cheek, the day's beard stubble prickling the palm of her hand.

"I *won't* give up," she said softly.

Heat flared in the depths of his eyes and he pressed against her hand for a brief moment before he stiffened and pulled back. "Thank you," he said quietly as he stared straight ahead.

Unsure of exactly what had just happened, Lexy sat still for a minute before literally biting her tongue and starting the car. She had one more card to play before they called it a night on the search. Aiming the car toward downtown her mind began to race as startling emotions smacked her upside the head. As much as the heat in Devon's gaze told her he was still affected by the attraction between them, she couldn't shake the feeling that he was unhappy with her—and that caused her own anger to flare.

What right did he have to be unhappy with her? Why was he unhappy with her? Was he mad because she couldn't magically find Theresa? Or was it more personal, because of their little chat back at Theresa's apartment when she'd admitted she enjoyed sex but sucked at relationships?

Professionally, she could only follow the leads they were given. Personally, those weren't things she could change about herself. If she could, she would. Not the enjoying sex thing—she loved it and did not regret that.

The relationship thing though . . . deep down inside there was a part of her that wanted that to change. A part of her that Devon called to.

3

Devon ignored the emotions roiling about inside him as he sat in the passenger seat of Alexis's 1964 GTO. There were too many of them to deal with right then: guilt, worry, frustration, determination, and even lust. Christ, how could he be lusting after Alexis when he'd failed to get to Vancouver in time to help Teri?

The classic muscle car was the perfect fit for his girl. His girl? He bit back a derisive snort and stared out the window.

A year ago he'd dropped her off at the Edmonton airport after helping her catch a killer and keep her uncle out of jail. She'd kissed him good-bye and whispered the words, *"I'll be seeing you again."*

Only it hadn't happened.

He'd called her a couple of times, and they'd had some great chats. It seemed that the talking thing came a lot easier for them when the temptation of physical closeness wasn't even an option. The last time they'd talked, less than six months ago, he'd invited her back to town to go to his parents' anniversary dinner with him. She'd said she'd think about it, and then promptly stopped taking his calls.

He'd thought they were getting closer. Who the hell knew what she'd thought?

At first he'd worried something had happened to her, and that was why she hadn't gotten back to him, but when her uncle had confirmed that she was safe and fine, and still in touch with them, his worry had changed to frustration. There was no denying he'd been tempted to chase her down after a while. He'd never felt anything as *right* as the way that woman had felt in his arms, but his pride had him work on forgetting her. He'd never had to chase a woman before.

It didn't surprise him that there were still sparks between them. Despite telling himself he'd moved on, he'd never really stopped waiting for her call. Seeking Alexis out had been in the back of his mind ever since he'd hung up the phone that morning with Theresa, but this was not what he'd had in mind at all.

"We're here," she said, dragging him back to the present.

"A nightclub?"

"It's Kane's night off, he'll be hanging around in here until the club gets too busy."

Devon got out of the car and followed Alexis as she strode past the security at the front door with nothing more than a smile.

She stopped just inside the door to gaze around the club. "There he is," she muttered and started off again, hips swinging in a way that kept his temperature at a steady simmer. He was used to seeing her in tight jeans, skimpy skirts, or nothing at all. All sexy and always looking good, nothing like the simple slacks and blouse that currently covered up her body. Simple or not, the dress pants cupped the full curves of her ass in a way that made his palms itch to touch.

Devon followed a few steps behind, scanning the nightclub. Dull golden lights gleamed behind a long wooden bar that stretched the length of the room, making the various bottles of liquor sparkle and shine like a rainbow. The bartenders were both men, and naked to the waist. The waitresses wore black shiny PVC outfits and only stood out from the crowd because of the trays in their hands.

There wasn't a lot of people in the club yet, but the ones there were enough to give him an idea of exactly what type of place The O Club was.

Most of the partiers were dressed in all black. Some were Goth looking with heavy eyeliner and black nail polish, and others were of the black leather and kink variety with corsets and collars. Some lounged indolently on the couches and over-stuffed chairs that were arranged throughout the club and along the far wall, others were strutting around, as if on parade.

Devon caught sight of a corseted woman sitting primly on the back of a kneeling man in a getup made of studs and straps that barely covered his ass, and he wondered if he knew Alexis as well as he'd thought.

If it were anyone else leading him through that club after he'd asked for help finding his cousin, he'd wonder what the fuck they were doing. But it was Alexis . . . and he trusted her.

She made a straight line through the small crowd and leaned against the bar next to a big blond guy and whispered something to him.

Devon stopped beside her in time to hear the guy say, "Hello sexy, you're looking very . . . *nice* tonight."

The familiarity in the guy's voice, and the warmth in his gaze as he looked at Lexy, made Devon want to growl.

She grimaced. "I was on a date, trying to look normal."

Devon had to work to keep from snarling at that. He slid onto an empty barstool and pulled Alexis between his spread thighs, staking his claim. The blonde speared a glance at Devon standing next to them. "This your date?"

"Date's over. This is a friend." She stared at the blond guy. "A friend in need."

Devon tensed as he watched a little silent communication happen between the two. When the guy finally nodded, Devon's possessive urges settled a bit.

The bartender stopped by and they all ordered a beer. "Kane, this is Devon Kaye. His cousin is missing, and I need you to check into a few things for me. Devon, this is Kane Michaels, Vancouver P.D."

The men shook hands, and Lexy got straight to the point, handing Michaels a piece of paper she'd pulled from her pocket. "Here's Theresa's information. Can you keep an eye out for anything that comes up in connection, maybe even do a little digging?"

The bartender put the beers down and Devon slid a twenty across the bar, waving away the change as the cop studied the details Lexy had compiled.

"I doubt I'll find anything that you haven't already uncovered." He slid her a glance. "I'm not going to ask how you got even this much."

Lexy held up her hands and laughed. "Completely legal search programs."

"Uh-huh. Tell me the rest. Why are you coming to me?"

Devon sipped his beer and sat quietly while Lexy filled her friend in on the situation. He kept the beer in one hand, but the other hand automatically settled on the curve of her hip. As she spoke, she sank back against him, a natural fit in the cradle of his thighs that made simply being near her hit home.

When he'd left his duffel at her place, it was with the unspoken understanding that they'd be sharing her bed. She'd made it clear at Theresa's apartment that she'd be happy to indulge in the carnal side of things. It was the emotional part she was quick to turn her back on.

A busty blonde sauntered by, her smile a clear invitation as her eyes ate him up with blatant desire. Even though he ignored her, Lexy's hand tightened tellingly on his thigh. She wasn't as casual about them as she pretended. Because he'd had her back when she'd been trying to keep her uncle out of jail she might help him out with Theresa, even if she was only interested in sex, but she wouldn't be feeling possessive.

Right then, as he looked around the club, the apathy of the crowd brought home to him just how much he wanted the connection with Alexis to be real and lasting. He knew it could be. Deep down he'd known from the moment he met her that she was the right one for him. He just had to find a way to get her on the same page.

When he'd checked out the customers at the dimly lit restaurant, La Scalia, he'd gotten a sense of romance, of intimacy that the couples in the club lacked. It brought home the difference between the sexual relationship Lexy said she was open to, and the real one he wanted.

Stroking his hand over her hip, he pushed his personal desires aside and refocused on the conversation she was having with the cop. She was telling Michaels about going over to Theresa's apartment and handing over the photos she'd found in the bedside drawer. "You think you can run one of these through your system and see if the guy pops?"

"That her?"

"It's recent," Devon said.

The cop nodded. "I can get her photo from the city's employment files, but him . . . he looks familiar."

He tensed. "You know him?"

"Not *know* . . . but I'm pretty sure I've seen him before."

He pocketed one of the Polaroids and handed the others back to Alexis before meeting Devon's gaze over her shoulder. "I'll see what I can find for you."

Devon nodded. "Thank you." Even if the guy couldn't tell them who the geek in the picture with Theresa was, the more people looking for his cousin the better.

Alexis tilted her head back and looked at him. "There's not much else we can do tonight. You want to stick around here or go home?"

"Let's go."

Lexy said good-bye to the cop and they headed out of the club, weaving through the growing crowd.

Devon's gaze practically burned a hole in her back as they left the club. And it felt good. Lexy was sorry that his cousin was missing, and she was going to do everything she could to find out what happened to Theresa, but she wasn't sorry Devon was back in her life—and would soon be back in her bed.

Anticipation of a long sleepless night wrestling between the sheets with Devon had her insides trembling in eagerness as she drove back to her apartment. Once inside, she closed the door to the apartment and leaned back against it, just taking in the sight of Devon in her front room.

With his cell phone in hand, he stood in the middle of the room, staring at the floor as he dialed. Tension built in the lines of his body as he dialed the phone and waited. He closed his phone and raised his head, his turbulant gaze meeting hers.

"Still no messages?" she asked.

His lips pressed together and he shook his head once. He took a deep breath and deflated in front of her eyes, dropping onto the sofa with a big sigh. "I have to call my family."

Lexy's chest tightened, and her heart went out to him. He

was beating himself up over Theresa's disappearance. She could almost see the blows land. *I was too late. Why didn't I ask what was wrong? What am I missing?*

Pushing off from the door, she walked over to the sofa and climbed onto his lap. Straddling him with her knees next to his hips, she rested her hands on his shoulders. Their eyes met and she smiled.

"It's nice to see you again," she said softly.

He didn't answer, just looked at her, hunger slowly taking over his expression. God, it was good to feel him beneath her again. Devon had always been like magic to her. Sexually inexperienced she wasn't, but the man touched her in a way no one else ever had, and she wanted that again. She wanted his touch, his taste. She wanted to feel him buried deep inside her body, she needed that connection again. But more than that *he* was hurting, and she wanted to take that pain away. She might not be able to do that completely, but she was sure as hell going to take his mind of it for a while.

She shifted closer, so close that a deep breath would make her breasts brush against his body, and cupped the back of his neck. Pulling him down for a kiss she whispered, "It's more than nice to be touching you again."

Their lips met and opened. It was as if the last year had never happened, as if they'd never been apart. There was no adjustment period. Devon's tongue speared between her lips and took control, dueling with her, stroking her to a fever pitch within seconds. She clutched at him, her fingers gripping his silky hair as she tried to get closer still.

Large male hands covered hers, stilling them as he pulled back with a groan and buried his face in her neck. He nuzzled her neck for a minute, and a shiver ripped down her spine as she fought for some semblance of control over her body. Devon kissed her behind the ear, and then stood up and set her on her feet, letting her go completely.

"I'll take the sofa."

She gaped at him. "Excuse me?"

"I'll sleep on the sofa tonight."

Chaos reigned within as her brain tried to make sense of what she was hearing. "What? Why?"

"You don't 'do' relationships, and I want more than sex from you, Alexis."

She noted his flushed cheeks, his rising and falling chest as he struggled to breathe, and there was no denying the hard-on pressed aggressively against the button fly of his jeans. What the hell? "Are you telling me you haven't slept with anyone since me?"

"That's not what I said."

Of course not, she thought. Confusion turned to anger and she snapped, "So it's just me you won't fuck?"

He started toward her, hands out, then stopped short. "It's just you that I want more from. Don't you get it? You're special. Do I want to fuck you six ways from Sunday? You bet your sassy ass I do. But even more important than that is the fact that *I like you,* Alexis. And I think we can have something really good together."

She planted her hands on her hips. "Sure, we can have a damn good time."

Devon's mouth turned down at the corners and he shook his head. Something tightened in Lexy's chest and she stared at him blankly. He was serious, he was going to sleep on the couch, and leave her alone in her bed!

4

She left him there, in the middle of her living room with a sheet, a pillow, and no more words. It was all she could do to not stomp her feet and throw a temper tantrum that would do her Italian heritage proud.

Damn the man, it always had been all or nothing with him.

She stripped off her clothes and threw herself on her bed. She tossed and turned, until finally, she lay there staring at the ceiling.

Kane's comment on her outfit had reminded her that she'd actually been on a date earlier that night. A boring date, but what did she expect? Dating was new to her, and it showed. She wasn't used to sitting across from a guy and playing twenty questions unless she was trying to get specific information out of him for a case. That's not to say she was inexperienced with men, just with dating.

She'd never dated Devon. She'd met him and within hours they were rolling around naked and sweaty. Sure they'd talked some. Not as much in person as they had after she'd come back to Vancouver and they'd only had the phone as a way to connect. But they'd talked a bit. She certainly felt like she knew him, and he knew her. Which is why his saying no was so fucked up.

He knew what she was like. He knew she wasn't exactly your typical girl who wanted dinner dates with flowers and good-night kisses.

Dating had never been a priority for her before, she'd had other things to deal with. First, it had been hunting down her parents' killers. By the time that was done, she was focused on her solitary life of helping those who needed it. When she wanted sex, she went out and found a man who could give her what she wanted, and that was that.

Only recently she'd started to wonder about what she'd been missing out on with her single-minded lifestyle. What would it be like to have friends, fun, and a man around for more than just sex?

It was all Devon's fault. She'd been just fine living her life her way until she'd met him. Even that brief stint with him in Edmonton had been okay, but he hadn't left it at that. Oh, no. He'd called, and they'd talked. He'd given her hints at what it would be like to share more than her body with someone. He'd created this freaking yearning to have *more* in her life.

But he'd been so far away, and yet in other ways, too close. So she'd started dating. God, what a mess that was. It was so *not* worth the effort. Which was maybe a good thing because if her date earlier that night had been going well, it wouldn't have been very nice of her to dump a guy the minute she saw Devon on her doorstep.

And there was no doubt in her mind she would've done exactly that. Not just because the man only had to look at her to get her heart pounding, but also because he'd been there for her when she'd needed backup. There was knowledge of each other between them, a trust that went beyond that of a lover.

She flipped over again and punched her pillow before burying her face in it. But they were lovers. And he still wanted her, it had been clear in his eyes. She wanted to connect with him again because she knew he was hurting. She wanted to comfort him in the only way she knew how and he'd thrown it back in her face!

"Screw this," she muttered and jumped up from the bed. She was already talking as she strode into the living room and flipped the lights on. "I don't do relationships because I've never had one. I don't know *how* to have a relationship!"

Devon sat up on the couch, completely awake. "Tony? Jimmy D? Those are relationships. And what about Michaels tonight? You have some sort of relationship with him."

She tried not to notice the fact that he had no shirt on. Devon was by no means a boy, he was a man's man all the way through and it showed in his body. Lean hard muscles, a light pelt of hair that enhanced those muscles, not hid them. Giving herself a mental head-slap she focused on what he'd said.

"They're my uncles! And Kane is married, it's not what you think."

He stared, his eyes burning in a way that suddenly reminded her that she was completely naked. She slept in the nude, and she hadn't even thought about it before storming into the living room.

Finally, Devon stood to face her, his voice rising to match hers. "They're still relationships, Alexis. You share yourself, your life with them. Sleeping with a person doesn't make it a relationship, *sharing* does!" He scrubbed a hand through his hair. "Hell, we were well on our way until you decided to clam up and shut down."

"Family is different and you know it." Anger fueled her arousal as she moved forward until she stood directly in front of him, chest-to-chest. Her heart was pounding and hot blood was racing through her veins. "Relationships aren't my thing, Devon. Especially a long-distance one."

"You saying you don't 'do' relationships is just an excuse. You cut me out of your life because I was getting too close. You were starting to care, and that scared the shit out of you."

He waved an angry hand around her apartment. "Just look at this place."

"What's that supposed to mean?" Her apartment was hardly a penthouse, but she kept it neat and clean. What the hell was he talking about?

"Your place is full of photos of family and people you've loved. I see Tony and Jimmy, you and your parents when you were a kid. I'm guessing that's you and your first boyfriend." He pointed to one of her and Mike. "You know how to have a relationship, Alexis. You've proven you understand what family is, and loyalty is a core part of you. You're just too damn stubborn."

Desperate to make him understand, but too angry and aroused to try and form coherent words, she just grabbed him by the head and pulled him down for a kiss.

Like putting a lit flame to gasoline, they were ablaze within seconds. Strong male hands roamed over Lexy's body, pulling her closer, stroking down her back, cupping her ass and squeezing, lifting. She wrapped her arms and legs around him and whimpered.

So good, he tasted so damn good. *Felt* so damn good, so right. They fit together perfectly, hearts pounding in time as Devon moved, turning and setting her on the sofa, sliding to his knees on the floor. He dragged his lips away from hers, nibbling, sucking, and biting his way across her jaw to the sensitive spot behind her ear.

"Ahh," she cried, arching her back and tilting her head to give him better access. "God, Devon. I've missed you."

Hot hands cupped her breasts and he moved down her neck to suck a rigid nipple into his mouth. He tongued one, then the other, going back and forth as she writhed beneath him. Lexy clutched at him, trying to get closer still, to get her hands between them and get to his zipper. She discovered the top snap of his jeans already undone and she grasped the tab of the zipper only to have him pull back.

"Noooo," she moaned. *Not again.*

"Shhh," he crooned, rubbing his denim-covered cock against her hungry sex.

"Fuck, Devon," she cried out. "Please, please . . ." She didn't even know what she was begging for, she was so lost in sensations she couldn't think. Didn't want to think. She just wanted to feel more, to have him inside her where he belonged.

As if sensing this, Devon pulled away from her and suddenly she was completely bereft and aching. A whimper rose in her throat but before it could escape her lips, Devon shifted back and shoved his jeans down his hips, baring himself to her gaze. His cock was hard and thrust proudly into empty air.

"Shift forward," he said.

She wiggled forward but she wasn't quick enough and he grabbed her hips and hauled her forward. When her ass was on the edge of the sofa he lifted her legs and put them over his shoulders. The position had her curved awkwardly against the seat and back of the sofa, but she didn't care because before she could suck in a full breath he thrust home, filling her cunt with eight inches of hard, thick, throbbing cock.

Their eyes met and her heart jumped at the fiery emotion in his gaze before he lowered his head and kissed her deeply. He never slowed or stopped, his hips pumping as he filled her up, stretching her inner walls and claiming her as no one else could. Muffled groans and whimpers escaped her and he ate them up as he plunged in and out, hitting deep inside with every stroke.

Her insides tightened, the tremors of pleasure multiplied and suddenly Lexy was digging her nails into his back and crying out as pleasure exploded from deep inside and spread throughout her body. Her pussy clenched and unclenched in ecstasy as Devon threw back his head and let out a triumphant roar as his hot cum filled her core.

5

Devon lay on top of Lexy, his head buried in the sofa cushion next to her head, his heart pounding. She ran a hand down his back and he shivered, an uncontrollable reaction.

Without speaking, he pulled out and sat back on his knees. Her legs slid to the side, her feet to the floor and he rested his cheek against her belly as he tried to steady his breathing. One of her hands trailed lightly over the back of his head and his shoulder and every couple of seconds another tremor would ripple through him.

He'd always thought they were good together—a perfect match. But that had kicked ass on any memories or fantasies he'd ever had.

Alexis stirred beneath him. "That was . . ."

"Yeah."

No more words were needed. He loved that about them. They had a connection deeper than words. They had since the first time he'd set eyes on her back in Edmonton, if only she'd admit it.

Part of him wanted to say, "Are you happy now? I fucked

you." And then spend the night on the sofa anyway. But he couldn't do it.

He couldn't deny the power between them, and he knew then and there that if she still denied it when it was time for him to head home, he'd do his damndest to forget about her forever. He wanted her, and he was willing to chase her, but he wasn't willing to force her. Which meant that while he was there, he couldn't deny himself the joy of having her in his arms again.

And he was going to use every trick in the book to make her see that they belonged together that way, forever.

He stood up, stretched, and then slid his arms under her.

"What—" she said as he lifted her against his chest and started toward her bedroom. "You don't have to carry me."

"I know I don't have to." He smiled down at her. "But I like having you in my arms."

Devon laid her out on the bed then got rid of the rest of his own clothes before climbing in next to her.

He was in *her* bed, *her* apartment. He sighed and gathered her close. They'd met when she was in Edmonton, working undercover at Jimmy D's bar. A man she considered an uncle even though they weren't related by blood, Jimmy had been accused of killing a junkie behind his bar, and Alexis, who had a solid mistrust of the justice system, had gone back home to catch the real killer. Jimmy and her Uncle Tony had hired him to protect her while she searched for the killer, unknown to her. So he'd watched her a few times from afar until he was unable to resist making contact.

The minute their eyes had met, the attraction had been off the charts. And within minutes he knew that they were on the same page. Spoken communication had always been minimal between them.

Even now, as they lay there, there was no pressure to speak. Her hand skimmed over his abs and down to his groin. Her fingers tickled at his inner thigh for a minute before she cupped his balls. He spread his legs a little wider, loving her touch. She rolled them, weighing them, stroking them, squeezing a little, and he lay back, enjoying it.

Soon, Lexy shifted, moving between his legs, her breath hot on his thighs. His cock twitched as she teased. She took him in her mouth and the blood started to flow south again, hardening him as she sucked gently.

Amazingly his cock was rock hard in less than a minute. He shouldn't be surprised, Alexis always got to him, and despite having other lovers since she'd stopped returning his calls, none had compared to what she made him feel.

Weaving his fingers into her long soft hair, he relaxed into the mattress and enjoyed her touch. She rolled his balls in one hand while the other caressed his hipbone, her mouth moving on him steadily. Up and down his shaft she moved, her tongue swirling around the head, riding the ridge, then pressing against the underside as she slid to the base again. His skin tightened all over his body, pressure built in his cock and his hips started to move.

Her hand left his hip and circled the base of his cock, stroking with her mouth as she picked up the pace. Pleasure sizzled along his spine and his body jerked. This wasn't what he wanted, not right then. He gripped her shoulders, pulled her up, and flipped her over in one smooth move.

"As good as that feels, I'm not looking to use your mouth tonight, babe." He got on his knees and flipped her over again so she was on her stomach. "On your knees."

Christ, what a sight! Her round ass cheeks tilted up; her pink pussy lips, all shiny and full, were framed beautifully between her thighs. He leaned down and bit her ass cheek lightly. A sharp yip rang out and he smiled. His Alexis liked things a little rough and raw.

Spreading her plump pussy lips with his thumbs, he licked her from clit to asshole, loving the way she shivered and how goose bumps arose on her skin. He loved that she was so sensual, so sexual. Nothing was held back when they were together like this.

Alexis tossed her head and blond hair flew over her shoulder as she looked back at him.

"Whatever you want, sexy," she purred, wiggling her ass in the air.

"So tempting." Her ass? Her pussy?

He ran his hands up and down her legs, and then over her rounded hips, the feel of her soft skin so different from her hard personality. As smart and tough as she was, she was still a woman to the core. He leaned down and blew hot air on her exposed pussy a split second before moving in and spearing his tongue deep into her creamy pinkness. A joyous cry leapt from her throat and her knees trembled.

Devon gripped her hips and showed no mercy. This was no gentle seduction, this was him claiming her again. She'd ignored his calls, shut him out, and he was determined to show her that she could never do that again. She was right, *they* were right, and he wasn't going to let her go again.

Ever.

Hungry to taste her again, to make her come, to imprint himself on her, to make her cry out his name, he kept her spread wide, his tongue thrust deep, and his teeth nipped teasingly. He felt the trembling start in her, her moans filling the room, her body pressing back against him, grinning against his mouth. He slid a hand between her thighs and started in on the rigid button of her clit. He circled it as his tongue toyed with her entrance, dipping in and out. His cock bobbed against his belly, hard and demanding to be part of the action.

The spasms started in her sex, rippling around his thumb, so he slid it up from her pussy lips to the little puckered hole of her anus. He pressed against that circle of nerves, barely breaching her entrance, and she screamed her release, her body shaking as she ground back and down on him. He lapped up her cream, then when her shakes turned to sporadic trembling he shifted, surging up and entering her from behind. Her cunt was hot and slick, welcoming him as he thrust home again and again.

Bending forward he reached around and palmed her swinging breasts. He gripped her nipples between thumb and forefinger, and began to pump his hips.

"Devon," she panted. "God, yes, Devon. Fuck me."

She braced her hands on the bed, her breasts swinging, her nipples pulling, her cunt clenching around him as he pumped. His chest filled, his belly slapped her ass, and his eyes crossed as he fucked her hard and fast.

Alexis whimpered, her pussy tightening around him as she came. Devon groaned, his balls tightened, pulling up as his cock swelled, expanding inside her until he couldn't hold back anymore. Every muscle in his body tensed and he let go, his head spinning as pure sensation swamped him.

He collapsed on his side, pulling Alexis into the curve of his body. He was still inside her, his cock twitching as they both worked to catch their breath.

"I've missed you," Alexis whispered.

"I've missed you too," he replied.

She snuggled back against him, and he relaxed.

So much had changed in less than twenty-four hours, and he was tired. Worry trickled back into his mind, but he shoved it away. He had Alexis, and together they were going to find Theresa.

6

Lexy woke up as the sun was starting to peek through the curtains. Birds were chirping outside her window and the muted sounds of cars driving past told her the world was already awake.

A heavy arm was draped over her waist and she eased out from under it. Standing naked by the bed she studied the man there. It was August, and hot enough that he'd done nothing more than pull a sheet over their bodies sometime during the night. He was such a stud. He'd always known when it was right for him to take control, and when he needed to sit back and let her do her own thing.

Devon was man enough that a strong woman didn't threaten his masculinity, not in bed or out of it. Which is why he'd come to her. She turned away from him and headed to the shower, loving the little aches and pains that came from a night of hard core lovin'.

As much as she wanted to climb back into bed and wake him up the right way, he'd come to her for help, and she was going to give it to him. The relationship stuff was going to have to wait.

She got her head in order while she showered and by the time she hit the kitchen, she had a plan. Just as she was cracking eggs into the frying pan, Devon wandered into the kitchen. She froze, dripping eggshells in her hand, and stared. Rumpled and shirtless, the belt and top two buttons on his jeans were undone. Desire flooded her system and Lexy forgot all about breakfast.

He scratched his head, walked over and kissed her on the lips. "Morning."

"Morning," she replied.

He smiled and moved past her to the fridge. When he'd poured himself a glass of milk, he nodded toward the stove. "The eggs are going to burn."

Giving her head a shake she tossed the shells and grabbed the spatula from the countertop. Stirring them up she decided scrambled eggs were better than burnt eggs. With that in mind, she grabbed the jar of salsa from the fridge and dumped some into the frying pan. There, now the eggs definitely wouldn't taste burnt.

The microwave pinged and she glanced at Devon. He was leaning against the sink, watching her with a thoughtful expression. Not wanting him to bring up their conversation from the night before, she spoke before he could. "Want to get the bacon from the microwave and put the toast down?"

His lips twisted in that half smile that made her heart jump and he nodded.

"Sure." He opened cupboards until he found the plates, and then set two down on the counter, side by side, where she could reach them. "You eat like this every morning?"

"Nope."

"So you're cooking for me?"

She smiled. "We're going to have a busy day. Need to fuel up."

His movements stalled, toast in one hand, butter knife in the other. "Have you heard something?"

"Not yet." She shook her head as she scooped the eggs onto the plates he'd set out with the bacon on them. She set the frying pan down and met his gaze. "But I have a feeling we will."

Devon's lips pressed together and he nodded sharply. Some people would scoff or laugh, but they both knew her instincts were sharp, and in their line of business, be it body guarding or investigating, a feeling was as good as a tip. Sometimes better.

"I've got a job this morning," she said as they moved to the small table with plates in hand. "I was going to cancel it, but I don't think we should. You can come with me, and we can do some phone work as we go."

"What's the job?"

"Cheating spouse. Follow with a camera and get the money shot."

Frustration flashed across his face and she reached across the table, covering his hand with hers. "I know you just want to find Theresa, and we will. But I think we need to go with this job for now."

Devon nodded, and they ate the rest of their breakfast in silence. Lexy loaded the dishwasher while Devon showered and changed and they hit the road within the hour. As they were driving along the highway, heading toward the airport, she noticed Devon kept looking at his cell phone. He wasn't checking messages or texting on it. He was just looking at it.

"Have you called your family yet?" she asked softly.

He shook his head. "I know I should, but I can't do it just yet."

Her heart went out to him. When they were still talking, their phone conversations had revolved around family and what was important to them. Devon had a big family, with plenty of uncles, aunts, cousins, and three brothers. They all lived in Edmonton or the surrounding area, except for Theresa—the lone female cousin.

Lexy didn't have a big family. Her parents had been killed

when she was young, and her uncle had raised her. It was just her and him, and his best friend Jimmy D. But they were tight. Family was everything, and she knew it was killing Devon that Theresa had called him and not the others, and that he didn't have any good news to share with them.

"There's no point calling them until I know something, anything," she told him. "If you called them now, they'd all be out here quicker than you can blink, and we both know if too many people get involved, this will just turn into a cluster fuck."

"I know."

They continued in silence as she wove her way through traffic, and they crossed the Arthur Laing Bridge. The airport wasn't far now, and traffic had thinned to a steady stream. Devon wasn't constantly looking at his cell phone anymore, he was staring out the window instead and she just knew he was beating himself up some more.

Determination swelled within Lexy. Devon was so strong, so solid. Sure, he was also the big bad biker dude. He rode a beautiful Indian Spirit bike, wore leather chaps that made her pussy melt, and knew how to kick ass. But there he sat, looking a little lost, and she couldn't handle it.

She reached for her cell phone and dialed Kane. She saw the car pulled over on the shoulder of the road, but it didn't quite register with her until Devon shot up straight in the passenger seat.

"Stop! That's her car." He swung his head to look at her. "That's her car back there. Pull over!"

Closing her phone she did a quick shoulder check and whipped over the right lane to the shoulder. The road was narrow, and not a good place to stop, but she slowed to a stop in front of a shiny gray Nissan Sentra that was parked at an odd angle on the side of the road.

Devon was out of the car before she stopped completely, and she slammed the GTO into park and followed him quickly.

By the time she caught up to him he had the driver's side door open and was looking inside. When he straightened up he was holding a ladies' purse.

"Hers?"

"Yeah," he said, his expression stone cold. "The keys are still in the ignition and her cell phone is on the floor."

"Fuck!"

Lexy moved around the car slowly, checking for body damage and finding none. "It doesn't look like anyone hit her." She opened the passenger door and took a good look around the interior. "No signs of blood or an injury."

She opened the glove box and checked the registration just to be thorough before standing up and looking at Devon. He stood still at the side of the road, hands on his hips, head down. Thinking? Breathing? Fighting for control? She didn't know what was going through his mind, but it probably wasn't good.

She flipped her cell phone open and hit her speed dial. "Diego, I've got a cheating spouse job to pass on. You got time right now?"

"Lexy, chica!" His raspy voice was a grumpy growl. "It's not even nine o'clock yet. You know I don't function well before noon."

"Do you want it or not? I'm in the middle of something and don't have time to dick around." Diego was another private investigator in town she worked with every now and then. Sometimes things came along that took more than one person. He was a good guy, but he drank too much and was usually useless in the morning.

"Shit!" he said. "I wish I could help you, but I got work already this afternoon. No way I can make it."

They hung up and she stood there for a brief second. She'd made a commitment to a client to follow his wife when her plane landed. He thought she was cheating instead of doing business in town, and he wanted proof for the divorce lawyers. Being a successful P.I. meant having a good reputation, and she took that seriously. She should continue on to the airport to do her job, but instead, it took less than thirty seconds for her to decide what was more important.

"Fuck it," she muttered. Devon was more important than any job.

Pushing the cheating spouse to the back of her mind, she dialed Kane. "We found Theresa's car." She told him where they were and hung up before walking to Devon's side.

He turned to face her and she wished he wasn't wearing sunglasses. Shit, she didn't need to see his eyes to know he was upset, worried, pissed off, and even worse, scared for his cousin. "Grab her things and let's go."

He didn't question her, just picked up the purse and pocketed the cell phone. "I left the keys where they were."

Lexy went back and took a quick look at them. Only two keys on the ring—door and ignition. There was nothing there for them to work with. She started to walk away, then hesitated. Pressing her lips together she reached in and popped the trunk.

Praying there wasn't a body back there, she moved quickly, before Devon could see what she was up to.

She lifted the lid and a sigh of relief gusted out. Nothing but a spare tire and a gym bag. She grabbed the gym bag and slammed the trunk closed. "Let's go."

They moved quickly to her car. Soon they were on the road again.

"Check her purse for her apartment keys, make sure they're in there," she instructed Devon as she drove. "Then look in that gym bag and see if there's anything interesting in it."

"Keys are here." He lifted the gym bag onto his lap and shuffled through it. "Clothes and running shoes. Water bottle. Nothing special."

The dead tone of his voice told Lexy that Devon had shut

down his emotions. As much as she wanted to comfort him, she understood the need to shut down. Still . . . "This is a good thing, Devon. If someone had wanted to hurt her, her body would be there. But they took her. They need her for something."

He didn't say anything, and she moved on. They were heading back into the city now, Lexy wanted to visit Theresa's office. Chances were good that this wasn't personal, not with Theresa being a parole officer.

"Has her phone got any juice?"

Devon flipped it open and nodded. "It's low though."

"Check her last number called." The phone beeped, signaling the battery's slow death. "Write it down."

Devon dug into Theresa's purse and pulled out a pen and paper. He wrote the number down, and the phone was still beeping. "While there's still juice, check her call log, see if any numbers are familiar."

The beeping stopped, and Devon flipped the phone closed. "It's dead."

"You got the last number called?"

"Yeah. I don't recognize it, though."

"No problem." She flipped her phone into his lap. "Call it. See who answers."

"Voice mail," he said, shaking his head at her. "The generic repeat of the number sort. No name."

Shit. "It's okay. We'll keep trying until we get someone."

They hit the city limits and she headed downtown. The car was quiet, and Lexy wondered if she should worry about Devon. Most people would be second-guessing her and asking annoying questions. It's why she worked alone. Well, that and the fact that she had trust issues and she knew it.

She glanced at Devon again and this time he was looking at her. He gave her a small nod and that was all she needed. He was coping. He was doing okay.

7

It was still early enough that traffic was heavy, so it took them a while to get back into the city and downtown. Adrenaline was flowing and Lexy knew that they were on the right trail. She could feel it.

Traffic got heavier as they got closer to downtown. She found the building she was looking for, and started to circle around and around the boulevards looking for parking. She didn't mind driving downtown, it was trying to find parking that was the bitch.

She found a lot and pulled in just as her cell phone rang. Snatching it up, she grimaced when she saw the caller I.D. She knew what was coming.

"Where the hell are you?" Kane growled when she answered.

"We're heading into the parole office Theresa worked out of. I want to talk to her boss. See if I can get a look at Theresa's files."

She could practically hear Kane grind his teeth over the phone line. "Do it quick. We've got the registration from her car and as soon as I call it in, it's going to be an official missing person's case. Then you'll be interfering."

"Fuck that."

"Just be quick," he said. "And while you're at it, make sure you ask about Steven Salter, he's the guy in the picture you gave me last night."

"That was quick." Something tickled in the back of her brain and she leaned her head back against the car seat, closing her eyes. "Why does his name sound familiar?"

"You might remember him from a few years ago. The hacker that made all the headlines."

It clicked, the images she'd seen on the news during Salter's court case, the face in the picture pressed against Theresa's. "Shit."

"Yeah, him. He's on parole . . . and Theresa Williams is his P.O."

"Shit. Shit. Shit." That guy had led law enforcement on a merry chase with his identity thefts and misdirections. If he'd taken Theresa on the run, they were going to be very hard to find. "Okay, I gotta go, we're here."

"Hey!" Kane shouted before she could hang up.

"What?"

"Did you find anything else in the car?"

He knew her well. "We've got her purse, and cell phone. Purse was on the car seat, cell phone on the floor." No need to mention the gym bag.

She hung up and got out of the car. Devon was right behind her. "What did he say?"

They strode toward the office building and Lexy filled him in on the way. "So is this good news? Salter is a hacker, but he hasn't got a violent history, right? And they looked real cozy in those pictures. So maybe—"

She grabbed his arm and they stopped in front of the glass doors of the entrance. "He's not known to be violent, no. But we still don't know what's going on here. Don't start thinking about what they're doing just yet, Devon. Right now, we're just gathering as much information as we can, and following the trail. Don't try to jump ahead or you'll miss something."

His jaw firmed and his eyes darkened. He nodded. "Information gathering, got it."

"We're on the right track, Devon. And things are moving at a good pace. The police will be actively looking for them both now as well. We'll find her." She wanted to add *Don't worry.* But she knew it was not only impossible, it was bad advice. Of course he should worry, his cousin was missing, possibly taken by a criminal. It didn't matter if Salter was white-collar crime, even the most sedate person could become violent under the wrong circumstances.

They entered the Correctional Services building and took the elevator up. Lexy took the lead as soon as the doors opened and they stepped onto the floor where Theresa worked. Devon stood back and watched Lexy work as she was put through almost the same paces as he'd been through the day before. Except the day before no one would talk to him, Theresa's cousin.

A private detective was another matter. Within minutes they were escorted to Mary Briggs's glass-enclosed office as the workers in the cubicles watched.

Briggs's air of impatient tolerance was thin, and her eyes were cold as she positioned herself in the back corner of the small room. Her office was neat, organized, and the ego wall to her right was full of photos of her shaking hands with "important" people.

Typical self-important bureaucratic supervisor, he thought.

"Ms. Briggs," Lexy began, "I'm looking into the disappearance of Theresa Williams, and I have reason to believe it could be tied to one of her parolees. I'd like the opportunity to look at her case files."

Briggs's cold eyes flicked to Devon. "I was unaware that Theresa was officially missing."

"Since yesterday."

She nodded slowly, looking back and forth between him and Alexis. Finally she focused on Lexy. "Unless you have a warrant, Ms. Signorino, I'm inclined to keep those files private. I'm sure you understand, even convicts have rights."

"No, I don't understand. Do you not care that one of your case P.O.'s has gone missing?" God, he loved that she didn't pull any punches. Alexis was a woman who got things done.

The woman waved a hand blithely in the air. "I doubt she's missing, she probably just partied too hard yesterday and is sleeping it off."

Before Devon could open his mouth, Alexis did. "You're wrong. Theresa is missing. Her car was found not long ago, and the police will be by soon to speak with you, but when a person is missing, time is of the essence."

Briggs nodded her head. "Then I will wait for the police."

Lexy glanced back at Devon, her eyes flicking over his shoulder for a moment, before she turned to face the supervisor again. "You wasted time by not listening when Theresa's family came to you yesterday, and today you're willing to wait and do nothing for even longer? Wow, you really don't give a shit about your staff, do you?"

"I think it's time for you to leave, Ms. Signorino."

Frustration surged forth and Devon took a step forward. "Miz Briggs, my cousin—"

Lexy grabbed his arm and spun him on his heel, "Let's go."

"Damn it, Alexis—"

She cut him off again, pulling him out of the office. "*Now*, Devon."

She strode before him, but instead of going to the elevator, she went into the stairwell. He followed her through the door. "What the hell, Alexis? We need to see Salter's file."

"We might already have it," Lexy said, pointing down the stairs. Standing on the next landing in the stairwell was a chubby brunette with a very big frown on her pretty face as she waited for them.

"I don't have his file, but I can give you his phone number and address," she said.

"What else can you tell us about Steven Salter?" Lexy asked, as she went down the steps toward the girl.

The brunette fidgeted, glancing from Lexy to Devon, before handing a piece of folded paper to Lexy. "Steven is a hacker. The best hacker in North America, possibly the world. He's hacked everything from government systems like the DMV and health care, to corporations like Shell, Motorola, and Bell."

"How dangerous is he?"

"That's just it. He's not."

"What do you mean?"

"He's a hacker," she said. "He says it was fun to break into systems that are supposed to be unbreakable, but he did it all for the rush, not for money. He didn't steal a corporation's secrets to sell, he did it because he *could.*"

"But he's done more than that," Lexy said.

"He didn't get into identity theft until he went on the run. Even then he didn't go in and start hacking credit cards and running them up or bilking people's money. He did it for the thrill, the adrenaline." She shrugged. "Most of the really good ones do."

Devon couldn't keep quiet anymore. "So you don't think he's got my cousin tied up in the trunk of his car somewhere?"

She shook her head, her lips pressed tight together. "No, he wouldn't hurt her. I think he loves her."

"If Theresa was his parole officer why do you know so much about him without his file?"

"I'm Tracey, Theresa is a friend of mine. I know all about her and Steven."

"When did they become a couple?"

"About three months ago. He's been working real hard at staying out of trouble. He's not even allowed to have access to a computer, so finding a job has been hard for him. Theresa and him always had something to talk about, and then finally a few months ago she admitted they were seeing each other on the sly."

Alexis put a hand on the girl's arm and stepped closer. "Tracey, do you know where Theresa is?"

Tracey looked at them, a small frown puckering her brow.

"Tell us," Lexy commanded softly. "What do you know?"

"I don't know where she is." Tracey's shoulders drooped. "But Theresa did say that Steve was nervous lately. He thought someone was following him."

"Did he have a reason to be nervous? Who would be following him?"

She shrugged again and Devon's tension rose. Didn't she know anything? What was with all the damn shrugging and frowning?

"I don't know, she only mentioned it a few days ago. I didn't connect her not showing up yesterday afternoon with it until I saw you here, looking for her."

"Why didn't you tell me this then!" His question came out more growl than anything and he took a deep breath. No need to scare her.

"I didn't know you were her cousin until after you left!"

Devon bit back another growl and turned away from the girl. Goddamn it! If people would just pay attention then they could've been looking at Salter yesterday!

He stopped listening to what the girl was saying to Alexis as his pulse started to pound and he worked to control his temper.

What the fuck was wrong with these people?

Briggs didn't give a shit, Tracey thought there was no way the felon ex-con boyfriend could possibly hurt Theresa, and she'd known Theresa was nervous about something, yet she'd not said anything to anyone when Theresa hadn't shown up for work. What did it take for people to start paying attention to what went on around them?

He stood silent and still as the girl edged past him and went back up the stairs to her floor. He really had nothing more to say to her. When Lexy's hand touched his shoulder, he just looked at her. What was there to say?

But he didn't need to say anything to her, Alexis knew what he needed.

She stepped closer and wrapped her arms around him in a quick, hard hug. "We're getting closer, Devon. We'll find her, and she'll be okay." Then she pulled back, smiled grimly, and held up the piece of paper Tracey had given her. "Let's go visit Steven Salter, shall we?"

8

Steven Salter lived in a small apartment complex in East Vancouver. It wasn't the best area of town, and Lexy had a moment's hesitation at leaving her car unattended at the curb. Her GTO was her baby, and the classic muscle car would be a temptation for many.

With a quick prayer for someone to watch out for her car, she reached over and took her Taurus from the glove box before climbing out. Devon raised his eyebrow at her as she shoved the gun into the waistband at the small of her back.

"What?" she said. "Couldn't bring it into a government office, but I'm sure as hell not going in there without it."

"It's got a pink handle," he said. "I've never thought of you as a pink kind of girl."

"Oh yeah? What kind of girl *do* you see me as?"

He grinned. "Red. Bright, fiery, and hot red."

Pleasure rushed over Lexy and she chided herself. *Stop thinking with your hormones, girl. You've got work to do.*

When she'd showed the paper Tracey had given her to Devon earlier, he'd confirmed that the phone number was the last one called on Theresa's phone, so they knew they were definitely on the right track. Chances were likely she wouldn't need the gun. She'd only had to use it once before in her life, but she hated walking into a questionable situation without a little backup.

Devon followed her into the crappy building and up the stairs. Her heartbeat kicked up as they went up the stairs, and she breathed deep and slow, trying to control the rush of adrenaline that hit.

Salter lived in apartment 210, which was a corner unit at the end of the hall. They got there and she gestured to Devon to stand to the side of the door, out of sight. If Salter was in, and looked through the peephole, he'd only see her, a lone female. Hardly a threat—or so he'd think.

She knocked, and it echoed through the crappy building. No sounds from inside. She knocked again just to be sure, and then pulled out her pick. In less than thirty seconds they were in the apartment, the door shut behind them.

It was a small one-bedroom place; mostly clean except for the dirty dishes in the sink. Without a word she headed for the bedroom, to make sure Salter wasn't just sleeping, and found nothing but an empty bed.

They began to search the apartment, silent and smooth, working as a team. Devon searched the living room while Lexy did the bedroom, then they switched to double check.

"Check this out," Devon said, as he came out of the bathroom holding a scrap of paper.

He handed it to her and she saw it wasn't a piece of paper but a business card. "Davidson Corporation. Security Division?"

Devon held up the piece of paper he'd written on hours earlier, and she immediately saw what he'd seen.

"Where was it?"

"The trash can."

"Okay," she said, her brain kicking into gear. "So the first question is why would an ex-con have the business card for a security contact at a big corporation? And why would the phone number on that card lead to an automated voice mailbox? And why would that same number be the last one to call your cousin? If Salter somehow stepped over the line with this company, they'd call his parole officer but it's unlikely they'd call her private cell phone. Also unlikely he'd have their business card." She shook her head. "And it doesn't explain the voice mail. Big corporations don't have automated voice mailboxes. They have receptionists."

Devon shook his head. "It's possible someone who's uptight about security uses only an automatic voice mail. It's a smart thing actually, for private citizens, for personal protection. It's unusual for a business line to use such a screening process, but not completely unrealistic."

Something hit the wall in the apartment next to them and rapidly rising voices had them both staring at the wall for a second.

Lexy nodded toward the door. "Let's get out of here."

What Devon had said made sense. If someone was paranoid enough, then the automated voice mail made sense, even for a business thing. And in her experience when someone was that paranoid it was because they had something to hide.

They left the apartment, Devon waiting while she closed the door, locking it behind them. Lexy took three steps to the stairwell but froze at the top step, her instincts screaming. She looked down just in time to see two thugs enter the building.

It didn't matter that they wore expensive black suits, or maybe it was because of the suits, whatever the reason there was no hiding the fact that they were hired muscle.

Before she could back up, they looked up and saw them.

Maybe it was the way she'd frozen, but the first guy looked

at her, looked at Salter's nearby apartment door, then back at her as he reached beneath his jacket.

Lexy saw the gun and scrambled backward at the same time Devon grabbed her by the back of her belt and pulled.

The first shot missed, lodging into the wall where they stood only a split second before. "Go!" Devon tried to shove her up the next set of stairs ahead of him but she balked.

Pulling the Taurus from her waist she glared at him. "You go, I'll be right behind you."

Another shot barely missed her head and they both moved, Lexy twisting at the waist to get a shot off at the two pursuing thugs.

"Goddamn it, Alexis! Just move!" He grabbed her free hand and pulled as he ran up the stairs.

Lexy barely watched her step as she ran behind him. Trusting him to lead, she kept her body twisted and her gun up in case the thugs continued to follow them.

Which of course, they did. Their heavy footsteps echoed in the stairwell as Devon hit the third floor and pulled her down the short hallway. She was amazed she could hear them after the loud rapport of the gunfire, but she could.

They reached the end of the hall and Devon didn't hesitate. He kicked the door of the final apartment open, his boot connecting right next to the lock and popping the door open.

She heard the heavy pounding of their steps as they finally got to the landing and she spun, aiming at the corner they'd yet to round, and squeezed off three rapid shots.

Curses filled the air, and Devon tugged at her free hand. Lexy didn't bother to stick around to see if the thugs had stopped, she followed Devon to the window and out onto the fire escape.

"Get going." Devon stepped back and pushed her toward the ladder.

She knew he wanted to protect her, but she was the one with the gun. She was the one who could fire back. "Devon—"

"Now!"

A shot shattered the window next to him and Devon ducked. Lexy's heart stopped, then kicked hard against her ribs when he lifted his head. "Move your ass, Alexis!"

She moved, rushing down the steep metal steps, holding onto the rail with one hand to keep from falling face first.

"Keep going, I'm right behind you," Devon urged.

She got to the final landing and jumped on the last rung of the ladder, hanging on as the ladder swung down to the pavement.

A couple of shots came from the third-floor window as Devon landed on the pavement beside her.

"Are you hit?" she asked, grabbing his arm and pulling him up.

"No, I'm fine," he growled, grabbing her and starting to run down the alley. "Now move!"

They ran and the shooting stopped.

They jumped into her car, and Lexy tossed her gun in Devon's lap. "Watch for them, in case they follow."

Silence filled the car and Lexy worked to steady her breathing and lower her heart rate. Her pulse wasn't pounding because of the run, she knew that. It also wasn't pounding strictly because they'd been shot at. She'd been shot at before, and she knew how it felt. Her heart was pounding because Devon had been shot at, and suddenly, she couldn't imagine life without him in it.

"Fuck," she muttered.

"Who were those guys?" Devon asked, assuming that was why she'd cursed. "Fucking hired muscle of some sort that just saw us and started shooting. They didn't give a fuck who we were!"

Lexy didn't say anything, still too shook up by her freakin' epiphany. She thought the thugs were connected to Salter somehow since they'd glanced at his apartment door before they'd started shooting. It wasn't concrete proof, but her gut told her she was right. She just didn't know what the fuck it meant.

Devon was a mess.

He didn't care that he'd been in danger, but the thought of Alexis getting shot, or killed, made him see red. He wasn't sure if he was more pissed at the assholes who'd shot at them, or at her for putting him in front of her while she shot back.

Never mind that he was pissed because Salter hadn't been there, and he just knew the guy was behind Theresa's disappearance. His cousin was no dummy. Growing up as the lone female with three brothers and seven male cousins had taught the girl how to handle herself. Not to mention as a parole officer she had to know what was out there. Yet somehow, this con had wormed his way into her life, and now she was gone.

He sat in the passenger seat, staring at the cityscape as it passed by him, and emotions threatened to overwhelm him. He'd been in town twenty-four hours, and he'd put Alexis smack in the line of fire, and he still didn't know where the hell Theresa was.

"We're getting closer, Devon," Alexis said from beside him. "Small steps, but closer."

He nodded. She was right, they were getting closer, but not close enough. "I can't put off calling her family any longer."

"Your family," she said.

Yeah, and when they found out he'd known she was missing for more than twenty-four hours and he hadn't called, they'd beat the shit out of him and then disown him.

Families like his didn't live in each other's pockets, but when there was trouble, they stuck together.

Aware of the heavy weight of his cell phone in his pocket he glanced at Alexis. "What now? Where are we going?"

She shot an assessing glance his way. "My place isn't too far away, so let's go there. I want to make a few calls and check some things on the computer anyway."

Anyway. She knew how hard this call was going to be and she was working to give him some privacy to make it. Her actions just went to prove that while she might think she didn't do relationships well, she really did. She was sexy and smart, and she cared. No matter what she said or didn't say, it was clear she cared. Now he just had to find a way to show her that it could all work out.

It had never entered his mind that them living in separate cities could be a relationship killer. To his way of thinking, physical distance was something easily overcome when the desire was there.

Lexy steered the car into a drive-through and asked him what he wanted for lunch. Once they'd picked up their burgers and shakes at the second window, they headed home. Lexy's place was just around the corner so the food was still plenty warm when they entered the apartment. He set the take-out bag on the table and reached for his cell phone. He couldn't put this call off any longer.

"Why don't you eat first?" Lexy said. "Let me call Kane and get an update before you call your family."

Part of him just wanted to get the call over with, but there was the small hope inside that if he waited another five minutes, just maybe he'd have something positive to report.

He grabbed Alexis's arm as she walked past him and stopped her. He leaned down and pressed a quick kiss to her soft lips. "Thank you," he said, and then let her go.

Lexy's heart literally ached for Devon. He was doing a great job of keeping his expression blank, except for his eyes. There was an emotional storm raging in those beautiful gray eyes of his and it killed her that she could do nothing to hold it off.

Well, maybe not nothing. She flipped her phone open and dialed Kane as she watched Devon unwrap his burger.

"Michaels here."

She turned away from Devon and spoke into the phone. "Kane, did your guys get anything from the car?"

"Nothing," he said. "Connors is at the parole office right now, did you get anything there?"

She told him about bitchy Briggs and Tracey the talkative. "We checked out Salter's place and found a business card for the Davidson Corporation. What do you know about them?"

He paused, the background noise becoming stronger, hinting that he was driving. When he spoke again he did not seem happy. "Rumored to have ties with the Chinese mafia."

"What? I thought the Asian gangs were into drugs and guns and street gang stuff?"

"Why are you asking about them?"

She told him about the phone number on Theresa's cell phone, the voice mail, the business card in the trash that stated SECURITY DIVISION.

"Where are you guys?"

"My place."

"Give me half an hour. Don't go anywhere or do anything until I get there," he said firmly. "We need to talk."

Lexy hung up and turned to see Devon staring at her. "Kane's on his way over," she said. "And I think we might be closer than we thought, so I think you should hold off calling if you can."

He glanced at his watch and nodded. "Until after we talk to him, no more than that."

9

Forty minutes later Kane walked into her apartment with a frown on his handsome face. He pulled up a chair at the kitchen table and got right to the point.

"Davidson Corporation develops and publishes video games. Rumor on the task force is that they borrowed from one of the Chinese triads to develop their new game Zulu, which is supposed to hit release in two months, just in time to catch the Christmas hype." He stared at them. "Only Croco Entertainment, another up-and-coming developer, has their game set to release at the same time . . . and their game is kicking ass, which threatens Zulu's success."

"Video games . . . electronics. So Salter is involved somehow?"

Devon looked skeptical. "How does this involve Theresa?"

"We think she got caught in the middle of something with Salter and Davidson. If Salter was hacking them and got caught, they'd either want to hire him to work for them, or take him out. They're not the sort of company to call the authorities. If

Theresa was with him . . ." Kane's words trailed off, his lips pressed tight together.

No one wanted to think about that possibility, not yet.

"How do we find out for sure what's going on?"

"You still have Theresa's cell phone?"

Lexy nodded at the kitchen counter where Theresa's phone was hooked up to Devon's charger. "Was out of juice when we got our hands on it."

Kane got up and got the phone. "I'm going to take it with me. You got that business card handy too?"

Devon looked at Lexy, a question in his eyes. She nodded. "Give it to him."

Devon pulled the card from his pocket and held it out to the cop silently. Kane took it and headed for the door. "Don't go anywhere or do anything for a while. The task force guys were pretty keen when I talked to them. They've scented something here with Salter's possible involvement, so just give us some time."

Devon jumped up before Kane could disappear. "You expect us to sit and wait? For how long?"

Kane stopped. He turned to face Devon and the men glared at each other. "For as long as it takes. I understand this is your cousin, but you have to let us do our jobs."

Devon stalked forward. "Theresa is more than a job to me."

Lexy watched the men, the tension snapping between them as they stood face-to-face. She was tempted to get up and step between them, but that would probably just make the situation worse.

"Kane is aware of that, Devon," she said from her seat at the table. "He has access to more information and resources than I do, and he's helping us as a favor to me. He's taking this seriously. Trust me if you don't trust him."

Devon ran a hand through his hair and turned away from Kane, leaving the room and heading into the bedroom.

Lexy stood and went to Kane. "You will tell us everything you find, right?"

"I will." He nodded. "I promise you'll be in on anything that goes down, when it happens."

Goes down? That sounded like he knew more than he was saying already. "Kane," she warned.

He put up a hand—stopping her from saying anything else. "We've got some leads, and I think there's a good chance you'll have his cousin back in the next twenty-four hours."

"So, you do know more than you're saying."

He nodded. "Stay here, I'll call you as soon as I'm able."

Lexy didn't bother to watch him go. She spun on her heel and headed for the bedroom . . . and Devon.

10

Devon stood in front of the bedroom window, staring at the ordinary street below. A lady walking her dog strolled past, cars were parked on the side of the road, nothing unusual was happening out there at all. Yet his world seemed to have dimmed drastically.

His emotions were boiling close to the surface, and his control was wearing thin. Intellectually he knew Theresa's disappearance wasn't his fault, but his heart was heavy with guilt for not being there sooner. Or at the very least making her tell him what was up when he was on the phone with her. If he had, he'd know if they were at least on the right trail.

He heard the apartment door close, and then Lexy's soft footsteps came toward the bedroom. Soon, he felt her behind him. The heat of her body close to his, the comfort of her hand on his back.

"You know I'm not one to put a lot of faith in the cops, Devon," she said. "But, Kane is different, and I trust him."

"She's out there somewhere, Alexis. Alone, maybe hurt . . ."

"It's barely been twenty-four hours, Devon. I know you

want to go bang on doors and look under every rock until we find her—and if I thought that would work I'd be right there with you. But she's not a teenage runaway, or a bail jumper. Someone *took* her, and that changes everything."

He turned to stare at her. "*That* makes me feel so much better."

"I've never been real good with words," she said as she stepped closer and rubbed her body against his. "But I know another way to make you feel better."

"I'm not in the mood, Alexis." He stepped back.

She stepped forward, bringing a hand up to the side of his neck. She stroked his cheek with her thumb and he thought, *She gets it. She wants to comfort me.*

And then she undulated against him, rubbing and grinding as she moved in and nibbled on his bottom lip. "Let me distract you," she whispered.

Disappointment, anger, worry, and frustration, all tied together into one big ball of emotion that finally exploded inside him. He grabbed Lexy's hips and shoved her away from him. "You just don't get it, do you? You can't fucking distract me from this! And would you stop trying to turn everything into something sex can cure?"

She stared at him, eyes round, color draining from her face. Regret hit him for his sharpness almost immediately, but he just couldn't deal with it, with her, until he got his own emotions back under control. He headed for the door. "I need some time alone."

He left the apartment and got as far as the front door of the building before he stopped. The anger drained out of him. Leaving only the heaviness of guilt and regret. For not being there when Theresa needed him, for not being able to find her, for not calling her family . . . and for what he'd said to Alexis.

At the same time guilt had been building and weighing his heart down, Alexis's presence had been warming it. There'd been no hesitation in her when he'd showed up on her doorstep unexpectedly asking for help. She'd ditched a job earlier that morning because they'd found a lead on Theresa, and he hadn't even had to ask.

With a deep breath he decided to go with his gut. Alexis had innate qualities that synched with his. Her sexuality was a big part of her, and he loved it; he had no right to imply otherwise. The real problem was that she didn't realize, or she refused to accept, that he loved more than just her sexual confidence.

He loved her.

Stunned, he leaned back against the wall. He'd always known she was special—she was both appealing and unnerving in a way that he found addictive. But love . . . he'd seen it in his future with her, deep down he'd known, but he couldn't pretend it was only a possibility anymore. It was a reality. He wanted to spend his life with Alexis Signorino.

He'd come to Lexy, and she was there for him. He trusted her, she trusted the cop. He'd give them time to work, and if Theresa was still missing after forty-eight hours, he'd call his family then.

Having made that decision, a bit of weight lifted from his shoulders and he stared at the building's door. Without setting a foot outside he turned around and headed back up the stairs. It was time to make things clear for them both.

Lexy sat on the edge of the bed, not sure what the fuck she was feeling. Shock was one thing for sure. Devon had turned away her advances for the second time, and this time she was not going to chase him down and make him face the fact that he wanted her.

Hurt crept past the shock and she fell back onto the mattress and stared at the ceiling. Her heart cracked and a big hard lump formed in her throat. He didn't want her.

Before she knew it tears were welling in her eyes and leaking down her cheeks. It was then that she realized she'd always thought Devon would be a part of her life. Sure, she'd cut off ties to him for a bit, but in her dreams she'd see him again. Some part of her had always thought he'd be hers in the end . . . after all, they were two of a kind.

She heard the apartment door open and sat bolt upright on the bed. She brushed her tears away in time to see Devon standing in her bedroom doorway.

He leaned a shoulder against the door frame and stared at her.

"That was quick," she said.

He nodded. "We need to talk."

"Okay." Feeling oddly vulnerable she stood up and folded her arms over her chest. "Talk."

"I'm sorry I snapped at you. You didn't deserve that."

She pressed her lips together, hiding her surprise before waving a hand in the air. "It's okay. I know you're really stressed about Theresa and all."

"Not just Theresa," he said with a slow shake of his head. He walked into the room, his lean body moving with an animal grace that made her pulse jump. He gazed at her intently, almost like he was stalking her as she shifted back a step. "Being around you again has had me turned inside out as well."

"Me?"

"Yes, you." He moved closer, following her as she backed away until her ass bumped into the dresser. He leaned in and planted his hands on either side of her hips, caging her. "When are you going to realize that I want you for more than sex—that you have more to offer than your body?"

66

"I know damn well I have more to offer than my body." She scowled at him, trying to ignore the pounding of her heart. Any second now it was going to go right through her ribs. "If I thought that was all I had to offer why the hell would I be trying to help you find your cousin?"

"I'm not talking about street smarts, or investigative skills, Alexis. I'm talking about your heart."

"My heart?"

"Yes. Your heart. That thing in your chest that I can almost feel beating for me. Mine beats for you, you know?"

"For me?"

He smiled, his full sensuous lips lifting at the corners. His eyes were no longer a dark turbulent gray, as he stared deep into her soul. They glowed almost silver with an inner light that she'd never seen before. One that made her breath catch in her throat and her heart swell.

"You knocked my world on its ass when you seduced me in that storeroom at Jimmy D's, and it's been off kilter ever since," he continued in his deep hypnotic voice. "Just being near you again has made it clear that you and I can *not* do anything in half measures. So this is it . . . all or nothing, Alexis."

Oh God. "What do you mean?"

He pulled back and gave her some space, but his gaze never lost its intensity. "I've given you time and space, but I'm done with that. I want more than sex from you, Alexis. Your parents were killed, your first love died and left you, then you ran from your family. Do you think I don't know it's tough? I do know. I understand. But I'm done waiting. I love you, Alexis, and you need to decide if you're going to keep running scared, or if you're going to accept that we have something worth fighting for."

Pulse-pounding heat whipped through her body. Her mind froze, and all her instincts came to the fore. He loved her! He hadn't rejected her, he wasn't walking away from her. He was

67

standing right in front of her—tall, dark, and dangerously hand-some . . . and he loved her.

Years of fear she'd never admit to hit her at once. Fear that she would love him, and then something would happen. He'd leave, he'd die, something would tear him away from her like something had torn almost everyone else from her life. It had always been easier to just not let anyone get close, but Devon had somehow done that. She loved him, too.

She'd let old pain and fear keep her from new people, but it had been in self-protection. Something she'd done automatically. Hearing him spell it out like that had her realizing that she'd been a coward to cut him off. She didn't like that at all.

She didn't like the thought of losing the chance to have him in her life—to love him and be loved by him.

Without speaking she moved. Jumping on him, she wrapped her arms and legs around him and kissed him with all the bottled-up emotion inside of her. Surprised, he stumbled forward, until she was sitting on the dresser, his arms still around her as they pressed together. Lips parted, tongues rubbed and hearts mingled as they sealed the deal. Finally, Lexy pulled back and pressed her forehead against his.

"I'm in," she said. "I just hope you know what you're get-ting yourself into."

Devon grinned. "I'm getting myself into you . . . for now and forever."

He gripped her hips and pulled her tight against him, and she squirmed. His rigid cock pressed against her hungry sex and the clothing between them just added to the tease. She needed to feel him, touch him, skin to skin. Reaching between them she tugged at his shirt. They parted so she could pull it over his head, and their eyes met again. Pleasure burst through Lexy and she smiled. It was so good just to have him there, to be with him. Devon put his hands on the front of her shirt, his hot knuckles brushing against her collarbones, and raised an eyebrow. Lexy grinned and he ripped her shirt open, buttons popping off and flying in every direction.

They laughed and she threw her arms around him, pressing her nakedness against him. Bands of steel wrapped around her and they just hugged for a minute, until Devon's hands unsnapped her bra.

"Sit back," he commanded, his hands encircling her rib cage and setting her back firmly.

He stripped her of her shirt and bra, then smoothed his hands over her naked skin. A shiver rippled through Lexy and her nipples stiffened to the point of pain while his touch skimmed over her ribs, up her back, and over her shoulders. Finally he cupped her breasts in his hot hands, holding their weight, lifting them.

"Devon," she groaned, throwing her head back and arching into his touch. "Please."

His head bent, his mouth surrounding one rigid nipple while his thumb and finger began to roll and pinch the other. He suckled, he stroked, he nipped with his teeth until she was rocking against him, her moans of pleasure filling the room.

Her nails scrapped against the bare skin of his back and he groaned. Trusting him to hold her, she leaned back and let her weight fall into his arms while his mouth moved from one breast to the other, and she reached between them, going to work on his belt buckle.

Once the buckle was undone, it only took one good jerk and the button fly of his jeans was open. His cock jumped out and she groaned. Commando, God she loved that! With a groan she wrapped her hand around his cock, stroking the hot hardness until he groaned and pulled away from her breasts.

"Fuck, your touch drives me wild," he said. "Hold on."

He cupped her ass and lifted, holding her tight to him as he turned. She wrapped her legs around his waist and buried her head in his neck as he carried her to the bed. She kissed his neck, and then nipped his earlobe before sucking it into her mouth.

He stumbled. "Jesus, Alexis, I'm going to drop you."

She smiled and left his ear alone, picking the spot between his neck and his shoulder to bite gently. He groaned and she sucked. The urge to mark him was too strong to resist.

Then suddenly she was airborne, landing on her bed with a bounce.

"Christ woman, you're asking for it." He put a foot on the edge of the bed, right between her feet. His hands were visibly shaking as he worked the laces of his boots.

She grinned and started pulling her slacks off. "You bet your ass I am."

He stood, kicked off his boots, and shoved his jeans down and off. Then he yanked off her shoes and the slacks and panties that had tangled around her ankles. He spread her legs and climbed on the bed between them.

"I'm not going slow," he warned her, his voice as harsh as his breathing.

"Who asked you to?" Her heart pounded against her chest, the pulse in her pussy matching it. "Just take me, Devon. Love me."

He levered himself above her and thrust home. His guttural groan of pleasure blended with her gasp. They stilled, eyes locked, foreheads pressed together for a moment. Lexy sucked in air, trying to fill her deprived lungs as she adjusted to his size, to him.

He kissed her, his mouth covering hers as he started to move. His hips pumped slow and steady, his cock sliding almost all the way out before thrusting deep again. Lexy closed her eyes and reveled in the sensations swamping her system.

Devon's lips slid off her, he kissed her cheek, her neck, bit into the muscle of her shoulder as she arched her back and moved her hips with his.

"Look at me," he commanded, bracing himself up on his elbows and putting his forehead against hers again.

She opened her eyes and fought for breath. There was so much emotion in his gaze, so much pleasure in her body.

"I love you, Alexis. You're mine now."

"I love you, Devon," she whispered. "And you're mine now."

She wrapped her legs around his waist, curving her back and moving with him, as he slid in and out, each thrust hitting deep, the ridge of his cock scraping along the nerves of her entrance, his groin bumping her clit. It was too much. She bit her lip and pleasure exploded inside her, radiating out as her pussy clenched, hugging his cock, sucking at him as he withdrew, only to weep with pleasure when he thrust deep. His groan matched her cry as he came, his cock jerking inside her.

11

Just before eight o'clock that night the phone rang and Devon tensed. He listened to the one-sided conversation as Lexy spoke to the cop, tension balling up in his gut.

Please let it be good news, he prayed.

He knew there was nothing he could've done that afternoon, but there was still a part of him that felt guilty for spending the afternoon in bed with the woman he loved when his cousin, who'd called him for help, was missing. She was out there, probably hurting and scared, and he was finding happiness.

They were in the kitchen having just eaten the pizza they'd had delivered earlier, while simply being together.

Lexy hung up the phone and turned to him. "They've found her."

He stood, heart pounding. "They have her? Is she all right?"

"They don't have her yet. They just know where she and Salter are." She strode to the bedroom and came back with his boots and hers. "Come on, they're going to raid the Davidson warehouse in thirty minutes. Kane said we can be there when they go in."

He jammed his feet into his boots and watched as she grabbed her gun holster and stuffed it into her waistband. She snagged the car keys from the counter and they raced out the door.

"Tell me," he said once they were in the car and on their way.

"The task force that's been looking into Davidson Corporation has surveillance and taps on most of their holdings. When Kane brought Salter and Theresa to their attention, they went over some video footage from one of the warehouses, and saw Salter and Theresa being taken in at gunpoint. They're not sure what they were up to, and they didn't want to go in until they knew what was going on. But I guess Kane's convinced them Theresa and Salter are victims, not accomplices to whatever is going down, and they finally got a warrant to go in. It's happening now."

"They're going in but they don't know what's happening inside?" He tamped down his fear. "They know Theresa is a parole officer though, right? That she's basically one of them, and a hostage or something. She's not a target."

Her hand moved from the steering wheel to his thigh. She squeezed. "They know what's going on inside, they just don't want to tell us. They for sure know who Theresa is, and that she's not a target."

They didn't say any more as she drove. Devon noticed that the lights and buildings were passing by at an almost alarming rate as Alexius sped through the city streets. Soon they were in the industrial district and she slowed. Devon saw the big black SUVs and cop cars up ahead, and started to sweat.

A sentry car tried to stop them a block away and Lexy glared at the uniform cop.

"We're here by invitation. Detective Kane Michaels has okayed it." She flashed her P.I. identification at him and waited for what seemed like forever as he radioed ahead.

She could practically feel Devon vibrating next to her as the uniform handed her I.D. back and waved her forward. "Don't go past the truck, ma'am."

As soon as Lexy stopped the car, she heard the explosions and saw the flash bangs go off up ahead. Devon jumped from the car and she followed, both of them running past the trucks only to be stopped by a line of uniforms.

"Damn it!"

Lexy stood next to Devon and reached for his hand. There was a lot of yelling and then two rapid gunshots echoed through the night air. Devon's fingers squeezed hers but his gaze remained trained on the building's entrance as they waited.

Things quieted down and the Tac team started filing back out of the building, one by one. A breathless moment later, Lexy saw Kane lead a pretty brunette out and she tensed.

The strangled sound that came from Devon confirmed that the woman was indeed his cousin, Theresa.

"Kane!" She waved her arm in the air and he saw her. And Theresa saw Devon.

"Dev!" she cried as she raced toward them.

Lexy led go of her man and watched as the two met in a fierce hug that had tears welling in her eyes again.

Shit, twice in one day. She smiled through her tears. She was turning into a real crybaby.

"So you applied for a job as a security consultant with them, and they tried to hire you to hack into a competitor's mainframe?" Lexy asked.

Devon, Theresa, Salter, and Lexy were all gathered around one of the police vans as the cops finished things off. He'd wanted to take Theresa directly home, but it wasn't going to happen until Theresa and Salter went downtown and put in their official statements.

Salter nodded, looking at Theresa with adoration. "I wanted to have a fresh start. To become a man Theresa could be proud of, and that meant doing more than clerking at the all-night convenience store. Since hacking is what I know best, I thought I'd take a run at it from the other side."

"I'm proud of you no matter what you do, Steven," Theresa said, cupping a hand on his cheek, careful not to touch the freshly stitched cut over his cheekbone.

Relief at finding Theresa unharmed rode Devon hard, but he was reserving judgment on Salter. "The other side?" he prompted.

The man ducked his head. "I figure if I know how to get into almost anything, I can go in and tell the company how to protect themselves from guys like me." He shrugged. "You know, use a thief to catch a thief sort of thing."

"Not that I was ever a thief," he added when he saw Devon's frown.

"He's the best hacker in the world, Dev," Theresa said, looking at him. "If anyone knows how to protect against cyber thieves, it's him."

"I'm not the best hacker, just the most well known," Steven said with a small smile. "The best hasn't been caught."

"And you called me because after he'd turned down their offer, he noticed he was being followed?"

"I knew you would come."

"I was too late," he said tightly.

Alexis snuck an arm around his waist and leaned against his side.

"Not too late," Theresa said. "Detective Michaels told me right off that if it weren't for you and Lexy they wouldn't have come in tonight."

"You should never have been here."

Theresa left Salter's side and went to stand in front of Devon. "Steven was done creating the virus they wanted. He was almost in the other company's mainframe. If they hadn't come in tonight, I have no doubt those guys would've killed us both as soon as he was done." She glanced from Lexy to him. "If you hadn't pushed the police, we might be dead right now. You both saved us, Dev. Don't doubt it."

She hugged him and Devon closed his eyes, swallowing hard against the emotion rising up. She was safe and sound. And he owed it to Alexis.

Clearing his throat he set Theresa back a bit and looked down at his little cousin. She smiled at him and familial love swelled within him. He was so glad she was whole and healthy. Now *she* could call her family and tell them what had happened.

Lexy was tired, and even though she hated to admit it, she was a bit scared. They'd found Theresa, and she was back at her apartment, safe and sound. Steven Salter had been taken into custody, but between Kane and Theresa and his promised testimony against the Davidson Corporation, he'd be free again soon.

It was all over and she didn't know what the fuck to do about Devon. She knew what she wanted to do, and that was what scared her.

"What a night," she said as she unlocked her apartment door.

Devon followed her inside, waiting until the door had closed and they were standing in the middle of the living room before he reached out and pulled her against him. "Thank you," he said.

"You're welcome." She wrapped her arms around him and hugged him tight. "I'll always be here for you, you know?"

He pulled back a bit and looked deep into her eyes. "Always?"

She looked up at him, her chest tight and her words sticking in her throat. Unable to talk, she let down her guard and her emotions floated to the surface.

Devon's eyes widened, and she knew he was seeing what she couldn't say yet. A slow sensual grin shaped his mouth and excitement, arousal, and love swirled in his eyes. She thought she'd panic at the promise of a future with any one person, but when she looked at Devon, really looked at him, her heart settled.

She loved him. And she wanted to spend the rest of her life with him. The year without his touch had been hard, but the real torture hadn't started until she'd cut off all communications.

"I'm sorry," she said softly.

His dark brows slanted down in a fierce V. "What for?"

"For not returning your calls, for being an idiot and a coward. I'd thought cutting off communication with you would protect my heart, but all it did was hurt us both."

He leaned down and covered her lips with his. Lexy didn't hesitate, she put everything she felt into the kiss. Her hand rose up and she cupped the back of his head, holding him still as she nibbled at his lips and seduced his tongue out of hiding the same way he had seduced her fears away from her, with raw passion and complete honesty.

When she pulled back they were both breathing hard and smiling. Without another word Devon bent low, picked her up, and carried her into the bedroom. Next to the bed he stopped and let go of her legs, and she thrilled at the way her body rubbed against his.

Once her feet were on the ground again, he gripped her hips and pulled her tight to him as his head lowered and his mouth descended on hers. Their lips parted instantly and their tongues tangled as Lexy undulated against him eagerly.

Her arms went around his neck and her fingers sank into his thick hair, tangling in the silky strands and grabbing tight. "I love you," she gasped against his mouth.

"I love you," he said, reaching for the hem of her top.

Arousal fired up her blood and she stepped back, out of his arms. Desire flamed even hotter in his eyes as she began to remove her clothes.

Devon toed off his boots and stripped with her, his gaze never leaving hers. When they were both naked they reached for each other. They came together softly and Lexy hissed at the pleasure of complete skin-against-skin contact. His large work-roughened hands cupped her shoulder blades, then skimmed lightly up and down her back, sending shivers of heat whipping through her body. She clutched at his shoulders as he lowered her to the bed.

The soft mattress welcomed her and she welcomed the weight of him on top of her. It wasn't enough.

She bent her knees a little, shifted her hips and Devon lifted up a bit, then slowly slid into her body. She let out a low moan at the pure pleasure of their joining. This was where she belonged, in this man's arms.

Devon pressed a kiss to her lips before pulling back and pressing his forehead against hers. Her hands gripped his shoulders and her legs gripped his hips as he began to move—pulling out, then sliding back in, his body moving over hers in an ancient dance that touched them both.

Her rigid nipples brushed against the hairs on his chest and her nails scratched lightly down his back to his flexing buttocks.

The whimpers escaping from Alexis and the wet warmth engulfing his cock was heaven to Devon. He'd dream about being with Alexis, forever, but even his dreams couldn't compare to the reality of their connection.

They didn't speak, they didn't need to. He could see everything he'd ever wanted shining in her deep dark eyes and his heart soared.

They were such a perfect fit—for sex, for love, and for life.

"Devon," she gasped, her nails digging into his skin, her sex tightening around him. "I'm coming. Come with me."

Her inner muscles spasmed, the shock of her orgasm rippling over his cock and through to his own insides. He picked up the pace, as the base of his cock tingled and he watched as she came. She threw back her head, her back arching and her mouth opening in a wordless cry.

Thrusting deeply into her, he followed her over the edge. Every muscle in his body tightened and the whole world narrowed to just the two of them, connected, and he groaned out his release before collapsing on top of her.

They were together, and that was never going to change again.

EPILOGUE

One year later.

Lexy parked the GTO in front of the small storefront and made a run for the entrance. It was early spring and the skies had opened up to dump on them once again. Despite the wind and rain that had whipped at her hair and clothes, she was grinning when she entered the offices of Deuces Security.

Once inside she strode past the clean and uncluttered reception desk that was front and center and around the curved privacy wall. Shaking off the rain that had landed on her bare arms, she kept moving past the two desks lining each wall to the offices at the back. She bypassed the door that had her name on it and turned left into the other one.

"Steven just signed another client," she said. "A big one."

The man behind the desk grumbled something but didn't look up from his paperwork and she bit back a grin. It didn't matter how many clients Steven signed for their fledgling security company, Devon would never admit to actually liking his new cousin-in-law.

She strolled around the desk and behind his chair to massage her husband's shoulders. "Don't grumble," she said. "It was your idea to start this company, and your idea to hire him."

"Well, since you didn't want to move back to Edmonton, and I wasn't going to let you stay here without me, I figured it was silly not to keep an eye on him."

"And what better way to keep an eye on him than to hire him," Lexy finished for him.

It was a familiar sentiment and she still smiled every time she heard it.

Life had an unexpected way of turning out. She'd finally stopped running from relationships, and now she had more than that. Not only had her family grown, she had a home with a man who loved her, a full-service security company that they shared, and a damn good sex life.

If grumbling about Salter made her man feel better, then it was okay with her. But she did know another way to make him feel better. Leaning forward she nibbled on his neck.

He growled his approval and spun his chair, reaching for her and pulling her onto his lap.

"I love you, Devon Kaye," she whispered before kissing him. Then she pulled back and grinned wickedly. "Now don't you think it's time we christen this desk properly?"

Large hands wrapped around her waist and lifted her until she straddled him. "I think this is the perfect time."

UNRESTRICTED ACCESS

Jack & Jill chase after their thrills, to see who gets on top.
Jack goes down and Jill doesn't frown, even when she's under the cop.

Jack is hard but also on guard, as Jill takes all control.
He'll take the spanks and always say thanks, especially if it gets him parole.

This isn't a tourney but a sexual journey, together they'll be in luck.
Jack and Jill use leather as tether, it's good they both like to fuck.

Jack let go and Jill starts to glow, no longer a matter of trust.
It's time to play, and this time with more than just lust.

Laurie Kapkowski
Sabrina Pugliese

1

———————

The heat from the August midday sun was nothing compared to the heat that washed over Jillian Furst when she pulled into the driveway and put her shiny red SUV in park.

She'd glimpsed her neighbor's mostly naked body as she'd pulled in, and that had been enough to tweak her need. Shit, who was she kidding? All she had to do was *think* of him and her body tightened with a yearning she couldn't deny. It had been that way for the last ten months, ever since she'd moved into the cute bungalow-style house on Parker Road.

She shut off the ignition and, of its own volition, her head turned. Like a woman dying of thirst, she drank in the sight of Jackson Barrows mowing his lawn.

A couple of inches over six feet tall, he was all lean sinewy muscle and fluid grace. Wearing nothing but long boarding shorts, sunglasses, and flip-flops, the sun gleamed off his sweat-slicked skin. If that wasn't enough to make her mouth water, the tattoos that covered a good portion of his body did the trick. They hinted at a dangerous edge, a craving for adrenaline, and maybe even the need for a little bit of pain. He was her ultimate fantasy.

If only he weren't such a complete macho alpha dog.

If only the cocky grin he flashed her as she climbed out of her Jeep Liberty didn't make the butterflies in her stomach take flight.

The man was totally hot, and he knew it. It wasn't just his looks—though the dark chocolate hair, bright green eyes, and athletic body definitely did their part—it was his confidence. He was strong and sure of himself in every way . . . and the challenge of him was almost too much to resist. But resist she did.

She'd made it clear when she first met him that she'd found him attractive, and he'd been nice, but distant. Friendly, but not flirtatious. So she'd respected the invisible wall he'd put up and stopped sending out the "I'm interested" signal and they'd become friendly neighbors who exchanged casual conversation about workdays and the weather over a drink on someone's deck every now and then. She was friends with his partner's wife, and they occasionally crossed paths socially. Never once had he been without a date on those occasions.

That didn't stop her from fantasizing about him when she was alone in bed with her favorite vibrator though.

After giving him a casual wave, she opened the back door of her Jeep Liberty and reached for the three brown paper bags full of groceries. Once they were balanced in her arms she used her hip to shut the door. She took two steps toward her door, one of the bags shifted and an orange jumped for freedom. Then a second one hit the pavement running . . . well, rolling as it were.

"Shit!" She shifted the bags again, and chased the little suckers only to stop sharply when two large male hands swooped down and grabbed them.

"Thanks." She hadn't heard the mower shut off, but Jack was definitely standing in front of her in all his sweaty glory.

"No problem," he said with a lopsided grin. "Happy to be of service to a damsel in distress."

Clearing her throat, she ignored the drop of sweat that was trickling down the center of his naked chest and focused on the playful tone of his voice. Then she replied in kind, "I was hardly in distress." And of course, that's when her cell phone went off.

They stood there looking at each other for a moment, and then Jack spoke, his voice full of suppressed laughter. "Your ass is ringing."

"Gee, thanks," she said with a laugh. "You going to help me out here or what?"

"Of course." He reached a hand out, but instead of taking a bag from her, he turned her a little bit and reached into the back pocket of her denim skirt himself. His hand wiggled and pressed against her ass. Her pulse fluttered, and she bit her lip against the moan that rose in her throat.

What the hell was going on?

Jack had always been friendly, even flirty, but this behavior was taking things to a different level.

Finally, he pulled her phone out and flipped it open before holding it to her ear.

"Hello," she said, blushing at the breathlessness of the one word. Her pulse was racing and suddenly, breathing was hard because every time she inhaled the scent of his clean male sweat, her head got a little lighter, her body a little tighter.

"Hi Jillian, it's Vanessa. And I need a favor."

The pleading note in her friend's voice would've been a clear warning, if Jill had been paying attention. But she was too aware of the grinning man in front of her, and she answered automatically. "Of course, Vanessa, whatever you need."

"I need you to do a show for me at the club."

That snapped her brain back into gear. "No way."

"You said whatever I need, and I really need you to do this."

"Uh-uh. I'm sorry, Vanessa, you know that's not my thing."

Her friend rushed on, as if Jill hadn't uttered a word. "O's giving a private party for some of her friends—friends that have never come to the club, and for whatever reason she wants to have someone on stage who can be trusted to read each volunteer and not take things too far. Mistress Miranda was supposed to do it, but she had an accident when she was hiking yesterday and is now laid up with a broken leg for six weeks. The party is in three weeks, Jill! Please? I wouldn't ask you if there was anyone else with even half as much talent as you, but we both know you're the best."

The pleading in Nessa's voice was clear and Jill squeezed her eyes shut for a moment. She knew she wouldn't say no to her friend, not when she begged. But there was no reason why she couldn't make her work for it a bit more.

"If I'm the best, why did you have Miranda scheduled in the first place?"

"Because I *do* know how you feel about public shows. I wouldn't even ask you now if it wasn't really important. *Pleeeeaase?*"

Jillian sighed and opened her eyes, surprised that for a moment there she'd forgotten about Jackson standing in front of her.

She really didn't want to do a show. But she'd been so busy with her Web design business that she hadn't been out to play in over a month. It would feed her spirit if not her soul to visit The O Club and spank a few virgins.

"Fine, I'll do it," she said. "But you owe me." She told Vanessa she'd call her later to set the details and said good-bye.

Jackson's full lips twitched as he closed the phone. "What exactly are you the best at?"

"Wouldn't you like to know." She smiled and put a little sass in her tone. "If you want to know what exactly, you'll have to find out for yourself."

His smile didn't change, but something subtle flickered across his face and she wished his mirrored sunglasses didn't hide so much from her. Something had just shifted between them, she felt it and tried to get it back.

"As you've seen, one of my skills is *not* carrying a bunch of groceries without dropping some," she said lightly.

He took the hint and moved quickly. Dropping the rescued oranges and her cell phone in one of the bags, he plucked them all out of her arms. "Your wish is my command."

Her pussy clenched and she had to close her eyes and take a breath for a moment. Those words, from that man . . . God, the images that started flashing through her mind had her creaming in her panties.

"Thank you," she said. He stood, waiting patiently, until she jerked herself back to the present and headed up the walk to her front door.

"No problem. You've got a lot of food here for one person." His smile was crooked and cocky, and his voice still playful, but it didn't ring true.

Deep-seated instinct had Jill biting back the invitation for him to come in once she had her door unlocked and open. Instead, she just smiled and shrugged. "I'm not much of a cook, so I tend to buy big once a month, cook a bunch of stuff, and freeze it for later."

His brow puckered and Jill got the impression he wanted to say something, but that invisible wall was back, leaving her slightly bereft. Talk about mixed signals.

Jackson set the bags he was carrying down just inside the front door and bowed his head to her before backing away.

"My work is done here," he said, a ghost of his earlier flirtatious smirk playing at his lips. "The runaway oranges are caught, the phone is answered, and the damsel is no longer in distress. Have a good afternoon, Jill."

"Thanks again, Jackson," she called out to his retreating form.

He waved his hand, and kept on walking.

Jill shut the door and leaned against it. What the hell had just happened? She'd flirted with him before, and it had gotten her nowhere. Yet, for a few minutes there, he'd been flirting with her, heavily too. The cocky smile, the playful manhandling—God, his hand in her back pocket had just about make her knees give out. The vibe he'd been putting out had definitely been a "let's be more than friends" one.

It seemed that maybe, just maybe, her pulling back these past couple of months tweaked some sort challenge reaction in him. One he'd been unable to resist. But then he had resisted. Sure, his parting comment had been playful, and even flirtatious, but his invisible wall had been firmly back in place, making her wonder just what kind of game he was playing.

Jillian's interest spiked higher than it had ever been, and a plan began to form. She loved to play games, especially those of the erotic sort.

2

———————

"You're going down, Barrows."

Shifting his weight Jack kept his muscles relaxed while he balanced on the balls of his feet, ready to spring into action in an instant. He eyed the blond—and some would say built—man in front of him. "In your dreams, pip-squeak."

"Fuck you." Kane Michaels threw back a split second before he lunged.

Jackson's chuckle echoed through the hollow room, bouncing off the walls and drawing attention to them. Not many people would call the almost six foot wall of solid muscle in front of him "pip-squeak," but Jackson had a whacked sense of humor. Besides, Kane might have twenty pounds on him, but Jackson was taller, and he was a dirtier fighter.

A solid punch landed on his cheek, and the fight began in earnest. Fists swung out, kicks were blocked and strikes were parried as the two men matched skills. Blood heated, chased through his system by fast and furious adrenaline as sweat began to break out on his forehead.

Sucking in his gut, Jackson jumped back just in time to

avoid a hard right to his solar plexus, his own left snapping out to connect with Kane's jaw. The lightweight gloves they used offered only minimal protection, and Jackson felt that connect all the way up his arm.

Using his forward momentum he stepped in, wrapped an arm around his opponent's neck and took him to the ground.

A loud *oof!* told him he'd timed it right and Kane would be winded. They grappled briefly but Jackson quickly got the upper hand with a combination arm bar–choke hold. He applied pressure slowly until Kane grunted and tapped the mat.

Jackson's focus widened and he became aware of the sporadic clapping and voices talking around them. The gym in the basement of the downtown cop shop was busy, and they'd gained some spectators during the sparring match, as usual. His and Kane's weekly sparring match had become a bit of a ritual, with some of the other cops placing bets on who would win.

Jackson ignored them as he stood and held out his hand to Kane. His partner took it and Jackson helped him to his feet. They'd agreed long ago to never bet on their own matches, or to keep score of who won more often.

"You were lucky," Kane said with a mock scowl.

"Your grappling skills suck, Kane. I'll win every time it goes to the ground until you admit it, and let me show you some techniques."

It was true. Kane was a good cop, and a good fighter. But he was a boxer. It was the classic boxer versus martial artist debate. Kane thought a solid punch was the best offense. Jackson was more of the "whatever works, use it" school of thought. If Jackson could get him on the mat, he had the upper hand.

"Ohhh, Jackson," a fake falsetto singsonged. "Flower delivery."

Jackson pulled the small towel he'd been using away from his face and looked around. "What the hell?"

Mitchell, the desk sergeant, was sashaying toward him with

a huge vase full of flowers. A cop . . . in uniform . . . sashaying with flowers. It was a fucked-up sight that got everyone's attention.

Mitchell stopped in front of Jackson and thrust out the vase. "Flowers were delivered to the front desk for you, pretty boy."

"Is it your birthday?"

"What'd you do to rate flowers, man?"

"You're supposed to send the ladies flowers, Jack. Not make them send 'em to you."

Kane nudged him, grinning and laughing. The comments and catcalls rang in his ears, but he ignored them, flashing a self-deprecating grin. Sure, he had a bit of a reputation as a player. Women liked the way he looked and he was a single guy who enjoyed their company. But he'd never had flowers delivered before, especially to the station!

He grabbed the flowers and set them down on the bench without looking at them.

"Aren't you going to read the card?"

He glared at Mitchell who'd lifted an envelope from within the bundle. He snatched the card from the guy's hand and opened it.

I look at you and fantasize about your body being my personal playground.
Do you like to be played with?

Your secret admirer.

Heat flooded his system. Not the heat of standing in a basement full of sweaty, panting men in the middle of August, but the heat of a desire long buried resurfacing . . . hard.

"Holy shit! Are you blushing?" Kane crowed, which of course made more heat rush up Jackson's neck. "He's blushing!"

"Fuck off," he muttered to his partner. He folded up the note and clenched it in his fist before anyone could try and grab it or read it. He flipped his towel over his shoulder and started to walk away. "I'm hitting the showers."

"Aren't you forgetting something?" Kane called.

"What?"

"These."

Jackson turned to see Kane three steps behind him with the overflowing vase full of flowers in his hands.

Jillian sat in front of her computer on Monday morning, the pages of html in front of her making no sense at all. One of the perks of being a freelance Web designer was being able to work from home, and dictate her own hours. However, that didn't mean the work could be ignored completely.

"Get your mind in gear, woman," she muttered to herself. If she didn't get this site up and running by the end of the week, she could lose a valuable client, not to mention her reputation for always being as reliable as she was talented.

But it didn't work. She kept glancing at the clock and wondering if the flowers had been delivered yet. And if they had, what Jackson's reaction was.

She'd thought about him constantly after he'd left her place the night before. That in itself wasn't really unusual, she always thought about him a lot after spending time with him. But this time she knew she was going to do something about her thoughts, and she had. Sending him flowers anonymously was fun, flirty, and calculated to help her get past that damn wall he threw up every time it looked like they might get closer.

Now she just had to sit back and see how he reacted.

For some in the BDSM community sex and submission were intermingled, but not for her. She was fully capable of enjoying sex without dominating her partner, just as she didn't need sexual contact to enjoy dishing out a little pain. Jillian didn't really believe Jackson Barrows was submissive; his words had been nothing more than his sense of humor at work. But it didn't really matter, because even without the kink aspect, she really wanted to get naked with that man.

An instant message popped up in the right-hand corner of her screen and she sighed. It was truly time to stop daydreaming and get back to work.

After showering, Jackson and Kane went to work. They sat at their desks and filled out paperwork—tons of paperwork. Jackson prayed that someday the police department would get with the program and figure out a way to cut back on the paperwork so they could just do the job they were meant to do. In his case, as a detective with the Robbery and Homicide Division, that would be to go out and catch some thieves and killers.

Kane got up from his desk, walked away, and came back with a stack of printed pages. "You done the Simms report yet?"

"Five more minutes," Jackson muttered, typing as fast as he could with four fingers.

"You really should take a keyboarding class one of these days."

"I'm a cop, not a receptionist. I get by."

Kane snorted and picked up the phone. Jackson tuned out the conversation as Kane talked to his wife. He finished the report he was working on and e-mailed a copy to the Simms's insurance company. Then he sat back in his chair and stared at the flowers on his desk. The vase was clear glass, and it was overflowing with big yellow sunflowers surrounded by a shitload of white daisies.

Every cop in the building had walked by his desk at some point in the last three hours. They'd sniff at the colorful things and ask who sent them, and he'd just smiled and acted like it was a big secret. And it *was* a big secret, even to him.

Once again he racked his brain, going down a mental list of everyone he knew, trying to think of who would send him flowers.

Did he have a stalker? Shit, no. He'd have noticed someone watching him. He thought about his last lover. Shelley had been a nice girl. Not so nice that she was against sex on the first date, but still a nice girl.

He'd made it clear to her, just like he did with any woman he got naked with, that he was a no strings attached kind of guy. The women he dated knew the score, and his instincts told him that whoever his secret admirer was, it wasn't someone he already knew.

He'd never played power exchange games with any of them, and whoever sent the flowers knew exactly the right thing to say to get his blood pumping straight to his cock. Only one woman in his past had gone down—no, *taken* him down that road, and there was no way in hell Lydia would ever send him flowers. She knew better than to try and contact him ever again.

Unease made his gut tighten and Jackson glanced at Kane. He was still on the phone, not paying Jackson any mind, so he opened up a Web browser and punched in Lady Lydia's Web site address. He flipped through the site until he found the blog, and the notice that said she was out of the country on a retreat. Relief washed over him and he ground his teeth. He was an idiot. The flowers were probably someone's idea of a gag.

He looked at the stack of case files on the edge of his desk and his muscles began to twitch. He'd done enough of that shit for the day, and he couldn't just sit there any longer. Opening the side drawer of his desk, he grabbed his gun and stood up. As he tucked the holster onto the waistband behind his back, he glared down at his partner. "I'm going to the bakery. Meet me out front in five."

3

They had to follow up with a couple of witnesses on two open cases, one a convenience store robbery that would probably never be solved, and the other a home invasion where the dog was shot dead. The homeowners were very upset at the dog's death, and since they were of the wealthy West-Van set, they were making a big stink.

Jackson figured the victims should be pissed at the gated community's security more than at the cops. After all, they were prevention, the cops were never called until *after* something went wrong, but some people weren't that smart. And Jackson needed coffee—good coffee, not station house slop, in order to deal somewhat cordially with stupid people.

"Morning, sugar," he said to the plump blonde behind the bakery's counter. "Two large coffees, please. One double double and one black."

She smiled shyly, not meeting his eyes as her cheeks turned pink. "Would you like a bagel, too?"

"Not today," he glanced at her nametag. "Linda. Thanks anyway."

She nodded and went to work filling the order. He wasn't surprised she remembered him. Either he or Kane made the trip into the bakery across the street from the police station house at least once a day.

"Here you are." Linda set two distinctive yellow and red paper cups down and slid them across the counter.

He held out a ten-dollar bill for her but she shook her head, blushing fiercely as she finally met his gaze. "They're on me today."

A lightbulb went on in his head and for a split second he wondered if she was his secret admirer. Linda was hitting on him for sure, but was she really bold enough to do something like send him flowers? Especially with a note like the one in his pocket? *No way.*

"I'm sorry, sugar. I can't let you do that." He put his charming smile on. "I appreciate the offer though."

They both knew he was turning down more than free coffee, but she smiled, made change, and wished him a good afternoon.

With steaming cups in hand he walked away from the counter. A pretty redhead was going in when he was going out and she flashed him a bold smile and rubbed against him slightly in the doorway. By the time he got to the car Kane had parked in front of the door he could see his partner laughing at him.

"What is it with you and women?" he asked when Jackson was settled in the passenger seat.

He shrugged. "They love me, what can I say?"

"They don't love you, they don't know you. For whatever reason, they find your ugly mug appealing, but I just don't get it."

It was true. Women liked the way he looked, they always had. But he didn't take them up on their offers nearly as much as he could've. Mainly because, aside from his hellish mistake with Lydia, he'd yet to meet a woman he wanted for more than a night or two, three at the most.

The image of a petite redhead in a short denim skirt and yellow halter flashed into his mind.

He shook his head. When Jill had moved in next door to him, he'd ignored the instinctive attraction she held for him as well as her subtle come-ons. He'd gone down the relationship road once before, and it wasn't going to happen again. Every time he went into the bedroom with a woman, he made sure she knew it was only for a good time, not a long time. He figured it was better to just be platonic and have good neighbor relations than to get laid. It was only natural she'd show up in his fantasies occasionally simply because she was off-limits.

It was normal to want what you couldn't have.

"Three more days, Jack," Kane said as he pulled out of the parking lot. "Then we get two weeks off. Can you believe it?"

"I'm ready for it, that's for sure."

"You got big plans? Don't forget we're having a barbecue for Nessa's birthday on Saturday. I expect you to be there, with a present for my wife."

A present for his wife? "Any suggestions? What does one give an ex-thief."

Kane glared at him. "There was never any evidence she was the thief."

But they both knew she had been. It didn't matter to Jackson, Nessa wasn't robbing anyone anymore. At least she wasn't a psycho.

The meeting with the home invasion victims had gone as well as expected, and Jackson was grumpy as hell.

"Idiots," he muttered as they got back into Kane's car.

"Not idiots," Kane said. "Just rich, spoiled, and used to everyone always making sure everything is perfect for them."

"They act like they pay our wages. Like they're better than us." He looked over at his partner, in his fashionable dress pants and button-up shirt. "Well, they act like they're better than me. They loved *you*."

Kane grimaced and put the car in drive. "Friends of my father, what can I say?"

Jackson didn't say anything. The two of them were from opposite ends of the social stratum. Kane's family was rich, well known, and political. Jackson's family was spread throughout multiple provinces, housed mostly in penitentiaries. He was a cop, the black sheep among the Barrows clan. Which is why he didn't much talk to any of them except maybe on Christmas.

Either way, he'd been partners with Kane for four years now, and he knew better than to judge Kane by his family connections.

They turned down Commercial Drive and Jackson thought about the note card in his pocket. He lived not far from here, and he'd recognized the name of the flower shop.

"Stop just up there, will ya?" he asked Kane.

With nothing more than a look, Kane pulled the car over and parked in front of the Best Buds Flower Store. Jackson climbed out of the car. "I'll be right back."

Kane was already pulling the keys from the ignition. "If you think I'm going to miss out on this, you're nuts."

Jack didn't argue with him. If he argued, it would just make his partner more stubborn. Plus, it wouldn't do any good. "Just let me do the talking."

He pushed though the glass door and went straight to the counter. There was a plump lady ordering flowers to be delivered to her mother in front of him, so he stood as patiently as he could with his hands in his pockets as Kane smirked at him from the doorway.

The girl working the counter was . . . distinctive. Her short black hair hugged her scalp and matched the black makeup circling her eyes. All that black, with her pale complexion, made her red lips stand out even more. The stark markup was almost enough to distract from the chain around her neck.

It was silver chain link, with a little padlock at the base of her throat. The sight of that chain made Jackson's pulse start to race.

Memories of a leather collar being put around his neck. The pride he'd felt in wearing it, the comfort he'd felt in his acceptance . . . and the trust he'd had for the woman who'd put it on him. The woman who'd seen him as nothing more than a piece of meat to be toyed with for her own amusement.

"Thank you, young lady," the woman in front of him said as she finally put her wallet away, picked up her overstuffed purse, and started for the exit. "You were much more helpful than I thought you'd be."

The clerk rolled her eyes and smiled at him so Jackson stepped up to the counter.

"Hi there," he said, flashing her his patented charming smile. "There were some flowers delivered to the police station earlier today. Did you handle the order?"

She folded her hands on the counter in front of her and smiled. "Yes, sir I did."

"I'd like to see it, please."

"Nothing to see, she paid cash."

"So it was a she?"

The girl's lips twisted into a smirk. "Yes, sir."

"Can you describe her?"

"Yes."

They stared at each other for a minute, Jackson impatient, the girl placid—except for the twinkle of merriment dancing in her dark eyes.

"Well?" he prompted.

"Well, what?"

"You said you could describe her."

"I can, but I'm not going to."

He shifted his weight, straightening up and leaning forward. "Excuse me?"

She widened her eyes and spoke as if she were talking to an idiot. "I'm. Not. Going. To."

A muffled snort sounded from behind him and Jackson turned to glare at his partner. Then he turned back to the counter girl and narrowed his eyes at her. "You're obstructing an investigation here. If you know who sent those flowers, you need to tell me. *Now*."

"Oh, come off it," she said with a wave of her hand. "You're going to ruin everything if you keep this up. She likes you, dude! And she's a good woman. Nice and classy, and sexy as hell. You should be thanking God she wants to play with you."

Kane laughed outright and Jackson folded his arms across his chest and glared—at them both.

"Do you know her?" he asked, flicking his eyes to her collar meaningfully. "Personally."

"She's a regular customer in here, comes in weekly to buy flowers for herself," she shrugged. "But yeah, I've seen her around outside the store as well. She's a lady."

Kane slapped him on the shoulder. "C'mon, Jack. Let it go. You've got yourself a secret admirer. Enjoy it." He nudged Jackson aside and smiled at the counter girl. "Do you have more roses in the back?"

"Sure, but there are some right there." She pointed to a cooler along the left wall.

Kane glanced at them then shook his head. "Do the ones in the back still have the thorns?"

Jill was just pulling her dinner out of the microwave oven when the phone finally rang. She snatched it up and answered before it could ring again. "Well?"

"He came in, just like you said." Grace's laughter was clear over the phone line. "You should've seen his face when I told him I could tell him who you were, but I wasn't going to. It was priceless!"

"But he let it go? He doesn't know?"

"He has no idea. His partner stepped in and told him to leave it alone. Then he ordered a dozen roses, *with* thorns, to be sent to the club for Nessa." Grace paused. "I had no idea her husband was such a hottie. It's no wonder she never brings him to the club."

Jillian laughed. "He goes in all the time, but rarely on members-only nights. He just sits at the bar and has a beer, so he can talk to her when it's quiet. Kane is not into the scene at all."

"Too bad. He could totally top me anytime."

Jillian wasn't going to get into that conversation with Grace. The girl was young, and very eager, and Vanessa and Kane's life was private . . . just like she preferred to keep her own. "Thanks for keeping my secret, Grace. I'll out myself to Jackson soon, but—"

"But he needs to be taken down a notch or two first. I get it."

That wasn't what she was going to say, but it worked. "Okay, so tomorrow your guy will deliver the coffee I left with you today?"

"Yep, I'll send it out with the morning run."

"Thank you. I'll be sure to tell Master Greg you've been a wonderful help."

"Thank you."

She hung up the phone and did a little victory jig around the kitchen. He got them, and he was hooked! The temptation to call Kane and see how Jackson had reacted was strong. So very strong, but she resisted. This was between her and Jackson. The less people involved the better.

It occurred to her as she sat at the breakfast counter and ate her microwaved macaroni and cheese that she was going through a lot of effort for what could be nothing more than a one-time experience. But some things were worth the time and effort, even if they weren't meant to last. Besides, having one night with her hot and sexy neighbor was something she'd fantasized about too often to not put a little effort in.

4

"Oh, Jackson."

The falsetto rang through the crowded room and Jackson cringed deep inside. It was Wednesday afternoon, two days after the flowers from his secret admirer had arrived. There'd been no delivery the day before and he'd done his best not to be disappointed. Now, that falsetto had him both cringing and cheering.

Yep, he was a little fucked up.

Mitchell set a wicker basket with a large handle on it on the corner of his desk. "Another delivery for you, pretty boy. And this one smells gooood."

Ignoring the small crowd that had gathered, Jackson sat forward and pulled the basket toward him. It did smell good, and when he lifted up the royal blue cloth that covered the basket's contents, he saw why.

"Aww, man. How come you're so lucky?"

"You're going to share right? You can't have that in here and not share."

The basket was full of cookies. Fresh, home-baked cookies with huge chocolate chunks clearly visible. Next to the open container of cookies was a bag of gourmet coffee, and tucked between the coffee and the edge of the basket was a distinctive blue envelope.

Ignoring the guys, he tugged the envelope out from the edge of the basket. Then he reached in and grabbed three cookies and the bag of coffee before pushing the basket away. "Help yourself."

The cookies were still warm, and when he bit in, he had to bite back a groan of pleasure. Some of the other guys weren't so quiet as they walked away with their hands and mouths full.

Once they were no longer standing at his desk, he opened the envelope and pulled out a small card.

You are going to come to me. And when you reach my door you will find a blindfold hanging on the doorknob and the door open a crack. Enter the room, close the door behind you, and put on the blindfold. Then wait there quietly for me.

I'll lead you into the center of the room. "Stand still," I tell you. "You are my personal playground . . . and I want to play uninterrupted."

My hand reaches out and I trail my fingers across your shoulders as I stroll around your body. I start to undress you at my leisure, stroking your muscles, nibbling on your ear, your neck. Pressing my body's full length against yours. The feel of your heart pounding in your chest is strong under my hand as I scrape my nails lightly across your nipple.

You feel my breasts against your chest, my nipples hardening as they rub against the hair on your body as I sink to my knees and examine your cock. Looking at it, breathing on it, I touch it lightly, lick it and—no! I won't suck it now . . . that will be your reward for behaving . . . if you continue to do so.

It is time for you to work . . . I lead you over to the couch and sit down.

"On your knees," I command.

I spread my thighs for you and tell you to get on your knees and use only your mouth to please me, no hands. Do you think you can do that? Do you think you can make me come with only your lips and tongue? I hope you can . . . for your sake.

Once you have gotten me ready I am going to lay you down and straddle you. Slip that hard cock into my wetness and ride you until I come. You may not come! Remember . . . you are MY playground.

If I feel you have behaved well I will reward you. What that reward is will be a surprise . . . one I know already you will enjoy. But if you misbehave . . . the punishment will be something I enjoy!

555-4378

Show me how good you can be, and don't try to trace my phone number. Just use it when you get home tonight.

Your secret admirer

Jackson stared at the number on the note and bit into another cookie. The second cookie tasted a little different—a little off. He flipped it over and chuckled at the slightly charred bottom.

So his secret admirer was smart, intriguing, and not the best cook. His mind whirled and a slow grin spread across his face. He knew who it was.

He went back and forth in his mind on if he was actually going to call the number on the note or not. And finally, just before the eleven o'clock news came on Wednesday night, he dialed.

She answered on the first ring.

"Hello Jackson," a husky voice said clearly.

"This is a little unfair, you know," he said, keeping his voice natural. He was pretty sure he was talking to Jillian, but he'd done as the note asked and *not* traced the number, so he wasn't one hundred percent sure. "I don't even know what to call you."

"What would you like to call me?"

"What's your name?"

"I'm going to make you a promise right now, Jackson. I'll never lie to you. And because I always keep my promises, I'm not going to tell you my name right now. You can call me whatever you want."

"Sneaky bitch?"

Her husky laugh made him smile, despite himself. "If you like."

"Naughty wench?"

"How about Miss J?"

His cock twitched. "That works."

"Did you like the gifts?"

"Yes, thank you."

"I know flowers are an untraditional gift for a man, but they always make me feel special. So, I thought maybe they would do the same for you."

Strangely enough, they had. It wasn't the flowers themselves, either. He could take or leave them. It was the way they were given to him. He'd never had anyone put so much effort into getting his undivided attention before. Normally women just flashed a smile, flaunted their cleavage, or offered to buy him a drink, whether it's coffee or a beer in a bar.

The deliveries didn't feel as superficial as the normal pickups.

"They certainly got my attention." He paused. She sounded

sane and normal, and very sexy. His instincts said she wasn't a psycho. However, he wasn't an idiot. He needed to know if it was indeed Jill. "The coffee was very nice, too. How did you know I drink coffee?"

There was that husky chuckle again. "I know you Jackson, Just as you know me. I'm not a crazy psycho stalker or anything. I'm just a woman, who finds you very intriguing and attractive."

Gotcha! "We know each other?"

"Casually, yes."

"Then why the secret admirer thing? Why not just talk to me?"

For a minute all he heard was her breathing, and he wondered if she'd answer honestly.

"You have a wall, Jackson. An invisible wall that you throw up every time it seems like the attraction between us rises. I wanted to go over that wall, and see if maybe we could explore that attraction for a night."

There was so much in that sentence that he wanted to deny, and even more he wanted to explore. He'd start with the important things first. "A night?"

"I told you, I know you. Yes, just one night. A night of erotic exploration . . . of fantasy."

He dropped into his favorite recliner and closed his eyes. "What kind of fantasy?"

"I've masturbated to fantasies of having your naked body at my mercy. Of blindfolding you before stripping your clothes off, bit by bit, then teasing us both with light touches. I want to search out your hot spots, play with them a little until you can't hold back a groan of pleasure. Then I'd move on, find another spot, touch you somewhere, taste you somewhere else. See what makes your cock swell and your breath catch."

Jackson pressed the palm of his hand against the straining fly of his jeans. "You seem to have found that already."

"Are you hard?"

"Oh, yeah." He pulled the button of his jeans open and had the zipper tab between his fingers when her next words froze him.

"Don't touch yourself, Jackson," she said sharply. "Not yet."

His mind slowed, his cock throbbed, and a shiver ripped down his spine. "Christ," he muttered.

"Jackson?" The sharpness had left her voice, and he could hear Jill now. The way she'd said his name was unmistakable. He'd heard that sharpness in her tone before, and he'd responded to it subconsciously.

It was why he'd always fought his attraction to her, it wasn't because she was his neighbor, it was because she had that vibe. Because she was a dominant woman, and she called to that part of himself that he'd buried long ago.

"Answer me, Jackson. Are you all right?"

Sucking in his breath he sat up straight and stiffened his mental reserves. "Yeah," he said. "I'm fine. You just caught me by surprise."

Rustling sounds echoed over the phone and he could imagine her resettling into her chair. Crossing her legs at the knee, the top leg firm against the bottom. No nervous bouncing for her. She would be still . . . in control.

"So . . ." When she finally spoke again, her voice was husky. "That's the start of my fantasy night with you. Does it appeal to you?"

"Yeah." It appealed to him on such a visceral level that it scared him. After Lydia, he'd sworn he'd never let another have that much control over him again. But he knew Jill. She was certainly strong and confident, almost serene in her own way. And she was only asking for one night.

One fantasy night.

Could he really say no?

He cleared his throat. "Would you like to come over, Miss J?"

5

Calm washed over Jillian as she stepped out of the shower. She was ready for this—she wanted this. Smoothing unscented lotion over her skin, she let her mind wander back over her conversation with Jackson. Sure, she thought her secret admirer seduction would work, she wouldn't have done it if she hadn't thought that. But it had worked better than she'd anticipated, on both of them. The plan had been to talk to him on the phone, feel him out, seduce him some more, and maybe even have phone sex. The first contact so to speak. But his invitation to come over to have their one-time fantasy night right then had been a surprise.

One she was unable to resist.

She had trouble deciding what to wear. Did she want to wear something sexy, or casual? Would sexy be too much, casual too little?

"You're so overthinking this. It's one night woman, wear something easy to take off, and get your ass over there."

After she'd dressed in a tank top and shorts, she slid her feet into sandals and double-checked her appearance. The excited gleam in her eye matched the adrenaline rushing through her system.

She grabbed the blindfold from her arsenal of toys and tucked it into her back pocket before heading out the door. Each step that brought her closer to Jackson's door brought home the worry that he would take one look at her and say, *"No way!"*

She didn't think he would, but there was the possibility. He had to have his reasons for always distancing himself from her when their attraction sprang up, and she could only hope that her promise of it being for only one night would get him past that.

Sucking in a deep breath, she pulled her shoulders back and pushed the doorbell next to his mailbox.

Before the last echo of the door chime had faded, the door opened and Jackson filled the entrance in nothing but soft faded jeans that had the top button already undone.

"Wow." The word came out a whisper of awe and he grinned.

"Are you going to come in, or just stand there and drool?"

Her gaze snapped up to his and she laughed. "Oh, I think I'll come in. My hands are already itching to touch."

"Tingling is good," he said, stepping back and letting her pass by him. "Touching is good, too."

She was surprised at the playful banter, at his lack of surprise and the automatic acceptance of what they were about to do.

She moved into the living room and turned to face him. "You're not surprised to see me." It wasn't a question.

He nodded. "I figured it was you."

"When? How?" She frowned at him. "You didn't cheat and trace my cell number or anything did you?"

"The cookies gave it away. You did a good job scraping the black off, but they tweaked my brain. The other day when you had all those groceries you said you weren't much of a cook,

114

and I remembered some of the cookies you brought to the Andersons' Christmas party were burnt on the bottom."

She should've known. Jackson was a cop, and a good one. No way would he invite someone he didn't know—or hadn't met in person—over to his house to have sex. "That didn't stop you from eating them all," she pointed out.

"And it didn't stop me from eating them this time either."

She shrugged. "I'm not the only woman who burns cookies every now and then."

His expression turned serious and he stepped forward, moving into her space and lifting a hand to brush against her cheek. "I'm sure. But you are the only woman I know who burns cookies, and can get me hard with just a look."

Something unexpected fluttered in her chest and she ignored it. This night wasn't about hearts, it was about bodies. And it was time to get it started.

"Then step back and let me look," she said, injecting some command into her tone.

His green eyes flashed and he stepped back, holding his hands out to his sides. "Your personal playground awaits you."

Pulling the blindfold out from her pocket, she slapped it against her thigh. His gaze flicked to it and his Adam's apple bobbed in his throat. "I did mention blindfolding you," she said as she moved around him, slowly.

"Yes, you did."

He turned with her and she put a hand on his shoulder. "Stand still for me, please."

He didn't say anything, but Jillian felt the ripple that went through him. Was it apprehension, or excitement?

God, she wanted to touch him. She wanted to scratch his back, pinch his nipples, and slap his ass. The need to strip him bare and make him hers was strong. But he was hers for one night only, and that meant controlling her needs. She had to remember that this was just for fun. Jackson wasn't some subbie boy she'd taken for a night of play at the club. He was her neighbor, her friend, and she wanted things to remain that way after their fantasy night. She had to keep things light.

Keeping her tone playful, she moved things forward. "Want to show me your bedroom?"

He grinned. "I want to show you more than my bedroom, Miss J."

She gave his shoulder a playful push and he grabbed her hand, leading her up the carpeted stairs to the second floor of his house. As she followed him up the stairs, his denim-clad ass was right in front of her and saliva pooled in her mouth. Lifting a hand she smacked a firm cheek. "Hurry up."

He laughed and picked up the pace. Seconds later she was in the middle of Jackson Barrows's bedroom, standing at the foot of a large king-size bed.

"Very nice," she said. She held the blindfold out to him. "Ready to play?"

Without a word, he took the blindfold from her and slid it on. Part of her regretted the loss of his eyes but it would be worth it. Losing one sense always heightened the others, and she wanted Jackson to be sensitive to every touch. Starting slow she kept up a steady stream of conversation as she touched him.

"You have a very nice body, Jackson," she said, reaching out and trailing a hand over the jungle scene with a black panther that covered one shoulder blade. "Lean, yet still muscled. There's no doubt in my mind that you're strong. And look at all these tattoos. Do you like them because of how they look, or how it feels when the needles dig into your skin?"

He shrugged. "A little bit of both. It doesn't hurt, and I like them."

"I like the tribal one that starts on this shoulder." She touched

116

the top of the deep black scrollwork, scraping her fingernail over his skin as she followed the ink work down over his chest to where it circled his nipple. She leaned forward and followed the scrape of her nail with the tip of her tongue. Down his hard muscle to the flat nipple. She licked the little nub and felt him jerk. She sucked the nipple into her mouth and his hands reached out blindly for her.

Pulling back, Jillian trailed a finger down the center of his chest to the waist of his jeans. "You're perfect you know, a little bit of body hair, but too much." She gave the soft fuzz on his lower abs a little tug. "You know what I call this? The treasure trail."

His lips lifted at the corner and she stepped forward, brushing her body against his, her lips against his as she spoke. "And this"—she moved her hand down and cupped him through his jeans—"is the treasure."

"Christ," he groaned. His hands slid up her back and held her to him, his mouth slanting over hers in a demanding kiss. She knew she should stop him. She hadn't initiated the kiss, hadn't given him permission to kiss her. But she couldn't pull away. Instead she savored his taste and the strong male moment of possession as his tongue thrust between her lips and danced with hers.

Slowly, oh so slowly, he pulled back. Their breaths mingled as she pressed her forehead to his. His heart pounded against her hand on his chest, and his cock throbbed through his jeans. She squeezed him, and he groaned again, the sound of his pleasure making her pussy cream. Regaining control of her senses she squeezed him harder until he froze, his body stiffening, his breath stopping. "I didn't give you permission to kiss me, Jackson."

"Sorry," he muttered, anger clear in his voice. "I'm sorry, Mistress. I couldn't help myself."

Breathing hard, Jillian let her grip loosen so that she was only holding him. Something had happened right then, and she realized she'd hit a button for him. His automatic use of the title "Mistress" surprised her, and beneath the anger in his voice, there was a thread of fear. She'd need to think about that later, for right now, she just wanted to get them back on the right track.

She kissed his lips gently, then pulled back a step and stood still. "You can make it up by undressing me," she commanded lightly.

He reached for the blindfold and she slapped his hand away. "Uh-uh," she reprimanded in a light and playful tone. "You don't need your eyes to strip me of a tank top and pair of shorts. Keep that on."

His mouth opened and then snapped shut. He shuffled forward one step and reached for her. She stood still as his hands found her rib cage, then hesitated there for a moment. She could almost see him thinking of reaching for her breasts, but he held back, and his hands moved to the hem of her shirt, lifting it off. He dropped her shirt on the floor and his hands skimmed down her naked front. She bit her lip, swallowing the gasp when his palms skimmed over her rigid nipples.

"Just checking for a bra," he said, lips twitching into a smile.

"No bra, and no panties. Just the shorts left."

His knuckles brushed over her belly as he searched for the snap on her shorts and she cursed silently. Why had she told him to strip her? He was moving so slow, and all she wanted was to get her hands back on his body!

"Now your pants," she said, her voice husky with repressed desire.

When they were both naked she pressed her body against his and they both groaned. His hands slid up her waist and over her back, pulling her tighter to him and she shivered. God, he felt so damn good!

She knew she should be going slower, she should be enjoying having this man naked in front of her, toying with him, teasing him and stoking his passion higher and higher until he begged. But right then, she was the one who was ready to beg.

Control, she told herself. *Restraint only makes it better.*

She only had one night, and she was going to make it last.

He reached up to remove his blindfold and she pulled back. "Stop!"

He froze, and a rush of adrenaline flooded her muscles. "Hands at your sides, Jackson. I'm not done playing with you."

She saw the struggle in the set of his jaw, the clench of his fists, but he did as she asked and pleasure swept through her. She looked at his body and wished she had her bag of toys. So firm, so strong, and so hard. Long and thick, his cock jutted out from a nest of black curls, already hard enough to be bouncing against his belly.

Bending down, she made sure he could feel her breath on his cock as she cupped her hands around his muscled calves, and ran them slowly up his legs. Up the back, soft, skimming him so lightly the body hair just brushed the palms of her hands. Bringing her hands to the front, she hooked her fingers like claws and scraped her nails down the front of his legs. Jackson hissed and his cock jumped.

"Ooh, you like that," she murmured.

He didn't answer, but he didn't need to.

Standing up, she put her hands on his naked hips and eased him back until his knees hit the bed. "Are you comfortable, Jackson?"

"Comfortable?" he asked. "I'll be more comfortable when I'm buried inside your hot cunt."

Said cunt clenched in response to his words and her lips twisted. She threw out a mental prayer of thanks for the blindfold he was wearing. His alpha tendencies were showing. "If you're good, you'll be feeling more than comfortable in a while."

"Good?"

"Yes. I want you to talk to me. I want you to tell me how everything I do feels." She pinched a nipple and his back arched off the bed. "How does that feel, Jackson?"

His mouth opened and closed and Jillian had the split-second fear that she'd misjudged. Then he spoke.

"Good," he said. "It felt good."

She pinched it again, adding a little twist. "Just good?"

"Fuck, yes," he gasped.

Moving her hand to the other nipple, she stroked a finger around the areola playfully. "And this?"

"Nice." His head rolled against the mattress. "But harder is better."

"That's it," she murmured, pinching and twisting the nipple in reward. "Have you ever thought about getting your nipples pierced? I think you'd enjoy that."

He didn't answer her and she stepped back, taking her hands off his body. He froze on the bed, and then raised his head up. "Jillian?"

She waited a beat before answering. "You didn't answer my question, Jackson."

His head fell back against the bed and she saw his jaw move as he ground his teeth. "No, I've never thought about piercing my nipples."

Figuring he'd had enough teasing and it was time to get serious, Jillian moved forward. Pressing her knees against the edge of the bed between his, she leaned forward. The tips of her breasts brushed against his chest and his hands once again went to her hips.

"I'm going to suck your cock now, Jackson," she whispered, her lips brushing against his ear. "I want you to keep your hands to yourself, and I want you to talk to me while I do this."

"Sounds good to me," he said, spreading his hands out at his sides. "I'm all yours."

Jillian smiled, her body scraping along his as she slid to her knees. Her shoulders nudged his legs apart and she reached out, taking his cock in her hands.

He sucked on a sharp breath and groaned. "So good, baby. Your touch feels wonderful." Pushing his hips a little deeper into the bed, he spread his thighs a little wider.

Jillian pulled his cock to the left and licked the soft skin where leg meets torso on the right. She tongued the soft skin of his sac, before sucking his balls into her mouth—and she wasn't gentle about it.

"Oh, God," he moaned. His thighs trembled and lifted a little, giving her more room, better access.

Her hand rode his cock as she rolled his balls around with her tongue for a minute before letting them slide from her lips. Licking up the underside of his cock she took him in her mouth, loving his groan of satisfaction.

She wrapped her lips around him and slid down as far as she could. It filled her up and her hand still had room to grip the base. She kept her head still and swirled her tongue around with a little suction. His hips started to slowly thrust in her mouth, his cock hitting the back of her throat.

"So good," he said. "So hot, so wet. Christ, Jill. I c-can't take much of this."

The stutter almost undid her. She closed her eyes, breathed in his scent, and began to suck in earnest. Putting her free hand on his hip, she made him still his movements as she began to rise and lower her mouth on him, picking up speed. Cum was leaking from him in a small steady stream and things were getting messy. Her saliva mixed with his cum, slicking him, coating her chin and her hand.

"Oh, god, don't stop. Please don't stop."

Her heart pounded and her pussy throbbed. Please, he'd said please so naturally and it got to her. Her breath rasped in and out through her nose and she went faster and faster. His cock hit the back of her throat and his moans and groans filled the room. Power sang through her veins, fueling her own lust as she worked his cock. She waited until it thickened even more, the heated throb intensifying as his balls swelled in her hand and then she pulled back, ringing the base of his cock with one hand and squeezing, holding back his orgasm.

"Arghhh," he groaned, his fists bunching in the bedsheets, but not reaching for her. "Christ, Jillian!"

She licked her lips, tasting him there, and struggled to keep her voice calm. "Breathe through it, Jackson."

His chest rose and fell, his breath panting into the room like a bellows. When she felt the change in his body and knew he wasn't going to blow immediately, she let go of his cock and leaned back on her heels.

"That's it, my man." She stood up, then moved onto the bed, straddling his body. "You did good, Jackson. Talking to me, and letting me play like that."

He was silent, and she sensed him struggling with something within himself. Part of her wanted to push, to push past that wall that he always built between them. She could feel it starting to grow again, brick by brick. But another part of her worried that they'd need that wall when the night was over, so she didn't push.

Instead, she gripped his rock-hard cock and rubbed the head against her slick entrance. "You said you'd be more comfortable buried in my cunt . . ."

She slid down, moaning as the head of his cock breached her entrance and filled her up. They fit together perfectly, and in that instant Jillian knew that Jackson felt it, too.

Leaning forward she braced her hands on his chest, kissed his open mouth softly, and spoke clearly. "Kiss me, Jackson. Fuck me."

With a low groan of surrender Jackson let go of the covers and slid his hands around her to cup her ass. He raised his head and covered her mouth with his. Jillian wiggled and squirmed against him, her tongue dancing against his, his unique flavor blending with the taste of his sex and filling her head.

He started to move his hips, thrusting up and matching his rhythm to hers as she rode him. She dragged her mouth away from his, sliding over his jaw to his neck. She nipped at his skin, bit his earlobe, and thrilled at his growl of pleasure. He groaned, his hips jerking under her as his hands moved up her back and around to wedge between them and cup her breasts.

Wrapping her fingers in his silky hair she tugged sharply, pulling his head back to gain better access to his throat. She zeroed in on the spot behind his ear and felt a tremor ripple through him when she licked it. Her pussy clenched and she ground against him in response, the nails of her other hand digging into his chest.

"Come on, Jack," she said, sitting up and bouncing on his cock harder. "I told you to fuck me, not just lay there."

His lips parted, showing his teeth gritted together in a silent growl as he braced his feet on the bed, and pumped his hips upward.

"God, you're an animal aren't you?" he gasped.

"I'm a woman, Jackson," she said. "And I want you to make me come."

His hands gripped her waist and he held her, his hips pistoning up and down as he panted like a freight train. His thick cock rammed up into her again and again and her sex tightened, the first tremors of an orgasm gaining power within her. "Yes, Jackson, like that. Just like that, my man."

"Jill!"

At the panic in his voice she closed her eyes and welcomed the rush of pleasure that washed over her. "Come with me, Jackson!" she cried out.

His guttural grunts filled her head as he pumped once, twice more and then buried himself deep as he came, flooding her sex with his hot semen.

More satisfied than she'd been in years, she collapsed on top of him and buried her head in his neck. His strong arms wrapped around her, holding her close as they both drifted off to sleep, still locked together.

Holy hell, Jillian thought as she stared down at the still sleeping man.

Dawn was coming soon, and he lay dead to the world in the middle of his very big, very rumpled bed. She knew she should wake him, say good-bye. Say thank you. But she couldn't do it. He'd surprised her in more than one way during the night. It had been better than any fantasy. He'd known who she was, he'd accepted her lead, and followed where she'd led. He'd been so ready for her, so responsive.

The blindfold, the sampling of submissive play, it had definitely been play for him, but his responses to her touch had been beyond play. She'd been a little rougher than she'd planned. And he'd relished it. Could he possibly have a submissive tendency? Maybe even a taste for sensation, for pain.

Jillian's heart pounded and her completely satisfied body stirred at the thought of really playing him. But it wasn't to be. They'd agreed on one night, and that night was over.

She blew him a kiss and left the room, and his house.

6

On Friday afternoon Jackson fought the urge to bang his head against the wall of the basement gym. What the hell was he doing? How could one tiny woman turn him inside out so damn easily?

He centered his weight and let his fist fly. The heavy bag bounced on its chain and swung back. Jab, cross. Jab, cross, hook. Duck, shuffle, jab, jab, cross.

"Jack!" Something hit his shoulder and he spun around, fist already in motion.

Kane leaned back sharply and held up his hands. "Whoa buddy."

Shit, he had to stop just reacting to things and get his fucking head on straight.

"Sorry, man. I was in the moment." What else was he going to say? *Sorry, buddy, I'm as strung out as a fucking addict so don't touch me?*

"You okay?" Kane asked.

"Yeah, I'm good." He looked at his partner. "What's up?"

"Nothing, I was just wondering why you're down here

hammering on the heavy bag when you already had your workout this morning."

"Just thinking some."

"Thinking about why you were such a moody bastard yesterday?"

"Leave it alone." He turned away and headed for the locker room.

Kane left it alone for all of two seconds before he followed, close on Jackson's heels.

"It's our last day on shift before a week off and you're spending your lunch hour in the basement gym working up a sweat. I know you're a moody son of a bitch, but this is more than that." He stopped before they got to the showers and grabbed Jackson's arm. "Tell me what's going on."

Jackson turned to his partner and snarled. "Leave. It. Alone."

"Fine," Kane said, and let him go.

He knew Kane was just trying to be a friend, but right then he didn't need a friend. He needed a fucking shrink.

Stripping off his clothes he stepped into the shower stall and cranked the water on, shaking off the first jolt of the icy spray. He could not get Jillian out of his head, and it was driving him crazy. Wednesday night had been amazing, and he hated himself for enjoying it so much. For being so weak as to get off on letting a woman control him in the bedroom.

But Jillian hadn't been controlling, not like Lydia had been. That was where things got all messed up in his head. Lydia Carson had been the only woman he'd thought he'd loved. She was also the only woman he'd ever let control him.

It had all started simply enough. They'd dated, and in the bedroom she'd liked to tie him up. It was ten years ago, and he'd been a young twenty-two at the time. Growing up in a small town hadn't prepared him for a woman like Lydia. He'd been a bit awed by her, an older woman, so strong and worldly and adventurous . . . so confident sexually. She'd taught him a lot about himself, with her floggers and paddles, her nipple clamps and cock rings. He'd fallen in love with her, and reveled in the joy of serving her, of pleasing her—until one night when she'd ignored his use of their safe word, ignored his shouts and his struggles against the ropes, and laughed while raping him with a strap on big enough to make him bleed.

After that he'd shut down emotionally. It had been easy to do. He set the rules with women, and they let him. He never got rough, and he never gave up control. Until Jillian.

She'd blindfolded him and played his body like a master musician. The scrapes and pinches, the talking, the teasing, the commands and the way she'd rocked his world all brought forth needs he'd thought were long gone. The craving for more had hit him the minute he woke up alone, and stayed with him for the past two days.

She'd dominated him, but she'd never once made him feel completely taken over. He remembered how in the middle of the night when he'd woken her with gentle kisses and slow sensual loving, she hadn't slapped him down or tried to take control. She'd laid back and let him love her. And then she'd left while he was still sleeping.

One night. They'd agreed on one night, and she'd stuck to it. Now he needed to.

"Kane sent me roses the other night."

"Nice." Jillian didn't mention that she already knew about the flowers. Nobody wants to know their private life isn't as private as they thought.

Vanessa flashed a wicked grin. "They still had the thorns."

Jill and Vanessa were sitting at the main bar of The O Club. It was just after six in the evening and the club was closed, so they were alone, drinking coffee and chatting before they went over the details for the party on Sunday that she'd stupidly agreed to do a show at.

"Is your cop kinky?"

"Well, he's not a top, or a bottom. And he doesn't have any fetishes beyond me." Nessa laughed. "But he's certainly not boring or staid. I'd classify him as . . . adventurous and exciting."

"Sooo, you're happy with that? I mean, you don't get restless, or feel like you're missing out somehow?"

Vanessa put her coffee cup down and regarded her carefully. "I can see how you might think that, but I'm not a domina. Sure, I know how to top someone. I *can* dominate someone, and I enjoy submitting from time to time as well, but it's not the same for me as it is for you."

"What's that supposed to mean?" She'd known Vanessa for years. Vanessa had helped Jillian come to accept that it was okay to enjoy having power over someone else. That it was okay to enjoy hurting them, if they got pleasure from the pain. That she didn't have to follow any rules or standards as long as both parties involved knew what was going on.

The last thing she'd ever expected was for the woman she thought of as a friend to judge her.

"It just means it's not a part of me the way it is you."

"So you've been faking it at the club for the past five years?"

"No!" Her eyebrows jumped and she leaned forward. "I manage a nightclub with a reputation as a BDSM hotspot. I host a monthly party for those, like you, who need the release BDSM offers. But I don't need it in my life."

Jillian sat still, her fingers fiddling with the coffee cup in front of her as she listened to her friend. She didn't know why she'd snapped at Vanessa, it's not like she didn't already know all that. They'd had many discussions circling the need, desire, or interest in BDSM when they'd first met.

"Yeah, I get it," she finally said. "You're *adventuresome*."

Vanessa relaxed and they both laughed. The conversation turned to other everyday things like clothes and movies. A while later the back door of the club slammed and Rob, one of the bartenders, came in. Vanessa glanced at her watch and they realized that almost two hours had passed and they still hadn't talked about the party, and exactly what sort of show Vanessa needed during it.

"Okay, time to get to it, I guess," Vanessa said with a laugh.

"The guests are going to be a blend of people familiar with BDSM and complete virgins. What they all have in common is O." O, or Ophelia, was the owner of The O Club, and Vanessa's boss. "Some are personal friends of hers, but most are potential investors. Ophelia wants to open another club, in Calgary, and with a slightly different twist. She's going for a sort of BDSM academy type feel, but as a nightclub."

Weird. "Sounds . . . interesting."

"Actually, it is. The idea for the new club is actually really cool. You'll get a taste of what she's trying to do at the party." She smiled, an excited sparkle clear in her eye. "But to get the backing for it we need to impress some high rollers so we can get them to open their wallets."

They talked some more, Vanessa explaining the concept of the BDSM marketplace theme they were going for. Stations that would ring the club, featuring various aspects of kink, where people from the crowd would be able step up and experience being spanked, or bound, or even try their hand at flogging. "Rob here has agreed—hell he jumped at the chance to be your bottom for the night, and you'll be on the main stage the whole time. I'll leave the details of what exactly you do to him up to you, but it would be great if you could maybe do some clothespins, and maybe caning?"

From behind the bar, Rob grinned and bowed his head to her. Jillian had played him a couple of times in the past year and knew him to be an obedient bottom, with a huge appetite for

129

pain play. They didn't have a great connection, but she knew him, knew his responses and his tolerance. He was a good choice since she didn't have her own partner.

"How well do you know Jackson?"

Vanessa's eyebrows jumped. "Kane's partner?"

"Yeah."

"Where did that come from?"

Heat crept up Jill's cheeks. "Just wondering."

"Being his neighbor you probably know him better than I do. I've rarely shared more than a few words with him."

"But you've been around him a lot, in social situations. He was Kane's best man at the wedding."

"And you were one of my bridesmaids, but you don't know Kane real well, do you."

She nodded and slid off the barstool. "Point taken." She knew Kane well enough to say hi to when they crossed paths, even to sit and have a drink or meal with if they happened to be in the same place at the same time, but she didn't really know him beyond the fact that he was a cop, and he loved Vanessa.

Vanessa cocked her head and gave Jillian *the* look. "Spit it out. What is it you want to know about Jackson. Why the sudden interest in knowing more?"

"How are things with Kane? Did the thorny roses do the trick for a night's entertainment?"

The two women stared at each other until Vanessa finally slid off her stool too. "Fine, I'll mind my own business for now, but I don't think this subject is closed yet."

Jill laughed and her friend walked her to the door. "Don't forget the barbecue at my place tomorrow. I expect you to come and eat cake with me!"

"I'll be there," she said, waving as she left the club.

Her pulse kicked up a notch. She'd bet money Jackson would be there too.

7

Saturday dawned sunny and bright. Jillian had finished the Web site she'd been working on late the night before, and she was ready to relax and enjoy the day.

After enjoying a breakfast of peanut butter toast and grapefruit juice on her back deck, she went inside to get ready for Vanessa's birthday party.

After piling all the ingredients on the kitchen table, she went to work making cupcakes. She wasn't the best cook in the world, in fact, she hated cooking, but she loved baking. And despite what Jackson had said about the burnt bottoms, she was good at it.

Jackson. She'd tried to catch a glimpse of him the past couple of days. Hence the breakfast on the back deck, but no go. The man was avoiding her.

She pressed her lips together and cracked another egg into the mixing bowl. She didn't know what to think about the whole thing. No, she knew what she should be thinking; it just wasn't working that way.

She should be glad the night had turned out the way it had.

She'd gotten to play with the man she'd been crushing on for months, and no one had gotten hurt.

It should be enough. She shouldn't want to see him again. She shouldn't want to make him hers. But a small part of her did. The part that enjoyed talking to him, flirting with him. The part of her that yearned for a man strong enough to accept her dominance in the bedroom, while still remaining her equal in other life aspects. The part of her that yearned for a true partner wanted Jackson Barrows.

But the part of her that lay within her head, and not her chest, knew it was wrong to want him.

Jackson was a strong confident alpha male cop. He was cocky, almost to the point of arrogance, and he'd never fully be able to give his obedience in the bedroom.

They'd fight, they'd make each other miserable, and then she'd lose him completely. It was much better that they let things be. A one-time fantasy night had taken place, and as adults, they could deal with that and move on, remaining friends.

She stopped stirring the batter and poured it into the little cups that were all set out.

After she'd slid the pan into the oven and set the time she became aware of the sound coming from the front yard.

The sound of a lawn mower.

After racing through the house, Jillian slid to a stop in front of her door. She fluffed her hair, smoothed her T-shirt down, and took a deep breath. With her insides jittering like a schoolgirl's she opened the door to see Jackson pushing his lawn mower over her grass.

Her heart went pitter pat against her ribs and she did a mental eye roll. She really needed to get a grip on herself. It wasn't like he'd never done her lawn before.

She stepped outside and waved. He waved back and then turned the mower off.

"Hey," he said. "How are you doing?"

"Good. You?"

"Good." He walked toward her, his stride easy and smooth. Confident. When he was only a foot away from her he stopped, and she saw the hesitancy in his gaze. "You left without saying good-bye the other morning."

"The night was over, and you looked like you were sleeping pretty good. I didn't want to disturb you."

"Before you came over, you promised you'd never lie to me."

She arched an eyebrow at him. "Yes."

"I'd like to test that."

Just then the timer on the oven went off and she jumped a little. *Relax,* she screamed at herself mentally.

"I have to get that," she said. "Do you want to come in?"

His lips twisted in a smile. "Baking again?"

She nodded, her feet shuffling back toward the door.

"Go." He nodded. "I'll finish the lawn first if that's okay?"

"Sure," she said over her shoulder as she rushed back inside. "Just walk in. I'll be in the kitchen."

She dashed back into the kitchen and quickly shut off the beeping timer. She opened the oven door and sent a prayer of thanks when there was no cloud of smoke rolling out. Snatching up a dishcloth, she pulled the tray of cupcakes out and went over to the cooling rack.

She had a second batch cooling and was just sliding a third one into the oven when the front door opened and Jackson's voice echoed through her house. "Jillian?"

"Back here," she replied.

He came in and filled the space with his masculinity. The scent of fresh cut grass and clean male sweat filled her nostrils and she licked her lips. He smiled at her, the gleam in his eye telling her he knew the effect he was having on her.

133

"The bathroom is just down the hall, Jackson. Go wash up and you can have a cupcake when you get back."

He left the room, smiling, and she smacked her forehead. She sounded like his freakin' mother!

Highly aware of his presence in her house she stared out the kitchen window and counted to ten. When her pulse was steady and she felt somewhat in control again, she turned and saw him standing in the doorway—shirtless.

"My shirt got wet," he said with a shrug. "So I took it off."

Saliva pooled on her tongue as she gazed at that sculpted chest, the colorful tattoos.

"Be honest, Jackson," she said with a wry smile of her own. "You took off your shirt because you know I love the sight of your body."

A small flush crept up his neck. "You said you liked my tattoos."

"Get yourself a drink and have a seat. There's beer and juice in the fridge."

To keep her hands busy, she reached for another mixing bowl and started in on the icing. An automatic smile came to her lips when Jackson opened her fridge and asked her if she'd like a drink as well.

"Nothing for me, thank you."

He pulled out one of the stools on the other side of the island and sat across from her. She watched as he peeled the paper wrapping off a cupcake and bit into the fluffy chocolate cake. He moaned his enjoyment and her nipples hardened. When he was done he sat and watched her spread white butter icing on the batch from the cooling rack. The room was quiet, and neither spoke, but the silence was comfortable. She'd expected some tension between them after their night together, but it wasn't there.

The erotic tension was there. She had to fight to keep her eyes on what she was doing, and to not reach over and stroke his arm, or tweak a flat male nipple, but there was no discomfort between them.

The timer went off, and she pulled the last batch from the oven.

"I thought you said you didn't like to cook?" he asked when she was done setting that batch out to cool.

"Baking isn't cooking."

"Yeah, you can burn baking and it still tastes good." He reached for one of the fresh-from-the-oven cakes with a grin.

She smacked his hand with a spoon. "No more, these are for Vanessa's party."

"Will you go with me?"

She stilled. "To the barbecue?"

"Yeah. Why not? I mean, we live right next door to each other."

She stared at him. "Is that why you're asking me, because we're neighbors?"

He met her gaze and they stared at each other for a minute. "Not only because we're neighbors."

She took a deep breath. "What's going on, Jackson? We agreed on one night."

"We did." He nodded. "But we were friendly before that, why shouldn't we still be friendly?"

She moved around the island counter and perched on the stool next to him. There was definitely something more going on. Her radar wasn't that messed up. "Is that all?"

He stood up and paced over to the window. Even with his back to her, she heard the anxiety in his voice when he asked, "Are you a dominatrix?"

So that was what he meant by testing her promise not to lie.

"I don't really like that word," she said casually. It hadn't been an easy question for him, but her instincts were telling her to keep things as light as she could. Jackson was suddenly strung tighter than a cat in a roomful of rocking chairs, and she didn't want to spook him. "I prefer domme or domina. Or even top, as I don't think of myself as a true lifestyle dominant."

He turned to her, but remained over by the window. "What's the difference?"

"I like to play," she said. "I like to play a person, male or female, even without the sexual aspect, but I'm not someone who has to always be in control."

"Play?"

She took a deep breath and let it out slowly. "Sensation play. Pain play. I like to spank, whip, cane, and even cut a person. I like to test their limits, see how much they can take, how far I can push them. But it's not always sexual, and it's never against their will."

"So you like to cause pain?"

She pressed her lips together and thought about it. It was easy to say she liked to cause pain, but that wasn't it. Not strictly. "I like to test people's limits. And I do that by blending pain and pleasure for them."

That sounded as comprehensive as she could make it. "Clear as mud for you?" she asked when he remained silent for a few minutes. He finally moved forward, coming back to the island and leaning against it.

"You said it's not always sexual, but you have to be in control in the bedroom too don't you? Like the other night."

"I don't *have* to be, no. I'm fully capable of enjoying sex without the power exchange." She saw his shoulders relax, and had to finish. "But I'd be lying if I said I didn't enjoy the sexual play more than the nonsexual."

His brow furrowed and he stared at her.

"You're very confusing," he said.

She smiled. It had taken her a long time to figure out her own likes and dislikes, and to become comfortable with all aspects of them. She didn't really expect him to understand her. "Let me sum it up this way. I, personally, like what I like. I'm not ashamed of the fact that I like to push people's buttons, or that I get a rush from the way they give themselves over into my hands. Getting that rush, needing that rush, is a part of me; it'll never go away. But it's not *all* of me. I'm a fully functioning normal woman who has sexual and lifestyle needs that have nothing to do with BDSM. Sometimes the two blend, but they don't have to blend for me to feed a craving or find satisfaction."

He was quiet, staring at her, his eyes bright, a light flush creeping up his neck. She saw the excitement rising in him, but she also saw the discomfort.

He didn't like that her words aroused him. She licked her lips and swallowed, her throat suddenly dry, her heart suddenly pounding. She had to break the tension. "Still want to go to the barbecue with me?"

His eyes widened, and his lips twitched. She grinned at him and batted her eyelashes, and he laughed. "Yes, I still want to go to the barbecue with you."

He pushed off the counter and stepped close, wrapping his arms around her in a hug. She had to bite her bottom lip to keep from nibbling on the bare skin in front of her, but she did it. He pressed a kiss to her forehead before letting go and heading for the door. "I've got to shower and get some stuff done. How does one o'clock sound?"

"Good," she forced the word out. "See you then."

When the front door closed behind him, she closed her eyes and let her head drop into her hands. What the hell had just happened? Were they going on a date?

* * *

At five to one Jackson left his house and headed to Jillian's. His step was light, and he was smiling.

He'd debated over and over if he should talk to Jill about things, but the simple fact was, he'd been unable to think of anything more than her for the past three days. Her and Lydia, and his past, and Jackson hated having shit hanging around in his head, clouding things up. He didn't like to dwell on things, and that had meant getting some answers. Moving forward.

He'd had a great time with Jillian, and he'd always liked her. There was no reason why he shouldn't see her again.

When she opened the door, the breath left his lungs. "You're beautiful," he said.

Her hair was a shiny cap, sleek and smooth, framing her face, her wide eyes dark and smiling. And her body, the strapless dress she had on was tight over her torso, outlining her round breasts, and the pointed nipples that made his mouth water. The skirt was light and floaty, swirling about her legs.

A vision of himself seated in a lawn chair in the middle of the party with her on his lap flashed through his mind. With that skirt, she could be riding his dick and no one would know but them.

He bit back a groan and took the huge plate of frosted cupcakes from her, leading the way to his car.

The afternoon went even better than he'd expected. They'd arrived together, and aside from a minute when Kane had stared at the cupcakes Jillian brought with raised eyebrows, things had gone smoothly. It felt natural. They each went their way at the party, meeting up to chat occasionally, sitting together to eat.

The only real surprise had come when he'd been helping Kane get the meat off the grill. Kane had flipped a burger onto the plate already piled high and smirked at him. "So Jill likes to bake, huh?"

"Yes, it was her sending the stuff. Did you know?"

Kane shook his head. "Nope. But I think it's about time you two got together."

"Why? Because we're all friends?"

He flipped a steak onto an empty plate. "That one's for Nessa. And no, I don't think you should be together because we're all friends. It's because you two have been dancing around each other ever since the wedding."

Jackson hadn't replied, but it bothered him. He'd felt they'd done a good job burying their attraction. Obviously he was the only one who'd thought so. The whole afternoon was casual. There weren't a lot of people, just some of the staff from Vanessa's club, and them. Fewer than ten people.

Vanessa had no family around, and Kane's family hadn't been invited. Jackson had watched as Jillian talked with everyone there, bright and social in her floaty dress, and it hit him. He really liked her. Not just found her sexy, or beautiful, but he *liked* her, and he wanted her to be his.

The drive home from the birthday party was quiet. Jackson was nervous, anxious, excited. He felt like he was on his first date again. One night, she'd said in her note. One night, she'd reminded him that morning. Why was she so set on one night?

He pulled into his own driveway, and rushed to get her door open and help her from the car.

"Thanks," she said. "It was fun, and not having to drive gave me an even better chance to relax."

"You don't like to drive?" he asked as they walked toward her front door.

She shrugged. "I don't mind it, but sometimes it's just nice to not have to deal with traffic. Especially on weekends."

"Is that why you work from home?"

"I work from home because I run my own business, and I can work from anywhere really."

They got to her door and she stopped. "Thanks for the company, Jackson. It was nice."

"It was." He reached out and stroked a finger down her cheek. Lifting her chin he stepped forward and leaned in—and she stopped him.

"No, Jackson." She grabbed his wrist and stepped back, her big eyes dark and confused. "We agreed on one night. That was it."

Frustration hit him. "Why is that? Why only one night? We know each other, we like each other. There's certainly chemistry between us. Why not see if it can go anywhere?"

"Because I already know it can't."

"How can you know that?"

"I know that because I know myself well. I know what I need, and I don't think you're capable of giving it to me."

It was like a fist in the gut. "You said you didn't have to have the play to enjoy sex. So why should it matter if I'm not into it a hundred percent of the time?"

"You don't have to be into it all the time. That's why one night is good for us. But for a relationship Jackson, I need more."

"What?" he snarled. "You need me to be your little fuck toy? A slave boy you can beat on and abuse and see how far you can push?"

The color drained from her cheeks and Jackson felt shame wash over him. He knew that she wasn't Lydia, and she hadn't deserved his anger. He turned away and dropped his head. "Fuck!"

"I think it's time for you to leave, Jackson."

Stomping on the jumbled emotions clamoring about inside him he turned to her, "I'm sorry. I shouldn't have said that to you. I didn't mean it."

Her expression softened. "You did mean it, Jackson. That's the problem."

"Listen, you should know I had an experience with a dominatrix in the past, years ago, that didn't end so well for me. It's her that I'm angry at, not you."

She smiled, stepping forward and cupping his face in her hands. "I understand."

He breathed a sigh of relief. "Then you'll forgive me. You'll see me again?"

"Forgive you, yes. Of course. But seeing you again, dating you . . . it's not a good idea." She moved to the wicker love seat to the side of her small front deck. "Come on. Let's sit."

He sat next to her, and she took his hand. "I had a relationship a couple of years ago with a submissive man. His name was David, and I loved him. He was very submissive, sometimes too much so for me. Like I said, I like to dominate and push limits, sexually and sensually, but with David, he was more slave than submissive. He wanted me to control everything. His only goal was to please me, and when I just wanted to be left alone, he was miserable. When I wanted to have vanilla sex, to have him hold me, I had to tell him what to do. I had to direct him, and reward him. It never really did anything for either of us, and as time passed it became clear to me that I was totally responsible for his happiness—and that was too much for me."

"I'm not like that!"

"I know, you are just the opposite." She sighed. "I'm not surprised you've been hurt, or that you were abused, and it breaks my heart to know that. You're so responsive, and a big part of me thinks I'm the biggest idiot in the world for saying no. But Jackson, when I have another relationship with a man, I want him to be okay with all that I do, all that I am. He has to accept that I need all those aspects in my life. The play, and the vanilla."

"And you don't think I accept that?"

"I think you will, to an extent. If we could date and have a casual relationship, then things would work as they are. But I

141

can't do casual with you. I've been half in love with you since the day I moved in, and with you, I want it all."

Stunned pleasure washed over him. She'd wanted him since they'd met! It hadn't been his imagination. "We want each other," he said. "We like each other. We can make this work, Jillian."

She shook her head slowly. "You have that wall I mentioned before, Jackson. That brick wall that you throw up, and it keeps everyone out. It'll always keep *me* out. In order to have a truly equal relationship, I need that wall to disappear."

He wanted to argue with her, to deny what she was saying, but he knew it was true. But . . . "Part of me craves what you're talking about. The play. Even though I haven't let myself think about it for almost ten years, part of me hears the command in your voice and wants to drop to my knees and give you whatever you want."

"But you don't accept that part of yourself, do you?"

He met her gaze. "I want to."

The clear struggle in her eyes gave him hope. She wanted him, he knew it. It had been her who sent him the flowers, the coffee, the cookies. Her who had suggested the one-time fantasy night. If she'd brushed him off that morning, and ignored him at the barbecue, he might believe the one night had been enough for her. But she hadn't. She wanted more too, he just had to convince her to give them a chance.

"You can help me accept that part of myself. We can make this work, Jill."

She stared at him, tears welling in her eyes. "I don't think so, Jackson. I won't be responsible for someone else's well-being like that ever again."

She stood and hurried into her house, leaving him sitting there, alone.

8

Three weeks passed, his vacation came and went, with him doing nothing but moping around his house. Kane kept out of his way at work, and even Linda, the pretty blonde at the bakery, stopped flirting with him. They worked their cases and days passed, and he missed Jill.

He'd left his house to head over to hers too many times to count, only to stop and go back inside. He sat in his kitchen and watched her have breakfast on her deck in the back, but hadn't stuck his head out to say anything.

It wasn't until he'd waited until she left her home to go over and mow her lawn again, that he'd realized what a coward he was being.

He was letting a woman who he liked, he respected, and yes, who he trusted, walk away from him because some bitch had hurt him a decade ago. Sure, it had hurt big time. It had taken him a long time to build that wall Jillian always mentioned. He'd buried his own need for attention, for acceptance so deep he couldn't even acknowledge it himself. But she was right. He was responsive to her play, he liked it. He was tough and strong, and he liked to be tested. He liked to push his own limits, and he could only ever be happy with a woman who would push those limits too, in all ways.

Enjoying that sort of play didn't make him any less a man than he already was. But being too scared to face his past, to move beyond it and find his own happiness . . . that made him less of a man.

Now all he had to do was show Jillian he was willing to push too.

Jillian had just stepped out of the bath when her doorbell rang. Her heart jumped in her chest and she froze. It was Sunday evening, who would be at her door, except Jackson.

She hadn't seen hide nor hair of him since their talk on the front deck, and she was a hurting for it. She'd never realized how much their little casual conversations had meant to her. How much a part of her life they'd been.

Wrapping herself in the short silk robe she'd set out, she rushed to the door. When she opened it, there was no one there. But there was a *huge* pile of flowers at her feet. She bent down and noticed that they were three large clear vases, with separate bouquets, just set together to look like one big one. She lifted the middle vase, and an envelope fell to the deck.

She made two trips, bringing the flowers in and setting them on the coffee table, before perching on the edge of her sofa and opening the envelope.

Dear Miss J,

You were right.
Not about us not being able to do this, but about me needing to find my own happiness. I've found it . . . with

you. I'm strong enough to try and knock down that wall from my side . . . are you strong enough to try from yours?

Jackson
Eager and ready

Jill's heart pounded and she realized she was smiling, and crying. That . . . That idiot was challenging her!

She'd been right, he did like to play games, and it looked like they might just be playing together.

She set the note down and sat back. She needed to think. If they went into this, and it fell apart, she would be heartbroken, and he . . . well he could be emotionally damaged forever. That wall he had built might get bigger and stronger and no one would ever be able to get around it, let alone knock it down. She needed him to be sure that he knew what he was getting into.

She picked up the phone and dialed his number.

"Do you like them?" he asked as soon as he picked up the phone.

"They're beautiful, Jackson. Thank you."

"I've missed you," he said.

"I've missed you, too." Her heart pounded and she took a deep breath. "I've been thinking as well. And you're right. If we both want this, we can maybe make it work. But before we go any further I need to know that you're fully aware of what my helping tear down that wall means."

"Okay." His breathing was heavy on the phone and she wondered if he was excited or anxious.

"I'm putting on a show tonight and I'd like you to come and watch. To see just how I like to push a person's buttons."

"A show?"

"At The O Club."

He groaned. "It has to be there? At Nessa's club?"

She heard the panic in his voice. "Yes, at Vanessa's club. I'm not a fan of shows, Jackson. I'll never ask you to do one, but I want you to see one."

"I thought we'd keep this private, between us."

"It's a private event."

"But Vanessa will be there. Shit, what if Kane's there?"

"Do you trust me, Jackson?"

"Yes."

"Then trust me, and come to The O Club before ten. I'll be on the main stage. If you show up, and still want to pursue a relationship with me, we'll talk afterward. If you don't show up, then I'll know you don't trust me enough to make this work."

And then she hung up on him.

There was no point in talking more if he couldn't even trust her in this.

9

He had no trouble getting into the club. He told the monkey at the door his name and he was waved right in. Part of him hated giving his name, but the other part was glad the guy didn't recognize him. He'd been there before, with Kane when he went to see Vanessa.

He walked in and stepped to the side of the door to survey the club. It was packed. Busier than he'd ever seen it. He saw areas sectioned off and spotlighted with people crowded around each one. The music was techno, with a steady beat that was almost hypnotic. Trance music, they called it. The crap that the kids liked to play at raves when they were partying. Give him good old rock and roll any day.

Shit, the music was the least of his worries. Nervous anticipation had him strung tighter than a virgin's ass. He laughed at himself and shook his head. Bad choice of words.

Sucking in a deep breath, he started moving through the crowd. He could see Rob behind the bar so he avoided that area and made his way to the sofas along the far wall. He could see the stage from there, and stay in the shadows.

A waitress in PVC short shorts and a corset took his order and he started to relax. When Kane was there, he was either in the back office or seated at the bar chatting with Rob. He wasn't at the bar, so there was a good chance he wasn't there at all.

He wasn't even sure why he was nervous of seeing his partner. It's not like Kane wasn't married to the woman who ran the club, an ex-con and thief. If Kane could see past Nessa's past, then it wasn't likely he'd care if Jackson liked to play things a little kinky now and then.

It was time he started trusting people a little more.

A movement out of the corner of his eye caught his attention and he watched as a lady in spike heels and a conservative business suit made her way toward him. She was staring very intently, and he knew what was coming. Shit, he was not in the mood to be hit on.

"Hi there," she purred. She raked her eyes over him in a way that made it clear she thought him already hers. "Are you a dom?"

He smiled at her. "No ma'am. I'm not. Is that what you're looking for?"

She waved a hand airily. "Oh, I'm not looking for anything in particular. I'm just . . . curious."

He nodded. No doubt about it. This wasn't the crowd he'd expected. The business suit was conservative, and her words said she didn't know what she wanted. But the look in her eyes made his stomach churn. She reminded him of Lydia. A queen bitch who wouldn't worry about including pleasure with the pain she dished out.

The waitress arrived just then with his beer and he flipped a ten onto her tray. She picked it and held it out to him. "Drinks are on the house tonight, sir."

He forced a smiled. "Keep it."

"So are you a regular here?" his new friend asked. "You're not wearing a collar."

"Mrs. Doucette, the show's about to start. Why don't you let Kevin here help you find a seat."

The woman looked at the clean cut and shirtless man in leather pants standing just behind Kane's wife and smiled, showing her teeth. "Very well."

Jackson glanced at his friend's wife, unsure of what to say. "Thank you." It was a start.

She smiled. "You're welcome. Most of these ladies are here as potential investors in a new club and have no idea what BDSM is." She glanced at the woman's retreating back. "And some think they know, even when they don't know the basics of the etiquette. She didn't mean to offend you."

"She didn't offend me," he said, even though he wasn't so sure she hadn't meant to. "To be honest, I don't really know the etiquette myself."

Nessa looked at him, and he waited for her to ask why he was there. Instead she just smiled and put her hand on his arm.

"The only thing you need to know is that this is a *private* club. You'll always be safe, accepted for who you are, and what happens here stays here." She leaned in and kissed his cheek. "Relax and let yourself go, Jackson."

He watched Nessa walk away, hips swaying, and his nerves settled down.

Lydia had fucked with his head along with his body all those years ago when she'd started tying him up and using a flogger on him. He was okay with enjoying the pain. He was a man, he was tough. It wasn't even really pain to him. There were times when she'd flogged him for so long everything else in the world faded away and all he was aware of was the hot flow of blood pumping through his veins. It was almost dreamlike, but it had ended as a nightmare.

Panic hit and his chest tightened. It had been a nightmare, and he was about to embark on it all again? He looked around the full bar. So many people, too many people. He didn't want this, not in a crowd.

He forgot about being strong and trusting, and he set his untouched beer down on the nearest table. He'd already started for the door when the lights went down even lower and a spotlight flashed onto the stage. Jackson stopped dead and stared.

On center stage stood a petite domina in full leather. *Jillian.*

The mask might hide her identity from the others, but he'd know her anywhere. She didn't talk, she just strutted from one side of the stage to the other, looking out at the crowd, and Jackson found himself moving closer. She was majestic, and magnetic. He didn't even notice the near-naked man standing in the middle of the stage until Jillian walked around him, trailing her fingers over his body lightly.

It was Rob, the bartender, whom he'd laughed with so much at Vanessa's birthday. He was naked except for a leather thong cupping his goods, and his wrists were tied together and strung up above him.

Jackson didn't pay any attention to the other people in the club; he was too focused on the woman running the show.

The bright blue corset and skintight mini skirt she wore showed off her curves to their best. Luscious flesh overflowed the top of the corset and inches of bare skin flashed between the bottom of the skirt and the tops of her thigh-high boots. Flesh that called to him, in a way no other had. He wanted to drop to his knees and lick that pale, pale skin, to taste her, to please her.

He wanted to go up on stage and tell Rob to back the fuck off, and take his place.

Entranced, he watched as she warmed him up with a flogger. With a slow and steady build, she swung it over his body—crisscross over her chest, then his arms, then his thighs. When the pink glow of his skin was clearly seen in the spotlight, she set the flogger aside and ran her hand over him. Jackson could see her lips moving as she walked around the bound man.

She'd be talking to him, coaching him? Calming him?

She glanced to the side of the stage and Kevin, the shirtless guy who'd led away the female shark earlier, came forward with a tray. He stood and held it while Jillian picked something off it, then she pinched a fold of skin just under Rob's arm.

Jillian shifted to get another thing off the tray, and Jackson saw it was a wooden clothespin. She picked up another, and another, pinning them onto her subject with slow steady moves. Soon, his torso was covered in them. Evenly spaced and spread up both sides of his body along his rib cage, and edging along the bicep of his lifted arms.

But Jillian wasn't done. Ignoring the crowd, the music, everyone, she knelt down and began placing more clothespins along Rob's inner thighs. When she stood, Kevin handed her a cane and she tapped it against her booted leg.

She leaned forward and said something to Rob. She flicked a pin with her fingers and Rob jerked. She flicked another, and this time Rob was still. She stepped back and began to slowly tweak the clothespins with the cane, like keys on a piano. Every now and then she'd rap him on the outer thigh or the ass with the cane, never losing the beat of her own rhythm.

"She's good, isn't she?"

Jackson started and turned his head to see Nessa standing next to him again. He licked his lips and cleared his throat, he'd been so wrapped up in watching Jillian that he hadn't even noticed her. "Yes, she is."

He was suddenly aware of the light sweat that had broken out on his own skin and the hot throbbing behind his own zipper. "She seems to know exactly what she's doing, and what it's doing to him."

"She does. I've never met a top that could read people as well as Jillian. I've seen her play complete virgins, and experienced slaves, and each one of them says it's an experience not to be forgotten." She glanced at him. "I know it's not one I'll ever forget."

That got his attention. He pulled his gaze away from the stage to look at Kane's wife. "She's played you?"

Vanessa smiled. "A while ago, before I met Kane, but yes. And I've played her."

Jackson felt his jaw go slack. "Really?"

"Jillian's not a bottom, not by any means, so don't go thinking that. But she does understand that the best tops are those who have experienced both sides of the coin. She understands what it takes to be a sub, and she respects it. It's what makes her so damn good."

He glanced at the stage, then back at the woman next to him. "You're not surprised to see me here."

"Not really, no."

"Why not?"

"Jillian brought you up in a conversation a few weeks ago. No, she didn't give any specifics, just asked how well I knew you. Kane told me you had a secret admirer. I put two and two together and got you and her."

"Do you think it's weird?"

She laughed. "Look around you and then ask yourself that. Besides, it doesn't matter what I think. It only matters what you think."

He nodded, staring at the powerful little woman on stage. He watched as Jillian stepped back from Rob and traded tools with Kevin.

"This is something you'll probably never see again, Jackson. Watch closely."

Jackson saw the long tailed whip in her hand and his breath

caught in his throat. Before he could think what she would do with it, she pulled back her arm and struck. Again and again, each flick of the whip snapping a clothespin off Rob's body.

The man's groans echoed through the club, blending with the music as his head fell back, but his body did not move. Each time a pin flew off, his body jerked once, but he stilled himself quickly. If he jerked or moved at the wrong second, that whip could hit something very vital, especially as Jillian snapped the pins off his thighs.

Jackson's head spun. That was trust.

When all of the clothespins were gone from Rob's body, the spotlight faded, and a curtain dropped.

"She'll be a while yet," Vanessa said softly. "She has to help Rob come down, and she won't leave him alone until she knows he's all right."

Jackson nodded and swallowed, his throat suddenly very dry. "Will you tell her I was here?"

Vanessa cocked her head and studied him. "I'll tell her."

He thanked Kane's wife and left the bar. He knew exactly what he wanted to do, and he couldn't do it in the club.

After helping Rob come down from the adrenaline high of their show, Jill left him sleeping in the club's private back room with a blissful smile on his face.

She rolled her shoulders and shook off her own aftereffects. Her muscles were pleasantly pliant, but she wasn't relaxed.

After changing into her street clothes she headed out into the club. Vanessa strode up to her as soon as she came through the doors. "Absolutely fantastic show, Jill! Thank you so much for doing it."

"Like I said, anything for you, Vanessa." She forced a smile to her lips and glanced around the club. "But don't ask me to do a public show again, okay?"

"He left."

Her gaze snapped back to Vanessa. "Jackson?"

She nodded. "He was here, he watched the show, and then he left."

"Did he say anything?"

"Just to tell you he was here."

Jillian's heart fell into her stomach and she tried not to cry. "Okay." She blew out a deep breath and forced a smile for her friend. "Okay. I'm going to go home now."

Vanessa gave her a hug and let her go without another word. It was a good thing too, because Jillian's throat had closed up with tears, and it was all she could do to walk out to her car and get herself home without breaking down.

She didn't bother to turn on the lights as she went into her house. She just toed off her shoes and went down the hall to her bedroom, already unbuttoning her blouse as the tears started to flow.

She walked into her bedroom, flicked on the lights and saw a completely naked Jackson Barrows kneeling on the carpet in the middle of the room.

10

It took a minute for the sight to register, but when it did, joy sang through her veins. The tears stopped and their eyes met.

He started to get up, to come to her, but she held up a hand. "No. Stay there. I'm fine." She grinned at him. "I'm better than fine."

"I figured it was time to show you I trust you and that I'm ready to start to work on that wall."

Her heart kicked in her chest at his words. Adrenaline, power, and desire rushed through her, but above it all, on top of the rush was the biggest high of them all. His trust.

Jackson Burrows was on his knees in front of her, offering himself into her hands, and her heart, with faith. She would not disappoint him. She would not hurt him. She would cherish him, love him, and accept him . . . as he accepted her.

She strode forward only stopping when she was directly in front of him. She bent down and brushed the hair back from his forehead before kissing him. She put her heart and soul into that kiss, and felt the answering heat from Jackson as he parted his lips and let her kiss him.

She pulled back and smiled. "Then I think we should get started right now."

Sucking in a deep breath, she stepped back and began to stroll around him, taking in his magnificent body from all angles, trying to decide how to play things out.

They'd talked, and he was making it clear it was time for action. It was obvious by the hard-on he had that he was excited about what was to come, and the slickness between her own thighs made it clear that her body didn't have the same apprehensions her brain did.

He'd told her he had experience, and that it had been bad. She hoped someday he'd share the details with her, but she didn't need them—a domina had abused him in the past, and as a result he'd buried his need for years. That was all she needed to know, for now. He was showing her all she needed right then.

What she needed to *do* was show him he could trust her with the gift he was offering.

An idea formed in her head and she went to her closet.

It took some time for her to gather all the things she needed and set them up. She didn't speak, and he didn't question her. He sat back on his heels, knees spread, hands on his thighs, palms up and open. His eyes followed her about the room, but he didn't move.

She set the video camera up directly in front of him, and uncertainty flickered deep in his eyes. But he still remained silent.

"Face forward at all times," she said. She stepped behind the camera and finished removing her clothes. She got rid of her blouse and skirt, but kept the stockings, high heels, and black push-up bra. Turning on her heel, she reached for the leather flogger she'd brought out of the closet and tapped it against her leg. "Does this make you nervous?" she asked.

"No, Mistress."

Her heart tripped a beat at the sound of that title coming from that man. He was everything she'd always dreamed of, the connection they had was already deeper than any she'd shared with another. Even David.

David had been a perfect sub, but he hadn't been a partner, and she knew that if she took things slow, Jackson would be the ultimate sub, and the perfect partner, *for her.*

"On your hands and knees," she commanded.

He was quick to move, sitting up and then leaning forward. When he was on all fours, she trailed the leather tips of the tassels across his back.

She swept them up and down his back, over his naked rump, slowly increasing the pressure and swing of the instrument. His skin started to flush as the blood rose to the surface and heat flowed through her bloodstream.

She moved into a better position and began to swing the flogger into a smooth figure eight motion. Not hard, not yet. She just wanted to get a rhythm going. Left to right across his back, right to left, then lower so the tassels struck his out-thrust ass, first one cheek and then the other.

Slowly she began to increase the strength behind the strikes, and in what felt like no time, his entire backside was an attractive rosy red. His head had dropped down and she listened to his breathing. Nice and steady, if a little fast.

She set aside the flogger and moved to stand over him. He tensed, and she stood still, her knees brushing against his ribs. He wasn't tied up, after what little he'd told her, she knew she wouldn't be restraining him in any way for quite some time. But he was still in a vulnerable position.

"Jackson," she said, leaning forward.

"Yes, Mistress."

"Lift your head and look at me."

He did as she asked, and pride filled her as she got a look at his sinfully green eyes. His cheeks were flushed, there was a light sheen of sweat on his skin, and his eyes were full of desire.

She leaned down and placed her lips over his. "You are mine now," she said.

He grinned, slow and lazy. "Yes, ma'am."

She realized she'd been more nervous than he was. His trust was there in his expression, clear as day. He was ready for whatever she wanted to do. He was eager to be her personal playground again.

Straightening up, she shifted her weight and placed a foot between his shoulder blades. She pressed down none too gently. "On your elbows, forehead against the floor."

What to do next? So many things she wanted to do to him, with him. She wanted to settle herself on the floor and have him inch forward until his face was between her thighs, his breath fanning the flames of lust that had her slick, wet, and ready to be devoured. But even more than that she wanted to play with those firm, round, and rosy cheeks of his.

This is just the beginning, she reminded herself. *What you don't do today, you can do tomorrow.*

Moving behind him she stroked the palm of her hand over him. She squeezed his firm ass, then dipped her hand low between his legs and cupped his balls. She tugged them away from his body a bit, thrilling at Jackson's hiss of pleasure.

Her mouth watered at the sight of his ass tilted high in the air and she knelt behind him. Stroking both hands across his cheeks, she used her nails as a weapon. Darker red streaks covered his ass and she ran her hands all the way up his back. One hand on each side of his spine, she dug in and raked her nails down his back. He arched, moaned, and shivered.

"So responsive," she purred. "You are so sensitive, my man."

She kept up the raking, alternating between gentle strokes of the palm of her hand, and hard deep digs with her nails. Pretty red and white welts rose up on his back and she grinned. He was being so good. His sighs of pleasure and groans at the pleasure/pain had echoed through the room, music to her ears.

Tenderly she bent over and licked up one ass cheek and all the way up his back, then down the other side. More shivers, and goose bumps popped out on his skin. "Oh, God," he moaned.

"You like that?"

"Is there any doubt?"

She slapped his ass sharply. "That's not an answer." She loved that he was still Jackson. He was still that smart-ass charmer she'd fantasized about for so long, but that didn't mean she would let him get away with much. "I want a proper answer, Jackson."

"Yes, Mistress."

She slapped his ass again, just because she wanted to.

He gasped. "I like it all, Mistress."

"Thank you, Jackson," she said. "That wasn't so hard was it?"

"No ma'am."

She slapped his firm ass again, just because she could. The palm of her hand stung, but she loved it. She slapped him again, and again, the top of his ass, the underside of his cheeks. A steady rhythm that had her soon wishing she'd brought out a paddle instead of the flogger. But she didn't stop, the fiery heat in her was nothing compared to the adrenaline running through her veins as his body rocked back into her strikes.

Finally she slowed. "You remember your safe word?"

"Yes, Mistress." He was panting by then, and she grinned.

Done toying with him, she spread his cheeks wide with her hand and trailed her tongue down his crack, skimming past his tightly puckered hole to where his balls were tight against him. She licked his balls firmly and then sucked first one, then the other, into her mouth. Pleasure and power blended in her mind and body as she cradled the most vulnerable part of him on her tongue. She rolled the sac around her mouth, sucking and even pinching a little, testing his trust before letting it fall from her lips.

She sat up and looked into the camera. Jackson's head was down, forehead on the ground, just as she'd ordered. But it wouldn't do, not for what she was about to do. "Lift your head up, Jackson. I want you to look into that camera, and keep your eyes open."

"Yes, Mistress." He did as she ordered.

It was awkward for him, to keep his head tilted up so far when he was on his knees and elbows, but she didn't tell him to adjust. She might not use ropes or cuffs on him for a long while, but that didn't mean he wouldn't be restrained by the positions she put him in.

She reached around him and gripped his engorged cock, pulling it away from his belly and using a fingertip to spread the juice oozing from the tip. A moan escaped his lips when she cupped his heavy balls in her other hand. She had a plan for that video. She wanted to show him what she saw. She wanted him to watch it with her, and see just how beautiful and strong he was in her eyes.

"Feel good?" she whispered in his ear. "Feels great to me. All hard and hot steel wrapped in velvet. I can feel your blood pumping into your cock. It's still growing in my hand. You're almost too big for my hand. Is that how it feels when you do this yourself? You know this cock belongs to me now, right?"

"Yes, Jillian. Yours."

"That means no more playing with yourself without permission."

"Only when you tell me to," he confirmed.

She squeezed his cock and pumped it a few more times. "Such a good man."

Knowing she had dominion over such a powerful masculine body gave Jillian an incredible rush and she nipped at his shoulder with her teeth as she pumped her fist faster.

Jackson's breath rasped in and out in the quiet room as she jerked him off. She moved her hand up and concentrated on the tip, fast, tight, jerky movements with a twist of her wrist that dragged her palm over the sensitive head. She put two fingers of her other hand in her mouth and coated them in saliva before inching them down between his spread cheeks to play around his puckered anus.

Jillian rimmed him a few times before gently easing a fingertip in up to the first knuckle. A few gentle thrusts with it, then his hole relaxed, and she was in. Timing her thrusts with the stroking of her hand on his cock, she knew he wouldn't last much longer.

She spread the pre-cum leaking steadily from the tip of his cock around to ease the friction and began full strokes, twisting up and down his cock. A loud groan escaped him when her fingers brushed over the sensitive head. The harsh sound of his breathing was only one signal of how close he was to coming. His body started to rock and she covered him, her chest to his back, and sank her teeth into his shoulder. He cried out, his body shuddering, and she thrust the second finger in his ass.

It was too much for him, the fingers fucking him in time with the hand stroking him, her body blanketing him, her teeth claiming him. With a guttural cry his cock throbbed in her hand, and warm liquid shot out, covering her hand and his belly.

"Yes, Jackson. Come for me. Give me yourself."

His cock twitched and jerked, as his body shook. She held him gently in the palm of her hand until his breathing slowed to normal. Then she slowly removed her fingers from his ass and wrapped her arms around him, pulling him up and back. She sat on her ass, spread her legs, and cuddled him between them.

They sat on the floor recuperating for a while before moving up onto the bed where they cuddled together, his arms cradling her close.

"This is just the beginning, isn't it?" he asked. "We're going to do this, together."

"Yes, Jackson. This is just the beginning for us."

"Thank you," he said, kissing her forehead.

"Thank *you*," she replied, snuggling deeper into his embrace.

NO ANGEL

1

————————

Anna Blair was special. She knew it, and accepted it. Her short, bouncy blond curls framed a face of fair skin, dark chocolate eyes, and lips that were naturally full and perfectly shaped. People often told her she looked like she was kissed by an angel. And they always looked at her funny when she replied that there were no angels in her life . . . but she had been blessed by the devil.

She thought herself a simple girl, living a simple life. The goal was to stay alive, and it didn't bother her that she often had to kill to do it. Emotions hadn't factored into her life for a long time.

Yet, walking back to her motel from the movie theater, she couldn't stop thinking about what a sap she was to get all teary over fictional characters that kept their friendship strong with a pair of "magical" jeans.

The stupid thing was that people saw the movie and laughed at the thought of magic. Anna watched the movie and saw the magic clear as the full moon in the night sky. The magic wasn't in the pants, but in the way the girls remained friends and accepted each other's differences with love.

That was the kind of magic Anna envied. She'd never had friends. Not even as a little girl. Her only friend had been her mother, but her mother had been killed when Anna was twenty-one, and now, nine years later, Anna doubted she'd ever have another friend. It wasn't safe for her to have friends. Being close to her put people in danger, and she'd been raised to protect people from the evil she knew was in the world.

She accepted it, as she did so many other things she had no control over. That didn't mean it didn't hit her in the heart when she saw others have what she'd always wanted. Even if it was just in a stupid movie.

Some people were born to lead a life full of love, health, and happiness. Anna had been born to a Catholic ex-nun, and raised to fight demons. As if to remind her of that fact, the wind changed and Anna caught a vibe on the air that had her muscles tightening, and her thoughts narrowing.

The tiny hairs all over her body stood on end—a sure sign that evil was nearby. Stepping to the edge of the sidewalk she placed her back against the building and closed her eyes. She'd gone to the late movie, and it was almost midnight, so the sidewalks were pretty much empty. It wasn't hard for her to tune out the few cars passing by as she concentrated on seeing the thread of energy she'd felt.

Among the blackness that formed when she closed her eyes Anna could see the energy that surrounded her. People gave off energy, plants and animals gave off energy. All living things gave off energy of different levels and different vibrations. Anna sorted through the colors in her mind and found the one that had made her skin crawl. It was pink, of all colors, and writhing angrily among the lazy ones of the plants and animals around her.

It was also fading fast. Anna opened her eyes and concentrated on using her powers to keep the alternate view of energy overlapping the one everyone else saw. She moved quickly, her boots silent on the sidewalk as she followed the energy trial.

She should've been prepared. She should've seen the energy thread thicken, strengthen. Her only excuse was that the thing had parked itself around the corner of a solid brick wall that blocked the trail. As she started around that corner, a long green arm reached out, grabbed her by the throat and pulled her into the alley.

Pinned to the brick wall by her throat she fought for breath and immediately kicked out, her steel-toed boot connecting with its stomach? She rolled her eyes down and saw that the thing that had her must be seven fucking feet tall!

"Anna Blair, you are wanted." Its voice was human, even melodious. Too bad it was big, green, and gross looking. Okay, and evil . . . don't forget it was evil.

Black spots started to float in front of her eyes as the creature squeezed her throat tighter, cutting off her air completely. Anna stopped struggling against the hand that held her so high up off the ground, and called to her first power. She opened her right hand and a flame leapt to life. With a flick of her wrist the fireball landed on the thing's head. The patch of black hair that grew in a long thick mohawk caught fire, and he dropped her.

Her rubbery knees collapsed beneath her. She rolled as she fell and landed on her hip. "Ouch!" That was going to leave a bruise, but at least she hadn't landed directly on her tailbone.

Without a second's hesitation she rolled again and stood up several feet away. She reached behind her and pulled two small, but very deadly knives from the hidden sheath in her waistband.

"Okay, big guy," she said holding the knives loosely in each hand as she looked the thing over. It was indeed over seven feet tall, heavily muscled, and vaguely human looking. It reminded her of the fictional Hulk from the movie she'd seen weeks earlier. Not quite as gross or slimey as she'd originally thought, but still evil. The energy coming off it was definitely evil. "You need to tell me what the hell you are, and who sent you?"

It roared and shook its head. "I am Maracas, sent by Focalor, Great Duke of Hell. He wished you to be brought to him, and I am his servant."

Yellow eyes gleamed at her from a broad, flat face. She tried not to focus on the small black horns that were visible now that he was bald. "You're not like any demon I've ever seen before," she said.

Throw the knives, you idiot. Don't talk to him. The little voice inside her head was drowned out by her training. Her mother had trained her that to know your enemy is to defeat your enemy. She needed to know. As long as she kept her distance, she could kill him with a flick of her wrist.

"You've not faced a true demon before," Maracas said as he stepped forward.

She took three quick steps back, shaking her head. "I've been fighting demons my whole life, you're not like anything I've ever seen."

She was a fighter for sure, but she wasn't an idiot. This guy was big and bad, very bad. If he hadn't been blocking the entrance to the alley, she'd have run for it. Since running wasn't an option, she needed to know what she was up against if she was going to stand a chance.

He took another step, she took another three, keeping a fair-sized distance between them. "I told you, I am sent by—"

"I know *why* you're here, you idiot. I want to know *what—ack!*" She scrambled back as he lunged, but he was quicker. And damn that long reach. His football-sized fist connected with her jaw and she flew back against the brick wall at the end of the alley. The knives left her hands when she landed and her head smacked against the brick. Everything started to fade and she fought not to black out. "Fuck!"

Without her blades she instinctively reached for her fire, and started throwing fireballs out in his direction, hoping to slow him down and give her vision a chance to clear.

Maracas batted at them as each one came close, blocking or dodging most of them and barely slowing his advance. The ones that landed would lick at his skin for a brief moment before flaming out on their own. Except where she hit clothing, but soon the materials were burned away and Maracas didn't even seem to notice.

Gathering her strength she straightened up, raised both her hands and threw, aiming at something much more sensitive than the hair on the top of his head. The fireball landed on his groin, and *that* one he noticed.

Definitely male, she thought with a snicker as she struggled to her feet. He got the flames put out at the exact time she reached back for another knife. She pulled it from behind and let it loose in one smooth move. The silver blade gleamed in the night and landed true with a loud thunk.

Maracas looked down at the little blade sticking out of his chest and laughed. "A knife to the heart won't work with a real demon, little human."

For the first time since she caught his vibe, true fear shot through Anna. "Oh, Deus," she murmured.

Maracas laughed. "God can't help you now," he taunted.

A prayer leapt to her lips and she scrambled back as Maracas lunged forward, his hands aimed at her throat again.

She tripped over an empty can that went spinning away and his hands wrapped around her throat as she fell, with him falling on top of her. She grunted, the wind leaving her lungs sharply and black spots danced across her vision once again.

When she finally got her wind back, she realized that Maracas wasn't holding her down, he'd just landed on top of her when he'd keeled over mid-grab.

Pinned under what had to be three hundred pounds, Anna let her head fall back against the pavement. It might've been delayed, but the knife had worked its magic on whatever Maracas was. Mostly.

What mattered was she was still alive, and Maracas wasn't.

She waited a few more seconds and finally decided the knife wasn't going to finish the job for her this time, so she prepared to wiggle out from under her captor. She braced her back, and pushed up against the body pinning her to the ground. It shifted with ease, and then suddenly burst into bright blue flame as the knife's magic kicked in and ashes rained down on her.

"Great," she swore. Hacking and coughing, she sat up and brushed demon ash from her clothes. "Just fucking great."

She tried to stand and got as far as sitting on her ass before the world began to spin from the crack her head had taken when she'd hit the pavement. Slumping against the wall she closed her eyes and worked on catching her breath . . . and tried desperately not to think about the ramifications of what had just happened.

Through no fault of her own, she'd been born with demonic powers. And the demons of hell were not happy about it. They thought it sacrilegious that a human have such powers, and had made it their goal to capture her and retrieve those powers . . . by killing her. Focalor was a new name, and Maracas was certainly a new thing, unlike any other demon she'd ever faced.

What with the horns and green fire-retardant skin, she had to acknowledge the knot growing in her gut. Maracas hadn't been a demon spirit in a human body but a full-on from-hell demon.

Every other demon she'd met up with had looked just like a

human, aside from the occasional flash from their goat's eyes, but basically they could've passed for human.

How the hell did a full-blooded demon get on her plane of existence? It was unheard of. The big green thing was a whole new deal, one she wasn't sure she could deal with.

Sometimes she wondered why she bothered fighting the supernatural bounty hunters that were sent after her. It wasn't like anyone would miss her if she died. Her father had died before she was born. Her mother was gone. She had no friends, no family. No magic jeans to help her form lifelong friendships with people who would accept her for who she was.

There were times she hated that her mother had raised her to believe. If she didn't believe in God, then giving up the fight wouldn't be seen as suicide, which was a sin that would send her straight to hell. Sometimes it seemed like no matter what she did, she was going to end up in the Netherworld.

Finally the world stopped spinning and she stood up, not bothering to bite back the moan of pain as she retrieved her three knives. Unzipping her hoodie, she shook off the demon ash then tied the sweatshirt around her waist so she looked reasonably clean in her jeans and tank top. She brushed the ash from her hair gently, careful of the goose egg growing rapidly on the back of her head, and then trudged out of the alley to find the nearest bar.

She needed a drink. Or five.

Ten minutes later she stomped into some dingy pub on the corner of Bernard and Wilson. With big screen televisions over the bar, team jerseys of all sorts hanging from the walls, and two pool tables in the middle of the room instead of a dance floor, she got the hint. It was a sports pub.

A waitress wandered over to the booth Anna had slid into and stood at the edge of the table. She wore a tight white V-neck T-shirt that showed off impressive cleavage and too much make-up. The bright red name tag just above her right breast said SALLY. Sally cocked her hip out and smiled wanly. "What can I getcha?"

All she needed to do was snap her gum and she'd be a total cliché. "Pint of draft and three shots of tequila. Gold if you have it."

Sally's eyes widened and she looked at the empty bench space on either side of Anna. "Expecting company?"

Anna smiled, baring her teeth. "Nope, it's all for me."

Sally walked away, shaking her head and Anna bit back a sigh. It didn't matter that she showed her teeth, shit, she could curse and growl and threaten, and people just looked at her and shook their heads, or worse . . . laughed.

It was her mom's fault. The silky blond hair and fair skin came from her. Mom said the full mouth and foul language came from her dad, but since he'd died before Anna was born, she didn't see how. Whatever. She was what she was, and she'd long since given up on caring what people thought about her.

Sally came back with her drinks and Anna paid cash, making sure to tip the girl. She'd waited tables before, and knew it wasn't an easy job. She slammed back the two shots of tequila immediately, one right after the other. The burn down her throat and into her stomach was not so welcome, but the warmth that spread through her veins and mellowed the throbbing pain in her head was.

Anna sat there, staring at the empty shot glasses, and wondered if the supernatural bounty hunters would ever leave her alone. She felt like crap. Her jaw hurt, there was a good-sized knot on the back of her head, and thanks to that sappy movie and lovely demon attack, she was feeling lonelier than ever.

It didn't seem to matter what she did or where she went,

they always found her. She'd only been in Pearson for two days!

Sipping her beer she scanned the pub. The crowd was sparse, and the clientele seemed to be made up mostly of the blue-collar type. The men wore jeans, T-shirts, and steel-toed boots, the few women wore denim shorts or skirts and tank tops that ranged in color but helped to showcase cleavage, even the ones with little to showcase. No one stood out as particularly dangerous, and even though most glanced her way at some point in those first few minutes, no one approached her table.

Anna watched two men move up to a pool table and get ready to start a game. In all honesty, it wasn't until the blond one kept glancing her way that she really took note of him.

He was good looking, in a cocky, king-of-the-world sort of way. His well-worn jeans hugged him in all the right places, his T-shirt was mostly clean, and his smile was seductive.

Anna watched him bend over the table to line up his next shot and a little tingle went through her. He had a very nice ass. Round, and firm. She could picture her hands on it, her nails digging in and urging him on as they flexed and filled with every thrust of his hips.

Ooh, she thought. *That would feel so good right now.*

He sank three more balls and then he was lining up the black eight ball. With a smooth sure stroke, he put that one in the corner pocket. He straightened up, looked over his shoulder at her, and winked.

The tingle in her belly spread lower and she smiled. He was just what she needed. Too wrapped up in himself to want more than one night, he would be the perfect distraction from her dismal thoughts.

She took a sip from her beer and put a little sparkle behind her smile the next time he glanced her way. His swagger increased as he moved around the table and Anna chuckled silently. Oh yeah, he was definitely what she needed to get her mind off her life.

When the second game was over, he set his cue stick down and made his way to her booth. He moved with a smooth liquid grace that had her blood heating and her mind stripping him naked.

"Hi there," he said. "Can I get you another drink?"

She glanced down and realized not only had she finished her beer, but the third shot glass was empty too. She didn't even remember drinking it, and her headache was pretty much gone.

"No, thanks," she replied. She better not drink anymore. Safety first, and alcohol slowed her reflexes and dimmed her control over her powers. "But you should join me anyway."

"I'm Gabe," he said as he slid into the booth. "How are you doing tonight?"

"Better every minute," she replied honestly.

His eyes widened and she noticed they were a nice deep blue . . . very pretty eyes for a man. When he chuckled his white teeth flashed and she thought they were pretty, too.

Funny, she'd never thought of teeth as attractive before. Maybe it wasn't his teeth, it was the lips that surrounded them. They were nice. Yes, very nice and full. Very kissable.

Without another thought she leaned forward and pressed her lips against his.

2

Gabe sucked in a breath at the soft touch of the woman's lips and then went with it. He leaned in, parted his lips, and slicked his tongue over her teeth. She tasted of tequila, and something sweet, but before he could deepen the kiss, she pulled back.

"You'll do," she said.

"Excuse me?"

"I'm looking for a distraction from my own thoughts, and I figure you'll do."

He sat back against the booth and looked at her. Really looked at her. Cute blond curls, pretty face, naughty smile. She definitely looked normal, even if she was slightly mussed up. The gleam in her dark eyes was sexy, not psychotic and he wondered if maybe he'd just misinterpreted what she'd said.

But there was really no way to misinterpret the kiss.

"Are you saying what I think you're saying?" *Smooth, Gabe.*

"What do you think I'm saying?" Her laugh was husky and seductive, not at all what he'd expect from such an innocent looking thing. Unexpected was good though, she was pretty enough to catch his eye, but that laugh, it stroked him all over and made his dick harden to hammer strength.

"That you've already decided to spend the night with me."

"Yes. That's what I'm saying." She looked at her empty glass pointedly. "Let's go, shall we?"

For the first time in his life, Gabriel Mann didn't know what to do. He wanted the woman. Hell, he'd wanted her from the second she'd stomped through the door. He'd been sharing some beer and some laughs with friends in another booth at the back of the bar and she'd caught his eye immediately. And while picking up women had always come easily to him, there was something off about how easy it had been this time.

"Maybe we should sit and talk a bit first." He couldn't believe he'd just said that.

"Why?"

Ignoring the hard-on pressing against his zipper he thought fast. "I don't even know your name."

"I'm Anna," she said. Then she smiled, her lips turning up at the corners slowly. "Did I scare you? I'm sorry. I'm just not that great with social skills."

Intrigued, he leaned forward. "Why not? You're beautiful. I'd think you get hit on all the time."

"Yeah, I do get hit on a lot." She put a hand to the back of her head and winced. She must've noticed his puzzled expression because she laughed again, this time a bit self-consciously. "Sorry, private joke. Let's start over, shall we?" She took a deep breath and he tried not to stare as her breasts rose and fell with it. They were the perfect size, round and firm and just more than a handful. He could already feel their warm weight in his hand. "I'm Anna, and I'd love another beer."

A little unsure what to do, Gabe waved Sally over and ordered

176

two more beers. When the waitress had walked away, he turned to Anna.

"So tell me Anna, why do you think you're not good with the social skills?"

"Isn't it obvious?"

His lips twitched. He couldn't help it, she was so cute when she scowled. "I don't know. I think your quick decision-making skills are an asset. I mean, I knew as soon as I saw you that I wanted to spend the night with you. I can hardly hold it against you that you did the same thing."

She beamed at him. "Exactly!"

Sally set their drinks on the table and he watched as the girl held out some money. "I've got them," he said, waving it away. "Sally'll put them on my tab."

"Thank you," she said.

"See? That was proper social etiquette and it wasn't that hard."

Anna's gaze snapped to his and he grinned. She saw that he was joking around and laughed. Relief hit him and he relaxed. Okay, so she was a bit different, but she had a sense of humor.

As they drank, they talked the small talk that people who really had nothing to say talked.

"Let me get this straight," he said a while later. "You went to see *Sisterhood of the Traveling Pants,* and it made you cry—"

"Sisterhood of the Traveling Pants *Two.*"

"Sorry, *Two.* The point being that it made you cry?"

"Yeah," she shrugged. "I know I'm a sap. But the magic of their friendship was so special."

He snorted. "Magic?"

She slid him a glance. "You don't believe in magic?"

Magic, psychic abilities, shapeshifters . . . all topics of conversation he desperately wanted to avoid. Time to change the subject, fast. "So you're new to Pearson?"

177

"Just got here yesterday," she replied. "It's a nice small city, but the people aren't very friendly."

"I'm friendly."

She eyed him. "You could've been friendlier."

"Friendlier?"

She waggled her eyebrows up and down lecherously and he laughed. It was truly rare for a women to catch him off-guard like that, but at least the initial awkwardness of conversation was definitely gone. And he *was* getting used to her bluntness.

Sure, she'd shocked the shit out of him, but he was kicking his own ass now for not jumping out of the booth and leading her out the door when he'd had the chance.

As if reading his mind, she finished her beer, smacked those luscious lips together, and met his gaze. "I have a room nearby, you ready to go?"

Excitement washed over him and his skin tightened all over his body. Oh, yeah. He was more than ready. "Definitely."

He slid from the booth, highly aware of the bulge in his pants. When she followed behind him, slapping his ass playfully when he stood, he forgot all about anyone else in the pub. He reached for her hand and wrapped his fingers around hers. "So where is this room you mentioned?"

Safety always being her first concern, Anna wouldn't normally bring anyone back to her hotel, but this time her impatient nature was getting the best of her. Plus, she'd scanned his energy with her second sight and his bright green vibe was all smooth and happy. The guy didn't have an evil bone in his body.

There'd been no hesitation in her when she'd climbed into his truck and directed him down Bernard and across two more streets to her motel room. It wasn't the Ritz, but it was cheap, close to downtown, and only a block away from the waterfront.

She used the old-fashioned metal key to open the door and ushered him in. Surprisingly, he took charge immediately. He pulled her to him and kissed her so passionately she was ready to burn the clothes off his body.

Large masculine hands ran down her back and cupped her ass, lifting and pulling her tight against him. Wrapping her arms around his neck she trusted him to take her weight as she lifted her legs and wound them around his waist. Their tongues dueled and she rubbed her hungry sex against the massive hard-on she felt behind his zipper.

His fingers dug into her butt and he dragged his mouth out from under hers. "Bed," he panted, as he stumbled a few steps into the room and fell forward onto the queen-size mattress.

They bounced and an inelegant *oof!* flew from her lips. Her bruised backside throbbed but she quickly forgot about that as his body rubbed against hers in all the right places.

"Sorry," he muttered as his hands reached down and shoved her hoodie out of the way.

He grabbed the hem of her tank top and swept it roughly over her head. She laughed, delighted to find a man who wasn't scared to get a little rough with her.

"Don't apologize," she said, panting and reaching for the hem of his T-shirt, matching his eagerness as she pulled it over his head. "Just fuck me."

Gabe hesitated when he unsnapped her cargo pants and discovered the weapons halter snapped low around her hips and belly.

"A girdle?" he asked, eyebrows almost hidden by his hairline.

She laughed and ripped the snaps open. Arching her back she tugged the harness out from under her while he was distracted by the naked breasts she'd shoved into his face. He sucked a nipple between his lips and she gasped, dropping the weapons to the floor next to the bed before going back to work on his pants.

Their arms tangled as clothes were shoved aside as much as possible.

When both their pants were around their ankles she raked her nails over the firm butt she'd admired earlier. "Condom," she said on a gasp as the head of his cock brushed against her slick sex.

He growled and she laughed as he made an awkward reach for the pants still around his ankles, and rolled right off the bed!

"Fuck!" he cursed.

"Well, we're certainly trying," she said as she sat up and looked down at him. Mostly naked he looked both adorable and ridiculously sexy at the same time.

He dug in his pants pocket before he toed off his boots, shoved his pants off his feet, and stood up triumphantly.

"Socks," she said, staring at the thick cock bobbing in front of her face. Maybe it was because his hips were so slim, but damn he looked big. Big and red and juicy. She licked her lips and he groaned. "No, don't look at it like that or we're going to be done before we start."

He bent forward, hiding himself from her view as he got rid of his socks. "Your turn now," he muttered.

She lay back on her elbows and giggled as he struggled to untie her boots. Then in one big flourish he pulled her pants and panties free and threw them on the floor before kneeling on the bed between her legs and rolling the condom on smoothly.

"My socks," she said.

"I don't care about your damn socks," he growled. He came down on top of her, smoothly fitting his hips into the cradle of hers. His fingers skimmed over her pussy lips and suddenly she didn't care about her socks either.

He pressed a couple of fingers into her sex and she arched against them eagerly. "More," she demanded.

"You want more," he said, pulling his fingers out. "You got it."

With one swift and sure stroke he filled her. She dug her feet into the mattress and arched into him with a moan. Their joking stopped as Gabe braced himself on his elbows and began to fuck her. His hips pumped steadily in a strong, smooth rhythm, and she happily dug her nails into his ass to help him along.

He buried his head in her neck, his hot breath sending shivers through her body as she moved with him. In and out his cock went, stretching her to the point that her sex burned with need. Her moans blended with his grunts as they worked up a sweat, straining to get closer.

Closer and closer she got to coming, her body getting tighter and tighter. "Faster," she commanded, digging her nails in.

Everything in her focused on the point of their connection. He picked up the pace, going faster, harder, deeper until he was hitting the sweet spot and her cunt started to ripple with pleasure. "Yes!"

"That's it, baby. Come for me. Come for me." He slammed into her and ground his groin against her, rubbing her clit and sending her off into spasms of pleasure as the world exploded into ribbons of color in her mind's eye.

She was vaguely aware of him throwing back his head and arching into her as his triumphant shout of pleasure blended with her cries.

Limp with satisfaction, she let her hands fall back to the bed and he collapsed on top of her. She couldn't bite back the cry of pain as she was sharply reminded of her earlier butt kicking.

"Sorry," he muttered and rolled off her. He lay beside her as they both fought to suck air back into their lungs. "You okay?"

"Oh, yeah," she said. "Very okay."

"Christ, you're hot," he said.

"I appreciate the thought," she said. "But please don't say His name like that."

Gabe turned his head and looked at her. "Huh?"

"Don't use the Lord's name in vain."

His eyes widened and she once again thought how pretty they were. Before he could say anything else she rolled onto her side and stroked her hand down over his sculpted chest.

"That was good," she said. "Will you fuck me again?"

3

Gabe had no clue what to think of the woman lying in bed next to him, but he did know one thing for sure. "If you give me a bit of time to recuperate, I'd be happy to fuck you again."

She smiled, her pretty face lighting up in a way that made his heart skip a beat. "Good. I'm going to go take a shower. You recuperate."

He didn't know if he should laugh or cry as he watched her slip from the bed and walk stiffly to the bathroom. He should feel bad for her stiffness, he'd sort of lost control and pounded her a little harder than he'd intended. But hell, her nails had been digging into his ass, egging him on.

He closed his eyes and lay there. What the hell was he doing? He was no stranger to one-night stands, but there was certainly something off about this one right from the start.

What woman decides right away if she's going to go home with a guy? Women take charm and effort. Not a lot of effort for him, but unless they're a total skank they take at least a little convincing before getting naked with a man they just met.

Anna did not strike him as a skank in any way, shape, or form.

She's just a little unorthodox, he thought to himself.

She said she lacked social skills, and it sure seemed like whatever she thought came out her mouth without being filtered by her brain. It was a good thing really. Maybe it was because he could see how happy his older brother was now that he was married, but he'd grown tired of the mating games he used to enjoy.

Caleb, his older brother, had become more serious and uptight after their parents had passed away. But Gabe, he'd seen it as an urging to enjoy life while he could. He'd worked hard and played harder, determined to enjoy all he could before he died. Until recently he'd been a big believer in the "live fast, love hard, die young" train of thought.

Then Gina Devlin had entered his brother's life.

The change in Caleb was definitely for the good. He'd been an uptight ass before Gina, but now his brother was quick to smile and way easier to get along with. Gabe admitted it had taken him a while to warm up to his sister-in-law, but when he'd finally seen how happy she made Caleb, when he'd seen the love shine between them, he'd opened his heart and his mind to her as well.

Caleb had told Gabe he'd fallen in love with Gina because after the night they met when Gina had pretended to be someone else, she'd never played games with him. She'd been straight up about what she was, and what she'd wanted from him.

The same way Anna had been with him.

Off-key singing come from the shower and Gabe acknowledged that as crazy as Anna seemed, it was indeed nice to meet a woman who liked the sex games without the head games. Maybe he'd see if she was interested in more than just the one night with him.

Rolling off the bed, he got rid of the condom and made his way to the bathroom.

He pushed aside the shower curtain and grinned at the sleek, wet woman in front of him. "Want some company?"

She welcomed him with a naughty grin. "You all recuperated?"

He chuckled. The woman had a one-track mind. He loved it.

"I just came to get clean . . . and play a little." He stepped into the tub and reached for the soap only to have her grab it first and wave it playfully in front of him.

"May I?"

He held his arms out to the side. "Go for it."

She soaped her hands up and started at his chest. "You have a very nice body," she said, skimming the soap back and forth over his left nipple.

Pleasure at her words, and her touch, floated through him. "Thank you."

"Very strong." Her hands moved over to one shoulder and down his arm, squeezing and massaging his bicep, then his forearm. When she lifted his hand and washed between each finger he groaned and his cock twitched, trying to come back to life.

She turned him around and did his back, the soap in one hand, while the other followed it, digging into his muscles with just enough strength to massage but not enough to hurt. Damn, she was good at this!

When she got to his ass, she used both hands at the same time, up and down, squeezing his cheeks, rubbing them. She parted them and her fingers trailed over his puckered hole, making him gasp and lock his knees. She didn't stop there though. Oh no, she bent her knees and soaped up his legs. Starting at his feet, she moved up his claves, then to his trembling thighs.

Her hand warmed and she dipped one between his legs to cup his balls briefly. Too briefly.

Her hand on his hip, she turned him without standing up and once again he saw her lick her lips and eye his cock. Before he could say anything she took him in her mouth and a groan ripped from his throat.

Oh, God, she was so warm and wet. Her hot little hand was cupping his balls again and her tongue was stroking his rapidly growing cock.

He reached out and braced a hand on the wall as he looked down. The sight of that angelic face stuffed with his rising hardness was the hottest thing he'd ever seen.

Blood rushed from every part of his body to his groin and he struggled to think. There was a reason he didn't want to come in her mouth. There was. What was it? Oh yeah, she wanted him to fuck her again.

With a groan he reached down and grabbed her by the shoulders. "Okay, that's enough of that."

She pulled her mouth away, and he had to fight not to cry when she looked up at him and asked, "Why?"

He lifted her to her feet. "Because you asked me to fuck you again, and if you don't stop now it's going to be a long time before I can recuperate enough again to do that."

"Oh."

He reached for the detachable showerhead and said, "I'm clean. Now it's your turn."

"Okay." She grinned and held her arms out the same way he had.

He laughed and turned her around so her back was against his front. The he held the spray on her breasts, loving her gasp as he directed it at one nipple and then the other as his other hand stroked her from shoulder to thigh.

"Lean into me, baby," he said, his lips brushing against her ear.

She shifted her weight so he was supporting her against his chest and relaxed into him. He brushed his hand over her neatly trimmed bush and slipped it between her thighs.

"You're not washing me," she said huskily. "You don't even have the soap."

"You were in here for a bit before me. You're clean enough."

Her pussy lips were all puffy and hot as he stroked a finger back and forth between the wet folds of her sex. When her hips began to move with him, he inserted a finger into her entrance, just a little bit.

"Ooh," she sighed. Her hands came back and clasped his thighs, pulling him even closer against her.

His hard-on pressed against her back and he groaned. Her skin was so hot and the urge to rub himself against her was strong. God, he'd love to fuck her tits. He lifted his hand away from her pussy and slid it up over her stomach to cup a breast.

"Hey!" she cried out, starting to straighten up. He pinched a hard little nipple and her cry turned to a gasp of pleasure as she settled back against him.

He smiled and smoothed his hand back down to her pussy. He found the hard little nub of her clit and teased it while keeping the stinging shower spray directed at the nipple he'd just tweaked. Her body moved against him, restless, eager as he nibbled on her neck and played.

"You want to feel this between your legs don't you? This hard spray pulsing against your hard little clit while my fingers slide inside your cunt and fill you up. Would that get you off?" he whispered. "I think it would. Should we find out?"

"Oh, yes!"

The finger teasing her clit abandoned its work and dipped into her slick opening again. "God, you're so wet already."

She stepped out a little, spreading her legs wider for him. He added another finger and her pussy tightened around him, grabbing at the digits as he began to thrust them in and out. Her eyes were closed and her head lay back against his shoulder, her body completely open to him . . . trusting him.

Gabe slowly adjusted his other hand so the spray moved from her nipples, down over her belly, to her bush. He shifted the angle of his hand, and brought the showerhead closer so the spray landed directly on her clit as his fingers wiggled inside her cunt.

Anna gasped loudly and pulled back sharply.

"Too hard, baby? Here, how's this?"

He changed the angle so the spray was just skimming over her hot button instead of spraying directly on it, and she gasped again—in pleasure this time.

"Yes, much better." Her breathing had turned to loud pants in the steamy air, and her nails were digging into his thighs again, pulling him close behind her.

"Oh, God," he muttered.

"Don't say—"

"You like that huh?" he said into her ear interrupting her. Sensations stormed through him as she rubbed against his chest. He bent his knees so that his cock nestled between her firm butt cheeks and groaned at the perfect fit.

"I can tell you do," he said as his cock rubbed against her rear entrance. "How would you feel about me taking your ass, huh? I can do it now, you know. Fill you with my cock in your ass and my fingers in your cunt. Oh, yeah, you like that idea, don't you? Your cunt is clutching at my fingers. You're close, I can feel it. I can feel you coming. Come on, come for me baby. That's it. That's it."

She groaned and shuddered in his arms. Her hips jerked and hot cream washed over his fingers just before her knees buckled. She started to slip and he let the showerhead drop to wrap his arm around her waist and keep her standing.

He didn't wait for her to catch her breath. Lust was riding him hard and he was done playing. He wanted that ass of hers, but his control was too thin to take it now. The last thing he wanted to do was hurt his little cutie.

With a quick twist of his wrist he shut the water off. He picked her up in his arms and stepped out of the tub.

He strode into the other room, dropped her on the bed and dug the other condom out of his jeans pocket. Her eyes slitted open and she watched him roll the latex on. She brought her feet up by her butt, bending her knees, and then letting them fall open.

He groaned at the sight. All pretty, pink, and shiny. She smiled at him as she moved one of her hands downward. She spread open those slick pink lips and rubbed herself . . . and Gabe lost it.

"I hope you're ready for a rough ride," he growled as he crawled on top of her.

She flashed him a devilish grin and lifted her arms to him. "Go for it."

Keeping a tight grip on the last thread of his control, Gabe slid into her welcoming body and fought not to come right then and there.

Perfect. She felt just fucking perfect.

He lowered his head and covered her mouth with his, thrusting his tongue inside her and taking everything she had to offer.

Her tongue taunted his, her teeth nipped at his bottom lip, and her inner muscles spasmed around his cock as he slid in and out. He reached back and grabbed her knees, lifting them, and pinned them beneath his shoulders. They both groaned at the angle change that took him deeper. He lifted his head and looked into her eyes, amazed by the storm of passion he found in them. With their gazes locked, he slipped a hand between them and cupped a breast.

Her nails dug into his shoulders when he squeezed and fondled the hot handful. "Christ, you like to use your nails, don't you?"

"And you like it," she said. Then she reached down and slapped his ass, *hard.* "Don't use His name."

"Fuck."

Her legs gripped his hips tighter and her hands roamed over his back, her nails leaving a trail of fire behind. "More," she whimpered, tangling her hands in his hair and lifting her head off the mattress to kiss him.

He drove harder, his rhythm picking up speed until the sound of their skin slapping matched the headboard banging against the wall. She was so tight, so hot, so fucking *good!*

Giving up any semblance of control he grunted and groaned, slipping over the edge as his balls tightened and his dick swelled. The orgasm started at the base of his shaft and took less than a second to blast off. Her nails dug hard into his shoulders as she lifted herself off the bed and bit into his neck where her scream of release vibrated against his skin.

He lay on top of her for minute, sucking air into his lungs and trying to get his brain back online. Her hands roamed his back and shoulders, gently this time, and she'd just placed a soft kiss on his neck when the door to her hotel room slammed open. She shoved him upward and he rolled right off the edge of the bed and onto the floor—again!

A triumphant shout filled the room. "I've got you now, Anna Blair!"

Adrenaline surged through Gabe's veins and he jumped up to see a tall slim black man standing in the doorway with a *broadsword?*

Quicker than he could blink Anna rolled off the bed and came up into a crouch completely naked . . . and with two flashing knives in her hand.

"What the hell?" he cried.

4

Anna ignored Gabe and focused on the demon that had stormed into her room. At least this one looked like a demon—a man that is, except for the glowing red goat slit eyes.

"You had to ruin my good time, didn't you?" she asked it as they circled. "You couldn't camp outside until morning? Let me have a night of oh . . . fun!"

"I care not if you have fun, Anna Blair. I care only of ending you." He stepped forward and swung the broadsword.

She ducked and rolled under the swing, slicing across his stomach with her right arm as she came up.

"Let me guess, Focalor sent you?" she said when he spun around.

"My master has waited long enough for you. It is time to stop running, Anna Blair."

"Why the sudden hurry?" she asked. She stepped to the left a little so it moved to the right to counter. She was trying to get it away from Gabe, but she could see Gabe behind it getting ready to make a move. *I guess I'll get answers another time,* she thought as she feinted a move to the right but shifted left, snapping out a front kick to its hand, then following through with a straight arm spear that had her blade sinking into its chest.

Before she could retract her arm, the demon burst into flame and ash fell to the carpet, leaving a naked Gabe frozen and gaping at her like a goldfish out of water.

So much for her fun.

Anna tried real hard not to lose her temper as she searched under the bed for her other boot. Some people claimed to have a hot temper . . . but Anna *literally* had a hot temper, and she really didn't want to set Gabe on fire. It wasn't his fault she was so pissed off.

"Let me get this straight," Gabe said. He stood in the middle of her motel room, with his jeans, T-shirt, and socks on, and both of *his* boots in his hands. "Demons hunt you and you kill them? That's your life?"

"Pretty much."

"Why?"

"Why what?" Aha! There it was.

"Why do they hunt you?"

She dragged the boot out from under the bed and slid it onto her foot before glancing up at him. "Why aren't you calling me crazy for thinking demons are real?"

He rolled his shoulders and sort of shrugged. "I've heard rumors."

"Well, they're true. And judging by the way they've picked up the chase on me, I've got to get moving." After she finished tying up her bootlace, she stood and grabbed the backpack that lay against the wall. "It was fun while it lasted, Gabe."

"Wait! Wait a second." He reached out and grabbed her arm before she hit the door. "Where are you going?"

"Away from here before another one shows up."

"But where to?"

The concern in his gaze surprised her, confused her. He cared where she went? "Why do you care?"

His eyebrows jumped and he stiffened. "Well," he said. "I like you."

A warmth washed over her that had nothing to do with temper. "I like you too, Gabe. But I have to go."

"It's almost five in the morning, where are you going to go?"

She didn't have an answer for that. All she knew was that she'd been attacked twice in one night, and she wasn't going to wait around for Focalor to be third-time lucky.

"Come with me," Gabe said suddenly. He let her go and quickly shoved his feet into his boots. "I know somewhere you'll be safe."

"Gabe, you can't protect me from my life."

His scowl was fierce as he tied his boots and stood up. He grabbed her arm and led her out of the motel room through the door that would no longer close. "Don't tell me what I can and can't do."

5

He was an idiot. That's what he was. Caleb was going to laugh his ass off when Gabe told him what he wanted, but it was worth it. He just couldn't stand there and let Anna walk out of the motel and his life. He wasn't ready for that.

He'd known her less than twelve hours, but he liked her.

Anna was gorgeous in such a cute and innocent way, but she was an animal in bed. She spoke her mind and didn't fuck with his head the way most women seemed programmed to do automatically. Not to mention she kicked ass. Not just any ass either, but demon ass.

Christ, demons were real.

Caleb had tried to tell him that. Demons, werewolves, shape-shifters. They were all real.

"Where are we going?"

Gabe turned to look at her. She didn't have a car so they were both in his truck as he drove to Caleb's house. She'd been quiet since they left the motel, giving him time to think he guessed, but that time was up.

"We're going to my brother's house."

"Why?"

"His wife is psychic, maybe she can help."

"I've been to psychics before," she said amiably. "They've never helped, but sometimes they can be fun to play with."

"Huh?"

She smiled at him innocently. "Most who claim to be psychic are not. I find their lying to people to be a bit annoying, so sometimes I play with them. Teach them a lesson."

He didn't want to know how she did that.

Actually, he did. "How do you teach a fake psychic a lesson?"

"I light the things around them on fire."

"What?"

"Oh, nothing big." She waved her hand. "Just candles or something small. Flowers in a nearby vase or the tablecloth maybe. Just something to show them that there are powers out there that should not be mocked."

Before he could ask her how she did that, he pulled up in front of Caleb's house and noticed that the house was lit up like a Christmas tree. All thoughts of how Anna started those fires left his head as he noticed the vehicles in the driveway.

"Oh shit," he muttered. Slamming the truck into park he shut it off and jumped out.

Anna was out of the truck and staring at the house strangely when he got around the front of the truck. He didn't give it a thought as he strode toward the house.

"Come on," he called out when she hesitated to follow him.

"What's wrong, Gabe?"

Without answering her he knocked, opened the front door, and entered his brother's house without breaking his stride. His heart pounded and for the second time in less than an hour adrenaline flooded his system when he saw Drake Wheeler come into the hallway to greet him.

"Everyone is fine," Drake said before Gabe could say anything. "Gina finally went into labor and they're all at the hospital."

"Not all," Melissa Montrose said as she walked up behind Drake. She smiled at Gabe. "You should turn on your cell phone if you want to be kept up to date on things. They called you hours ago."

Relief washed over Gabe as he gaped at the couple. "They're okay?"

Drake nodded. "Yes. Devil said he'd call as soon as the baby was born."

Angelo Devlin, known to his family and friends as "Devil," was Gina's brother. He and Drake worked for a ritzy security company as Hunters. The job came with free access to a private jet that had no doubt been used to get them there quickly.

"You want to tell your friend that *we're* friends?" Melissa gestured to the right of Gabe and he turned to see Anna standing there.

She was just standing there, hands at her sides, but she had one of her shiny little knives in one hand and looked ready to spring.

"It's okay, Anna, this is my family." He pointed to the big blond guy that had greeted him as soon as he'd come in the door. "That's Drake Wheeler, the lady is his girlfriend Melissa Montrose."

She didn't take her gaze away from the couple in front of them. "You didn't tell me your family was . . . supernatural."

Surprised, Gabe stared at her. "You can tell that? How?"

"Because she is too," Drake said softly.

Anna's hand tightened on her knife and suddenly the tension in the room cranked up to high. Gabe stared from one person to the next.

"Okay, I don't have time for this shit," he said. "Anna, he's an empath and she's a shape-shifter. Guys, Anna is, well, I don't know exactly what she is other than demons are hunting her and she kills them. We're all on the same side, so just get along, okay? I need to get a hold of Caleb."

He pulled his cell phone from his back pocket and cursed when he saw the battery was dead. No wonder he hadn't heard it ring. He strode over to the landline.

He glanced over his shoulder when nobody else in the room moved. "Anna, put your knife away, they won't hurt you."

"Caleb is probably in the room with Gina, you should call Devil," Drake said and rattled off a number.

"Who is Devil?" Anna asked.

Gabe ignored her for the moment and listened to the phone ring on the other end. "No news yet," Gina's brother said as soon as he answered.

"But she's okay?"

"She's good," Devil replied. "She's in pain, but apparently that's normal. Caleb is with her, he's been with her for hours."

Gabe could hear the worry in the guy's voice and he sympathized. Devil had practically raised Gina after their parents had died, the same way Caleb had done for him. Both sets of siblings had only had each other for so long, only to be brought together into one very unorthodox and slightly freaky family when Caleb and Gina had fallen in love.

"Hang on," Devil said, excitement in his tone. "I can hear her."

Gabe felt Anna step up behind him, her hand on his back as he tensed. Devil was a telepath, and he had no doubt that by him saying he could hear her, he'd meant his sister Gina.

Sure enough a second later he laughed. "It's a boy! She had a boy! I've got to go, we'll be home soon."

Gabe put down the phone and took a deep breath. He had a nephew.

* * *

Anna watched as Gabe's energy shifted from a tense neon yellow back to his relaxed blue. The vibe was nice and thick and she relaxed with him.

He turned and smiled at her, then glanced at the others. "She had a boy."

The pretty woman cheered and the big man nodded silently, a small smile on his handsome face. Everyone was happy. It was time to get back to her problem.

"Can you tell me why you think I'm safe here now?" she asked.

Gabe put an arm around her and pulled her to his side with a chuckle. He kissed the top of her head. "Yes, we can talk about you now. Let's all sit down."

Once everyone was seated, Gabe told Drake and Melissa about the demon attack at the motel.

"It looked human though?" Drake asked carefully.

"Yeah, except for the glowing red eyes."

He looked at Anna, his face blank. "And you stabbed it with a knife and it burst into flame?"

She nodded. Why was he looking at her like that? "He was a demon, with a sword. It was it or me."

"Him," the big blond corrected. "You killed a man possessed by a demon, not a demon. Demons can't manifest themselves in this realm."

Excitement rippled through her. At last, someone who had some idea of what she was talking about. He was wrong, but she could fix that. "Demons *can* manifest in this realm, but not without a lot of help from someone stronger, like one of the goetic demons." Like Focalor, the bastard that wanted her.

But that wasn't what they were talking about right then. Anna leaned forward, elbows on her knees. "The one who attacked me in the alley earlier tonight was a full-on demon. My blade didn't work on him at first. I thought I was a goner but it soon turned him to dust. It just took a bit longer than with the ones who possess humans."

"What do you mean the one that attacked you in the alley?" Gabe asked, his voice rising slightly. "You were attacked twice tonight? Is that normal?"

Drake ignored the questions, so she did too. He stared at her, hard. "So you're aware that the man in the motel was a human possessed by a demon, and you killed him anyway?"

"Yes. It was him or me." She smiled at him. "It always is. You can't reason with a demon, they want what they want, and by the time they are after your blood, there is no changing their minds."

"She's right about that, Drake. There was no reasoning with the guy that stormed the motel room." Pleasure washed over her at Gabe's defense. She didn't need him to defend her, but it was nice of him to do so. She smiled at him and put her hand on his leg next to hers. She liked touching him. A lot.

The man cleared his throat and waited for Anna to look at him before speaking again. "How do you know so much about demons? Why are they hunting you?"

Anna looked at the silent woman next to Drake, then at Gabe. Should she tell them? They weren't evil, none of them. Despite her initial unease around the new couple, she knew that. And she liked Gabe. He covered her hand with his and warmth went up her arm that had nothing to do with her powers.

Gabe smiled at her, his bright blue eyes serious. "Go ahead, Anna. You can trust us."

"I know so much about demons because my mother was possessed by one when she was pregnant with me. When she went into labor the demon did not enjoy the pain, and left her of his own will." That was enough. She didn't want to tell them everything. Safety first.

Gabe stared at her, his jaw slack and his mouth slightly open. She smiled. He really was handsome, even when looking a little stunned.

"Is your mother still alive?"

She turned back to Drake. "No, she was killed by a different demon nine years ago."

"So why are they after you?"

"I don't want to tell you that, yet."

Drake scowled and Gabe laughed. "She's not what I would call subtle, Drake. Get used to it."

"Your mother taught you about demons then?"

She nodded. "Demonology was part of my mom's studies at the convent."

Gabe stared at her. "Your mother was a nun?"

"Well, a novice, and it was before she met my father obviously."

"Obviously." The twist of his lips told her nothing was obvious to him.

Humor warmed her insides and she grinned at Gabe. "You're surprised because I like to drink, fight, and fuck?"

"Well, yeah."

She'd never bothered to explain herself to anyone before. She'd never needed to. The demons she fought weren't interested in anything more than her powers and the men she fucked didn't care beyond the fact that she was willing. It was a strange sensation, but she actually wanted Gabe to understand why she was the way she was.

She turned to face him and met his questioning gaze. "God didn't give me life, my mother did. And although He has seen fit to send some pretty good tools to help me deal, He can't tell me how to live it. Mom taught me to live with a good heart, and find happiness where I can. So I do."

Gabe's eyes darkened and his expression softened in a way

that made her heart pound. Suddenly the day, and the orgasms, caught up with her and Anna's muscles got heavy. She sat back on the sofa and leaned into Gabe's side, happy to feel his arm around her shoulders.

Drake looked at them and straightened up. "You guys should get some rest while you can. Why don't you head for the guest bedroom and we'll wake you when the others get back?"

That sounded real good to her. She turned to Gabe. "Are you sure I'll be safe here for a while?"

"Devil's wife, Jewel, is a gypsy. She set wards around the house a long time ago, so if a demon tries to get in we'll have plenty of warning." Drake met her gaze. "We've had a demon attack here before, too."

Gabe stood and pulled Anna up with him. "Night guys," he said and led Anna from the room.

Anna didn't question the wards, she'd seen them when they'd pulled up in front of the house, and had been relieved that they hadn't gone off when she'd entered the house. After all, her powers had come from the demon who'd possessed her mother.

They were a gift from hell.

6

Gabe led her down a short hallway with photographs hung along the walls. She held back and made him go slow so she could look at some of them.

She caught glimpses of Gabe at various ages, in a graduation cap and gown, in a snazzy suit with a drink in hand, and also dancing with a woman in a wedding dress. If it wasn't for the photo of another man on his knees in front of the same woman in the same dress right next to it, she'd wonder if he'd ever been married.

"Gina and Caleb's wedding last October," Gabe said when he saw her pause longer at the picture of a large group, all dressed formally. She recognized Gabe, Drake, and Melissa, and figured the others were Gabe's brother Caleb, his wife Gina, her brother Devil, and his wife Jewel. It wasn't hard to guess that Jewel was a gypsy, she had the long flowing tresses and curves that should be cliché, but were actually very beautiful. There was also a teenage girl there who resembled the gypsy.

Every one of the people in that photo wore a mile-wide grin. The photo was an inanimate object with no energy of its own, but Anna could imagine the phenomenal vibe that they'd given off that day.

Anna's chest tightened as she stood there.

They were a family. All of them.

"You all right?" Gabe asked.

She tore her gaze from the photos and smiled at him. He was a good man. "Yes, I'm okay."

He tugged on her hand and she followed him into the guest bedroom. When they were both in the room Gabe closed the door, then pulled her into a hug.

A hug.

No one but her mother had ever given her a hug before.

Strange new emotions rose up in Anna and she hesitated for just a second before wrapping her arms around Gabe. She simply held onto him and absorbed the energy that they created together. Warm, safe, honest energy that filled her mind's eye and flooded through her system.

When she pulled back from him, the tears welling in her eyes surprised her more than him.

"I'm sorry," she said.

She hadn't cried in a long time. Not since her mother's funeral. Not real tears, anyway. Movie tears didn't count.

Gabe smiled down at her and brushed a falling tear away with his thumb. "It's okay," he said. "You've had a rough day."

Which brought to mind some things she wanted to share. Things she'd never wanted to share with anyone before. She moved to the edge of the bed and sat down. "How tired are you?"

"I'm good. What's up?"

"We should talk."

Gabe nodded, his blue eyes serious. "Okay, but let's get comfortable."

When they both settled back onto the bed, their feet were

bare, Gabe's chest was bare, and Anna had gotten rid of her hoodie and weapons sheath. Gabe was stretched out on the bed with his back resting against the wall while Anna sat cross-legged facing him.

"What's up?" he asked.

Anna never had trouble saying what she wanted to before, but she'd also never told anyone her whole story before. Gabe had brought her there to keep her safe, and he deserved to know what he'd brought into their home.

"I have demonic powers," she said. Gabe's eyes widened and his jaw dropped, but Anna didn't stop talking. "The demonic spirit that possessed my mother when she was pregnant with me left them behind when he departed from her, and Focalor is a demon lord who finds it highly offensive that a human has retained the powers he gave an underling. He wants them back and has put a bounty on me, which is why the demons all hunt me."

By the time she was done talking Gabe had closed his mouth, and he stared at her. There was no fear or recrimination in his gaze, and Anna's muscles relaxed.

Until that moment she hadn't realized just how tense she was, how much she cared about his reaction.

His eyes suddenly lit up. "The fire thing!"

"Excuse me?"

"You said on the way here that you liked to play with phony psychics by lighting things on fire around them. But when we got here and I saw all the lights on in the house I forgot all about it. That's how you do it? You have some power, like the little girl in *Firestarter?*"

She laughed. If he was quoting movies, he was definitely someone she could get along with, even outside the bedroom. "Yeah, sort of like her, but instead of a big secret agency of some kind wanting to control me, the demons want the powers back."

"Cool." He nodded. "What other powers do you have?"

She explained to him about the way she could see and sense the energy of living things, including people. "So that's almost sort of like Drake's empathy thing. I don't know exactly how Drake's power works, but they could be similar. Emotion is energy. However, I think an empath *feels* other peoples emotions, while I only see them."

They talked about various psychic gifts and abilities, and Gabe told her how his sister-in-law had known from the minute she'd met Caleb that he was her soul mate.

"Do you believe in soul mates?" she asked him. He rubbed his hand on her thigh and thought about it. His brows drew together and his lips tightened briefly. Then his eyes cleared and he looked at her. "I think there are people that we all instinctively fit with, but I'm not sure I'd call them soul mates."

She uncrossed her legs and crawled on the bed until she could swing a leg over his. When she was sitting in his lap, she braced her hands on the wall behind his head and leaned close. "We fit together pretty good."

His eyes rounded and she kissed him before he could say anything more. She didn't believe in the idea of soul mates, but she did believe in enjoying the moment.

Blood heating and pulse pounding though his body, Gabe gripped Anna's hips and pulled her tight against him. He'd been up for twenty-four hours with no sleep, but he wasn't the least bit tired, all he could think about was sinking back into the woman in his arms.

She straddled his lap and rocked against his rapidly filling cock. He slid his hands up her back, loving the way her feminine muscles rippled and moved under his hands. She was such a strong little thing. So hard and firm in some places, and so irresistibly soft in others.

He cupped her head, tangling his fingers in her soft curls and pulling her head back so he could kiss the bruise he'd noticed forming under her jaw. She'd been attacked twice that day. He'd watched her fight and kill a man—no, not a man. A *demon-possessed man.*

The grace and speed she'd shown told him more than anything that she was a fighter—a warrior. Gabe relaxed his grip on her hair and she straightened up, leaning over him as if she sensed his thoughts. Soft blond curls fell forward, brushing against her cheeks as they stared at each other. Their breaths mingled and his heart thumped in his chest. The passion and soft wonder in her eyes made him want to hold her so tight that he never had to let go. He wanted to keep her safe so she never had to fight again, so that she only knew pleasure and passion for the rest of her life.

He cupped her cheek and pulled her down until their lips pressed together once again. He nibbled on her bottom lip, then sucked her tongue into his mouth. He caressed it with his own, wallowing in the flavor that was all her.

"You taste so good," he whispered. "Take your clothes off, I want to taste you all over."

Her eyes lit up and she jumped off him. "Oh, yes!"

Gabe chuckled at her eagerness as he watched her strip. God, how he loved the way she was so open. There was no shyness in her and her enthusiasm stoked his arousal. He stood up and quickly shucked his clothes. By the time he'd checked the bedside table and set out a condom packet, she was already back on the bed.

"You like the idea of being eaten up by me, do you?" He asked with a chuckle as he climbed back on the bed and arranged himself between her legs. "Put your hands on the wall," he commanded.

Her eyebrows jumped and she hesitated for a second before lifting her arms over her head and placing her hands against the wall. He shifted closer, breathing deep as her scent floated up his nostrils. Musky and slightly spicy, it filled his head and fired his blood up even more.

"Good girl," he purred. His fingertips brushed across her swollen pussy lips, stroking the soft curls there, and her whole body jerked in response. "Ooh, a little sensitive, are you?"

Her hips wiggled and Anna smiled down at him. "Very sensitive," she said. "Lick me, Gabe."

He quirked an eyebrow at her and fought to keep a straight face. "What is the proper social etiquette when you make a request of someone, Anna?"

"Please?"

He lowered his head, thrust his tongue between her pretty pink pussy lips and licked. He licked up and down, learning the dips and swells between the slick folds of her sex, until he nudged against her entrance. Slipping a hand under his chin, he moved his mouth up to the hot button at the top of her slit.

The soft pelt of her curls tickled his nose and he wallowed in her scent. He sucked her clit between his lips at the same time as he thrust two fingers deep into her and her hips bucked against him, her moans filling the room.

He nibbled and sucked, and her clit grew in his mouth, hardening for him. He tapped at the rigid ball of nerves with the tip of his tongue and her insides clenched around his fingers.

"More," she gasped. "Inside me, please."

He curled the fingers inside her and thrust a bit deeper, reaching for that sweet spot that would set her off.

It didn't take long. Her body tightened, her pussy clenched around his fingers, and her back arched off the bed as she came, her juices flowing faster than he could lick them up.

But he wasn't done. No way, he wanted more. He continued to lick her whole pussy gently until her shudders subsided, then he nipped one of the swollen lips sharply, and she yelped.

He glanced up to make sure she wasn't glaring at him, only to see her eyes closed and a blissful smile on her full lips.

Arousal and anticipation blended as he shifted again. His nose brushed against the tender knot of her clit as he worked his tongue against her entrance. He nudged her thighs farther apart with his shoulders and slid his cum-covered fingers between her butt cheeks to tease her rear entrance.

"Oooh," she sighed.

Any doubts he had about her willingness for a little anal play disappeared when she spread her legs wider and pressed down against his roving digits.

His dick jumped, bouncing against his belly as it throbbed to the rapid beat of his heart. He moaned against her pussy and she ground against him even more. Eager, but careful, he pressed a finger against her anus, sliding into her to the first knuckle.

"Oh, yes, Gabe. I like that!"

The surprised pleasure in her voice made his chest fill with pride. He pulled back, panting.

"Turn over," he commanded. "Get on your hands and knees so I can fuck that ass."

She didn't hesitate and he rolled the condom on while she turned over. When her ass was in the air, he knelt there for a moment, just staring as he stroked a fist over his hard-on.

She wiggled her ass and tilted her hips for him, and Gabe dove in. He spread her rounded cheeks with his hands and bent low enough to lick at her pussy again. He squeezed her butt cheeks and moved one hand so his thumb pressed against her puckered hole. His tongue delved deep into her juicy cunt and his thumb breached her anus. He panted for breath, her juices covering his lips and running down his chin as he pumped his thumb in and out, and his tongue worked her over. Fuck she tasted good. She felt good. Her legs trembled and her body pressed back against him as her panting gasps of pleasure filled the room and ratcheted up his own arousal to the point where his blood was pounding through his veins so fast and hard that his brain shut down.

He pulled his thumb out, thrust two fingers into her ass, and she screamed. He froze, at first thinking he'd hurt her, then the wash of juices on his tongue and the way she pushed against him hit him. His bit of roughness had set off another orgasm.

His whole body flushed with heat and he pulled back, withdrawing from her body. He slid his hand between her thighs and slicked her juices up from her pussy to her ass, lubing her up. He pressed his hips against her and thrust his cock between her thighs, sliding it back and forth between the hot slick come-covered pussy lips until he was well coated.

His hands gripped her hips and he lined his cock up with her puckered hole. He pressed forward slowly, using his tight grip on her hips to keep her from pressing back against him so hard. He eased into her, gritting his teeth at the hot tight fit, until he was hilt deep.

He froze, struggling for control. He didn't want to go too fast and hurt her. The only thought in his head was to not hurt this wonderfully open, sexy, sensual, amazing woman.

"Anna." He panted, trying to speak clearly, trying to *think* clearly. "Baby, you need to tell me if I go too fast. I don't want to hurt you."

"Move," she said, rocking back against him. "You're not hurting me. I want more."

He started slow, loving the long slow rub of his body connecting with hers. Neither of them lasted long. The tremors started in her first, and Gabe's cock swelled, throbbing hotly as her insides stroked him and she cried out again. Her ass squeezed his cock and his hips pumped uncontrollably as everything in him centered on the sensation ripping through his body.

When he became halfway aware of things again, he was collapsed on the bed, with Anna curled against his side. He squinted against the glare of the overhead light as he left the bed. He got rid of the condom, turned off the light, and crawled back into bed.

Anna was sleeping soundly, her lips parted in a little moue. Panic had hit him hard when she'd asked if he believed in soul mates, but at that moment, for the first time, as he looked down at the angelic-looking woman in his bed, he believed that just maybe there was such a thing.

He pulled the throw blanket from the end of the bed up and gathered the still sleeping Anna in his arms, covering them both before he drifted to sleep.

7

Anna woke up a few hours later to the feel of a lean male body pressed against her back and a hot thick cock rubbing against her butt.

She hummed her pleasure and rolled over to face Gabe. With sleep heavy eyes and mussed-up hair he was better than good looking. He was . . . heartbreaking. Anna's breath caught in her throat as she realized that somehow she had come to care for the man in front of her. A lot.

He'd been fun, and interesting. He'd talked to her, laughed with her, and he'd fucked her so senseless the night before she hadn't even noticed the demon approaching her motel room door.

Even more than any of that, he'd cared enough to find her a safe haven for the night, and to listen to her. It was more than anyone except her mother had ever done for her.

"Good morning, beautiful," he whispered. He lifted a gentle hand and brushed a curl from her cheek and she was suddenly awash with intense emotion and need.

The need to be connected, truly connected with him, face to

face, took over and she slid her hands through his thick hair. She tilted his head down and kissed him. Unable to put her need into words she put everything into that kiss and his fingers dug into her hips.

She rubbed against him, chest to chest, belly to belly, groin to groin as their mouths met hungrily. Gabe shifted forward and over her, his hands sliding up over her ribs to cup her breasts, her hands sliding down his back caressingly. Her pulse raced and her body warmed, softened, readying itself for him as he settled between her thighs once again.

Anna's nails scraped against his skin, delighting in the flexing of his muscles everywhere she touched. Her heart pounded as she wrapped her legs around his waist and rubbed against him, searching for the friction she needed.

A frustrated growl rose in her throat and she arched her back, rolling them over so she was on top.

Gabe laughed and cupped his hands around her ass. Heat swam through her veins as he squeezed her butt, making her grind against him in response. Shifting her weight, she moved lower until the length of his cock was sliding between her pussy lips. She moved against him and the head nudged her entrance.

She braced her hands on the mattress next to his head, and stared down into Gabe's eyes. Then she rolled her hips, up and down she rocked while the length of his cock slid back and forth along her slit. She bit her lip and rocked some more, each time the head of his cock nudged against her entrance, but didn't breach it. She held herself a millimeter too far from him for that, and the tease was exquisite.

"Anna," he groaned, his body arching beneath hers. "Please woman, you're killing me."

No matter how powerful and sexy his words made her feel, she couldn't resist the pleading in his tone. With a roll of her hips she had him right where she wanted him.

She froze, the head of his cock pushing against her. Losing herself in his gaze, she lowered her weight and his cock slid into her welcoming body. Neither of them moved for a moment. They just stayed there, absorbing the sensations, cementing their connection.

Then she sat up and felt him shift deeper. He was so deep she swore they would never come apart.

Gabe's hands rested on her thighs and she rolled her hips again. She leaned forward, balancing herself by placing her hands on his solid chest, and withdrew her hips. Then she slid back down the full length of him as pleasure rippled through her body. Slowly she rotated her hips, up and down. Savoring the feel of him filling her up again and again. Drowning in the emotion in his eyes, as he watched her take them both to the edge.

Soon, it wasn't enough. Anna planted her hands on the mattress next to his head and really began to ride him. She rocked back and forth, using him to forget everything but the knot of sensations building in her sex.

Their panting filled the air, erotic music in the utter silence between them. His hands skimmed over her rib cage to her swaying breasts. He cupped them, tugging at the nipples until she lowered herself enough so that he could clamp his lips around one of the rigid tips. He suckled briefly, and then nipped it sharply with his teeth and she ground down hard on him, seeing stars at the same time he dug his heels into the mattress and thrust up, lodging himself deep and shooting hot fluid into her, filling all the emptiness inside.

She closed her eyes and collapsed on top of him, their bodies slick with sweat and still connected. His heart pounded against his chest . . . and the rhythm was in tune with hers.

8

When Gabe woke up again, Anna wasn't in the bed next to him. He got up, stepped into his jeans, and headed for the kitchen. The sun was bright and shiny and his watch said it was almost eleven in the morning. The voices got louder as he got closer to the kitchen and apprehension set in. Anna was alone with his family, and they weren't always the easiest people to get along with.

"Good morning, everyone," he said as he entered the kitchen. Drake and Melissa were nowhere to be seen. Devil wasn't around either, but his wife Jewel was sitting at the table with Anna and Nadya, Jewel's little sister.

Anna had apparently showered before he woke up, and had on fresh clothes from her backpack. She was bright and smiley, and showed no signs of a person who'd had less than five hours of sleep.

Anna and Jewel smiled at him while he poured himself some coffee, Nadya just waved and stared at Anna.

"I was held captive by a demon-possessed man once," Nadya said. "Devil killed him."

Anna nodded at the girl. "Devil did the right thing."

"Did he really? I could feel the man still inside the body. He was a good man, a good soul." Her fingers twisted together on the tabletop. "I think they should've let me exorcise him. We should have at least tried to save the man."

Anna's shoulders lifted and fell in a delicate shrug. "Most humans aren't strong enough to survive a demon's possession, unless they themselves are evil. And if they're evil, then killing them is good."

"That's a pretty black-and-white view of things," Jewel said.

"Yes."

"Why don't good humans survive?" Nadya asked.

Gabe hadn't been around when Nadya had been kidnapped. He'd been in Vancouver attending a business seminar for a job that had lasted less than six months. He still got guilty twinges about Caleb paying for him to go to school to get a degree he didn't use. But they hadn't known that at the time. Caleb had wanted Gabe to be educated, and Gabe had wanted to do something other than work construction for his older brother. Or so he'd thought.

Six months after getting his degree, he realized he enjoyed the manual labor and the camaraderie of the construction crews, so he went back to work for his brother at Mann's Construction, and took on more of the administrative duties. It worked for them both, especially since Caleb was going to be raising a family.

Anna's sure voice brought him back to the conversation at hand and he listened as she tried to make the teenager understand why killing demon-possessed humans was necessary.

"Their bodies are made to do things when they're possessed that the soul of a good person can't always reconcile themselves with," she said. "If an exorcism *is* successful, the chances of the person being mentally and spiritually broken are pretty high."

"Your mother survived," Jewel said.

"The demon wasn't exorcised from my mom. It left her willingly after she went into labor to deliver me, which is less traumatic for the human. Or at least that's what we figure since it's the only time we'd ever heard of a demon willingly leaving a human body to return to hell." She looked at the sisters and Gabe saw her shrug again. "Plus, my mom had me. Raising and protecting me gave her a reason for living."

Wow, Gabe thought. *That was something pretty heavy to lay on a kid.* No wonder Anna's whole life view was demons. She'd really known nothing else.

"Let's go to the hospital," he said before Nadya could ask more questions about demon hunting. He didn't think Anna minded the questions, but he did. The sudden urge to show her there was more to life than drinking, fighting, and fucking was powerful.

After grabbing a quick shower, alone, and a pair of sweats from Caleb's closet, he was ready to go.

Anna felt almost normal as she rode in the truck beside Gabe. Jewel and Nadya were in the backseat of the cab and he was taking them all to the hospital to see the new baby!

"So your knives are blessed, that's what makes them special?" Nadya asked as she handed the pure silver blade she'd been examining back to Anna.

"Partly, yes. The convent my mom was a part of has a sect that makes weapons and studies demon patterns and such. They've supplied me with weapons since I was a child."

"What sort of weapons?"

Anna glanced at Gabe and saw his smile. She didn't mind that he found it amusing the women were talking weapons. His smile was nice and it brightened his pretty blue eyes.

She grinned back at him and listed the weapons she'd used

over the years. "Crossbows, swords, short blades and long blades, dart guns, and a variety of knives. I like the throwing knives. It's smarter to try and keep your distance when fighting evil."

"I think a dart gun would be cool," Nadya said.

Jewel shook her head. "What happens if you run out of darts in the middle of a fight? Blades are always better."

Anna listened to the sisters bicker back and forth, and wondered if this was what having friends felt like.

She hadn't been able to go back to sleep after her morning ride on Gabe, so she'd showered and dressed, and slowly moved through the house to the kitchen. Just being in a house instead of a motel room had filled her with a sense that things were changing. More things than the fact that she'd been tracked down and attacked twice the day before. She'd never been attacked twice in one day. Until a month earlier, the only time she'd seen more than one demon every couple of weeks was when she hunted them!

She glanced at Gabe as he pulled into the hospital parking lot. Yeah, more than one thing was changing in her life.

"Let's go, ladies," Gabe said as soon as he'd parked.

They all got out of the truck and headed to the door. Gabe's hand found hers as they walked side by side, and their fingers twined together. Nadya raced ahead of them and Jewel smiled.

"She's been so excited about that baby," Jewel said. "She plans to be the auntie that spoils that kid rotten."

"Caleb said she's been doing a lot better since Melissa has been working with her."

Anna listened with half an ear as they talked about Nadya learning to manage her shape-shifting abilities. She'd caught a hint of something strange on the air and tried to focus her concentration, but she couldn't nail it down.

"Anna?" Gabe tugged on her hand. "You okay?"

The sliding doors of the hospital entrance slid open and they went in. Different energies smacked her upside the head and she blinked, quickly getting rid of the swirling colors of her mind's eye.

"Anna?"

She squeezed his hand and smiled up at him. "I'm good."

It was so sweet of him to be concerned for her. She'd started to wonder if she'd ever find someone to share her life with, and it occurred to her that maybe Gabe was the reason she'd been drawn to Pearson. With his supernaturally eclectic family, she didn't really stand out all that much.

They rode up in the elevator and when the doors slid open on the nursery floor the four of them stepped out. Nadya and Jewel walked ahead and Gabe hung back with her. She saw Jewel embrace a tall dark man dressed all in black who stood with Drake and Melissa. Anna saw another man with his face pressed against the window, and knew instantly this was Caleb, Gabe's brother.

She let go of Gabe's hand and watched as the two men embraced. "Congratulations," Gabe said.

She took a step back and watched as they all tried to talk at once. The men slapped each other on the backs and the women rushed to the big window as a nurse held up a tiny blue-blanketed bundle. She didn't need to use her mind's eye to see the happiness and love that surrounded the group. She could see it in their faces, in the way they all constantly kept touching each other. Gabe turned from the window and saw her hanging back. He held out his hand and Anna felt their happiness, all thick and warm, reach out to her.

With her heart pounding and chest tight, she stepped forward and was introduced to the rest of the family.

An hour later they were all leaving the hospital, even Caleb. "You stink, my brother," Gabe said to him as they stood in the elevator.

Caleb grinned and rubbed a hand over the stubble covering his jaw. "Yeah, but I have a healthy baby boy."

"You need a shower."

"Yeah, but I have a son."

Everyone laughed and Devil nudged the other man. "That's going to be your answer to everything for a while, isn't it Caleb?"

"Yeah, pretty much."

The doors slid open and once again everyone exited en masse. Gabe stayed back and wrapped his arm around Anna.

"You okay?" he whispered, his lips brushing against her ear and sending a shiver down her spine.

"Of course."

"My family can be a bit . . . overwhelming at times."

"I like them," she said gazing up at him. "There's a lot of magic here. You're very lucky."

He looked like he was going to argue, but then he just shrugged and said maybe she was right. Then he kissed her.

His hand cupped the back of her neck and he held her close while his mouth moved over hers. It was unlike any kiss she'd ever experienced. It wasn't a passionate-fucking kind of kiss, but one full of . . . promise.

"Gabe," she said when he pulled back.

"Anna," he replied.

She didn't know what else to say. Somehow, in less than twenty-four hours, she'd fallen in love.

Stunned, she said nothing. Gabe pressed a quick kiss to her lips and then led her toward the parking lot.

The others were ahead of them, waiting by the back of Gabe's truck. When there was less than ten yards separating them, the hairs all over Anna's body stood up.

She pulled her hand free and reached for her blades. She wanted to close her eyes, to search out the energy that she felt, but she had nothing to put her back to.

"Anna?"

"Get behind me, Gabe. Now."

She saw him look at the knives she gripped and then swing his head around, his gaze searching the parking lot. "I don't see anything, Anna."

"What's wrong?" Drake called out.

"Nadya get in the truck," Devil's deep voice commanded. "Caleb and Mel, stay here."

Anna heard Nadya arguing with Devil's orders and worked to tune them out. She saw Drake approaching her, his movements slow and cautious. "What is it, Anna?"

"Demon," she said. "Nearby, I can feel it. But I can't see it."

"I can't sense anyone," he said.

Gabe stepped between them, as if to protect her from Drake. "If Anna says it's nearby, it's nearby."

"You're trying to sense the human soul," she said. "Focus on the demon essence instead."

As soon as the words left her mouth, she felt the ripple of evil wash over her and her feet were moving.

"Anna!"

She sprinted around Gabe and Drake but she was too late. Everyone had shuffled around as if Anna were the threat, putting Nadya the farthest away from her. Only she could see the thing behind the teenager as it materialized and reached for the girl.

"*Gloria Patri, et Filio, et Spiritui Sancto,*" Anna prayed as she dropped her blades, called to her inner power and threw two balls of hellfire at it in rapid succession. It batted the fire away as if it was nothing but that gave Nadya time to drop and roll under the truck.

Anna reached for another knife from her sheath, and Devil stepped forward, but the demon disappeared.

"Holy shit!" Gabe muttered from directly behind her.

"There's nothing holy about that thing," Anna muttered as she turned a slow circle. "It's still here."

She backed up until she was up against Gabe. "Keep watch," she said and closed her eyes. It took two seconds and she found the source of the vibrations bouncing over her skin. She opened her eyes and spun around Gabe, ready to fight.

The demon was standing between two parked cars, less than two yards away.

It was tall, golden skinned, and had wings folded along its back. It moved forward and without hesitation, and Anna stepped to meet it—only to be grabbed from behind by Gabe.

"No!" he said, his hand wrapping around her arm and stopping her.

She sensed more than saw Drake, Devil, and Jewel flank them.

The demon didn't even glance at them; he had eyes only for Anna. Staring at her, he smiled a grossly beautiful smile, then disappeared into thin air.

The vibrations disappeared and Anna jerked her arm away from Gabe to sheath her knives. "It's gone."

"What the hell was that?" Devil asked.

"*That*," Anna said with a glance at Drake, "was a fully manifested demon lord."

9

Gabe kept his mouth shut on the drive home.

So did Anna.

Since they were the only two people in his truck, it made for a quiet drive. He didn't care. He was pissed off at her and it took all of his concentration to keep from yelling at the top of his lungs. He needed to breathe, and drive. Breathe, and drive.

The family had split into three vehicles when they left the hospital and when he parked his truck, Caleb was the only one already home. Drake, Devil, and their crew hadn't arrived yet.

As soon as they entered the house, Anna turned to face him. "I'm sorry I put your family in danger," she said. "I'll get my bag and leave before they get back."

That made him lose his temper. "Like hell!"

Caleb took one look at the two of them and left the room.

Anna didn't even notice. Her pretty forehead wrinkled and she stared at him. "It's not safe for any of you if I stay."

"We're safer together than apart."

"I agree. You should stay with them."

Emotion boiled over inside of him and he lost it. "What the

fuck do you mean I stay and you'll leave? You're not going anywhere without me, Anna. I don't care what the hell you can do with knives or . . . or . . . fire or whatever powers you have. You are not going anywhere!"

"Don't yell at me," she said.

"Then listen to me."

"When you make sense, I will listen to you."

Gabe bit back a growl. He *was* making sense, she was just being dense.

He took a deep breath and held out his hands. "Okay, let's start this again. Anna, are you nuts?"

Okay, so that wasn't exactly what he'd meant to say.

"Me?" Color rose in Anna's pale cheeks and her hands clenched into fists at her sides. "It's you who is nuts. What did you think you were doing grabbing my arm when a demon is right in front of me? You think I can fight with you hanging on my arm?"

Devil's voice came from behind Gabe. "She's right, you know."

Gabe ignored the crowd that had followed Devil in and focused on Anna. "You weren't supposed to fight it! That's the whole point!"

"You think I should've just stood there and let him snatch Nadya? Or you? Focalor wants me, and he'll do anything to get me."

Gabe stilled. "Him?"

"That was no possessed human, Gabe. That was Focalor, the Great Duke of Hell himself! I don't know why he's suddenly stepped up the hunt. I don't understand why in the last week I've been attacked six times. Twice yesterday, on my first day in this city. Twice in one day, Gabe. That has never happened in my life!"

She pointed a trembling hand at him and the family spread

out behind him. "He will kill you all with nothing more than a laugh if you get in his way."

Silence fell on the room and Anna stood there, fists planted on her hips, cheeks flushed, chest heaving and it hit Gabe. She was afraid. His tough little warrior angel was afraid. And not for herself, but for *him and his family.*

Unable to speak past the emotion clogging his throat, Gabe stepped forward and pulled her into a hug.

"Shhh, it's going to be okay." He saw Caleb standing in the living room doorway, watching them. "It's going to be okay, Anna. My family is pretty hard to kill."

"You have a new baby coming home soon," she said against his chest. "I have to leave, Gabe. That baby needs to have a safe home."

Pride knifed through him at her words. She was hunted, had been hunted her whole life, and her first thought was to make sure his new nephew had a safe place to come home to.

She truly was an angel, and he was going to make sure she didn't go anywhere.

Hours later Anna sat at the dining room table of Caleb Mann's house and watched in awe as half a dozen people she'd known for one day worked to find a way to help her.

Melissa and Nadya typed madly on a laptop, searching for she didn't know what. Jewel paced in the corner of the room with a cell phone to her ear. Drake and Devil sat on the other side of the table with a map of the city in front of them.

Caleb sat on one side of her and Gabe on the other. Caleb leaned in and spoke softly so only she and Gabe could hear him. "They can be a bit much, can't they?"

"Are they always so . . . intense?" Gabe asked.

"Yeah, pretty much."

Anna looked at Gabe. "You don't know?"

He shrugged. "I've never been around when they worked.

224

Caleb's told me stories, which is why I didn't freak out when you told me demons really exist. He'd told me they did."

Caleb snorted. "You didn't believe me when *I* told you. You thought I was nuts."

Anna sat there as the two brothers leaned in on her from each side and argued back and forth.

"Well, you marry a psychic then tell me her brother is a mind reader and her best friend a telepath, and I thought whatever. But then you introduced me to Jewel and Nadya, telling me they were gypsies, and Melissa who you said was a shapeshifter, and they all look normal to me so I thought . . . well, I don't know what I thought."

"You didn't believe me."

"I didn't *not* believe you," Gabe insisted. "I just wondered if you were cracking up a bit."

Warmth flowed over Anna and she grinned. Magic was all around her. Robust magic full of love and strength. She leaned to the left and pressed a kiss to Caleb's cheek, then to the right to place one on Gabe's cheek.

The men stopped bickering and stared at her, puzzled. "Thank you," she said.

Caleb glanced at Gabe with a smirk. "She'll fit right in."

"I've got it." Jewel's words got everyone's attention. She moved toward the table, stuffing her cell phone into her back pocket as she stared at Anna. "You said this Focalor has been after you since you were a baby because it was one of his spirits that possessed your mother, right?"

"Yes." Anna nodded. "Because Mom was pregnant with me when she was possessed, and the demon spirit stayed inside her until she was in full labor, I sort of inherited its powers. Focalor does not like a human having one of his minion's powers. He's always wanted them back."

"And to get them back he has to kill you?"

"At first the bounty hunters he sent after me just wanted to take me to him in hell. Lately though, they've been trying to kill me, yes." She shrugged. "I'm not sure if killing me will get the powers back, but it would do just as well."

Jewel nodded. "According to my clan's wise woman, there is a legend about humans surviving possession by receiving demonic powers. Shuvani said that if you hold the powers for thirty years then they can never be taken away from you. Any bounty on you, and the powers you have, will be lifted."

Anna sat up. If they couldn't be taken away from her, the demons would stop hunting her. She could stop running. She could find a home.

She could keep the good-looking Gabe for herself.

"Why thirty years?" Devil asked, bringing her back from her own personal fantasyland.

"Because it's the number of the circle, and the circle is the geometric expression for infinity," Anna answered as she looked at Gabe, wonder making her heart light. "A full cycle."

It all made sense now—why the attacks had been so many in the last weeks. Why Focalor himself had shown himself on this day. "My thirtieth birthday is tomorrow."

One more night, she just had to live through one more night, and the bounty would be lifted. No more demons chasing her. No more—

What? No more Focalor? He wouldn't cease to exist just because she turned thirty. He might not be able to reclaim her powers for another of his demon spirits, but he'd still hunt her. He was a demon lord, and he'd still see her as an abomination. Not just a human with demonic powers, but a human who'd continue to hunt evil with those demonic powers.

She'd never stop fighting the evil in the world. It was what she was born for. And because of that, he'd still want to kill her.

Unless she killed him first.

10

"She's going to rabbit, isn't she?"

Gabe was in the kitchen with Devil and Caleb, putting away the last of the dinner dishes. He could see Anna and Jewel working on Jewel's laptop at the dining room table from where he stood. Everyone thought it best to get Nadya away in case of another demon confrontation so Drake and Melissa had left to go back to Mel's bookstore in Chadwick, taking Nadya with them.

Gabe felt more than saw Devil and Caleb share a look.

"Oh, yeah," Caleb said. "You've run true to the family in that way. Your woman is definitely stubborn and unwilling to back down or hide from a fight. Even if it's only for one night."

"She thinks we'll be safer if she's gone."

Devil spoke up. "We've all felt that we were a threat to our loved ones at one time or another."

"Not all of us," Caleb said.

"I'm not letting her hunt that demon lord by herself. Why does she have to hunt it at all? I mean, in less than twenty-four hours she'll be safe."

Devil frowned. "She'll never be safe. Not as long as that demon knows she's alive."

"Why? He can't take her powers away after tomorrow."

"He's evil," Devil said. "Sure he wants the powers back, but he also wants to make sure no human has them. He'll kill her even if he can't retrieve the powers."

Gabe glared at Devil, then met his brother's gaze. "This is fucked up."

Caleb smiled grimly. "Welcome to my world."

Guilt hit Gabe and he tried to smile at his big brother. "You should be at the hospital with Gina and the baby."

"You're my brother. I'm here for you."

"Don't be an idiot," Gabe said, loving that his brother would stick by him. "This is a fortress with Jewel's mystical wards and three experienced demon fighters here. You go be with your wife. And when I see you tomorrow my nephew better have a name."

Caleb was torn, and it was clear on his face. Finally he gave in. He threw his dish towel on the counter, slapped Devil and Gabe on the back, and left the house.

Gabe met Devil's gaze and forced a smile. "I think it's time for Anna and I to go to bed now."

Devil chuckled as Gabe headed for the dining room. "Bring some rope."

He took her breath away.

Lying in bed next to the man who'd changed her life in the space of twenty-four hours, Anna struggled with the knowledge that it might be the last time she looked upon his face. The last time she touched him. She'd known by the fire in his eyes and the steel in his jaw when he'd told her they were staying at Caleb's that night that arguing wouldn't be worth it.

He'd expected a fight, but he hadn't gotten one. She'd already had a plan, so she'd docilely followed him to the bedroom, and then proceeded to fuck him stupid.

They'd gone at it like animals, then again, like lovers, staring into one another's eyes, breathing each other's air, bodies moving in a well-synchronized dance until the earth moved and they fell asleep holding onto one another for dear life.

Now, as she stood beside the bed in the pitch black night and stared down at him, she had to fight the urge to crawl back into bed and curl into his big warm body. It had felt like home. She belonged there, in his arms, if only she weren't being hunted.

Fingers that gripped her worn backpack itched to run through his thick hair, to cup his cheek and feel the stubble of his morning beard. The need to touch him, to assure herself that he was there, that he was safe, was strong. The urge to ensure he was safe was stronger.

Good-bye, she said silently, then moved to the bedroom door and creaked it open. Unable to resist, she turned and took a final look at the man who'd claimed her love.

By the time the sun rose in the morning sky Focalor might have her powers, and God might have her soul, but Gabe would always have her heart.

11

Anna knew how to hunt, but she didn't need to hunt Focalor. All she had to do was pick a spot, and wait for him to come to her.

A deep sense of resignation filled her as she stepped outside Caleb's house. She'd been battling demonic spirits her whole life. When she was younger, she'd held hope that someday it would all be over, but that hope had died a long painful death after she'd seen her mother struck down.

It was back, though.

Gabe and his family had given her hope that she might be able to have a normal life. In them she'd found others who knew what was out there. They fought evil, and lived a life blessed with family, friends, and love. She wanted so much to be a part of them, but more than that, she wanted to protect them.

Devil and Jewel had been nowhere to be found when she'd left, neither had Caleb. Caleb was probably asleep in his own bed, but there was only one guest room in the house. With a mental shrug she started off down the street. Jewel and Devil probably had a hotel room somewhere. It didn't really matter.

They were safe no matter where they were, as long as they weren't with her.

She strode down the dark street, not knowing where she was going, not caring, as long as it was away from the house. As she walked, her voice echoed in the dark silence. *"O Deus, Ego queso thee, succurro mihi per vestri propitius inspiration quod fidelis vires in quicumque Ego operor. Amen."* The prayer that her mother had taught her flowed naturally from her lips. It was a plea for God's assistance, one she hadn't uttered in too long.

Fifteen minutes later she came across a park. The swings and merry-go-round were empty and there was plenty of open space with no houses too close.

"Perfect," she muttered. "Close enough so you can find your way back to Gabe if you survive this."

She picked a patch of grass and pulled one of her knives, took a deep breath, and without hesitation, sliced it across her left forearm. It wasn't a terribly deep cut, but her blood welled and flowed out of it.

She put the blade away and held her arm out, watching the dark crimson drops fall onto the dewy grass and soak into the earth. It looked like any other human's blood, red and thick, and life giving. Only there was so much more in her blood.

She felt him before she saw him. The cold chill that had all the tiny hairs on her body standing up, making her extra sensitive to the energy vibrations around her. She turned slowly, expecting to see nothing, surprised to see tall, golden, and winged Focalor standing ten feet away from her. He smiled at her, as if he'd just dropped by for tea.

She arched an eyebrow at him. "No invisible attack this time?"

"You were kind enough to call me, I figured you wanted to give yourself up, maybe make a deal to protect those new friends of yours."

Anger stirred in her gut but she tamped it down. She needed a clear head in this fight to have any chance of surviving. "I don't make deals."

"You've no wish to protect them?"

"I have a wish to end this, here and now."

"Come now, Anna Blair, you of all people should know there isn't much on earth that can defeat the power of hell. Why do you want to fight me? If you come willingly, I'll ensure you survive being stripped of your powers."

"Survive? And then what? You'll keep me in hell as a play toy to be poked and prodded at every now and then?"

His smile widened. "You've been a worthy opponent, I wouldn't do that."

"Worthy, huh?" She stepped to the right, and watched as he stepped to the left, circling her. "I'm surprised I'm considered only 'worthy' when it's taken almost thirty years for you to get even this close to me."

He flinched at that, just a small one, but she saw it, and she *knew*. He was worried. He didn't like it at all that she'd evaded his minions for so long.

Reaching into her backpack, Anna's fingers wrapped around the comforting handles deep inside and pulled. She tossed aside her backpack and unsheathed the lovingly crafted butterfly swords. The curved blades slid free of their leather sheath with a smooth hiss, and she stood facing Focalor with one in each hand.

"Enough talk," she said. "This ends now."

"Ah, yes." His smile was benign as he eyed her swords. "Your blades have felled some of my best soldiers. But do you really think they'll hurt *me*?"

"These ones will. Forged in my own hellfire, blessed by God's servants, and wielded by me, someone who has mastered powers born of evil." She bared her teeth as she moved to the right, watching him counter shift to the left. "Powers you gifted to a weak spirit."

"The spirit wasn't weak, the powers were." His wings expanded behind him.

Preparing for flight, she told herself. Out loud she laughed. "Powers are as strong as those who wield them, you know that. And I am not weak."

"Let's find out shall we?"

He lunged and she swung. Expecting him to fly, she'd swung high, but not high enough. The shiny steel of her blade just missed his foot as he flew over her head. She spun and crouched, but still took a solid kick to the head. She rolled with it, and came up swinging.

Focalor was on the ground now, on his feet, and throwing bolts of hellfire at her. Deflecting the flames with her left blade, she stepped into the fight instead of away from it, and swung the right.

The blade connected with flesh, slicing into thick meaty shoulder and sliding free. His howl of rage and pain was music to her ears and adrenaline soared through her veins.

She continued to swing, pushing him back and back as she used the foot-long twin blades to slice him open quicker than he could heal. She was winning, she could feel it. The taste of freedom, of victory, was sweet on her tongue.

Then Focalor jumped, flying up and somersaulting backward to land fifteen feet away. His laughter echoed in the dawn sky sending a chill down her spine.

"Prepare for hell, Anna Blair," he said, then a blast of hellfire the size of a soccer ball smacked her in the chest and she flew back to land on her ass. The world blurred and she gasped for air as it slowly faded to black.

* * *

Fear-fueled adrenaline had Gabe running ahead of Devil and Jewel. He knew Anna didn't have a car so she couldn't have gone far in the half-hour since he'd fallen asleep. Thank God, Devil and Jewel hadn't fallen asleep on watch. They were less than ten minutes behind Anna, and Gabe was pissed. He knew she'd run, he knew it!

It hurt that she'd leave without saying good-bye, but it hurt even more than she thought he couldn't protect himself, let alone protect her.

She hadn't trusted him to protect her, to protect *them*.

"She's close," Devil said, picking up the pace. "And she's in trouble."

Gabe knew where they were, and he knew there was a park just up ahead. Anna had to be there. She had to be!

He wanted to ask what kind of trouble, but asking what Devil was hearing with his telepathy would take too much breath.

They rounded the corner in time to see the human-looking demon with golden wings throw a ball of fire at Anna and score a direct hit. Dawn was hitting the horizon and the flames lit up the park. There was no mistaking the damage done as Anna flew through the air and landed with a sickening thud.

"No!" He ran forward and fell full body on top of the flame-covered Anna.

The sounds of Devil and Jewel fighting with the demon echoed behind him but he didn't even glance at them as he rolled with Anna, putting out the flames.

He stopped rolling and noticed that she hadn't grabbed at him. Her arms hung limply at her sides and her eyes were closed.

"Anna, Anna baby, talk to me." He cupped her face in his hands and begged. "Come on, baby. You're a fighter. You're fine, come on Anna. Wake up!"

Nothing. No response.

A yelp of pain and an anguished roar pierced the pounding in his head and he glanced up to see Jewel on the ground and the demon pick Devil up and throw him into a nearby tree.

A strange calm settled over Gabe as he watched the devil out of the corner of his eye. Focalor approached him slowly, confidently.

He spoke when he was directly behind Gabe. "You have a choice to make, human. You can back away from Anna Blair, or you can die where you are."

Rays from the rising sun glinted off something silver near Anna's out-flung hand and Gabe reacted instinctively. He grabbed the small sword and stood, smoothly spinning and swinging at the same time, catching the demon off guard and slicing through his neck like a hot knife through butter.

The golden head rolled off the shoulders and turned to ash before it hit the ground, the body following suit.

"Gabe." The breath of sound cut through the pulse pounding in his ears and he spun.

"Anna!"

"What . . . ?"

"Shhh, baby. Don't talk." He stroked a thumb across her soot-covered cheek. "We're going to be all right."

"Your family," she whispered.

"We're alive," Devil said from behind him.

"Bruised, but alive," Jewel confirmed.

Anna sighed heavily and her eyes drifted shut again. Gabe leaned forward, kissed her forehead, and stood with her cradled in his arms and close to his heart. Right where she would always be.

12

One Month Later

Anna sniffed and widened her eyes, trying to keep the tears from falling. The whole family was together again. Devil and Jewel, Drake and Melissa, Gina, Caleb, Nadya, and baby Michael—they were all gathered together for the Labor Day weekend, full of happiness and promise for the future.

A month had passed since Gabe had gotten rid of Focalor, and Anna had not been attacked once since. It had taken time, but her burns had healed, absorbed into her body, blending with the fire inside of her. And in that time it became clear to her that not only was Gabe never going to let her go, but his family already considered her a part of them.

"It's okay you know," Gabe said as he came up to lean against the tree next to her.

"What's okay?"

"To cry every now and then," he said as he nudged her away from the tree, then pulled her back against him. "Especially when they're happy tears."

He was right and she knew it. But she'd been crying too much in the past month. All happy tears, but still, she hated that she was such a sap.

Then again, if she hadn't been such a sap, she might never have gone to see that movie not long ago. She might've been in a different place when she'd been attacked, or a different state of mind when she'd walked into that pub.

Instead of worrying about how silly she looked, standing under a tree in the sunny backyard of Caleb and Gina's home, crying.

She let the tears fall.

Sinking back into Gabe's arms, using his body as a cushion against the tree, she felt his heart beat against her back and knew she was finally home. It didn't matter that the house wasn't the one she'd been living in with Gabe since the morning of her thirtieth birthday. Her home was in his arms, no matter where they were.

She closed her eyes, and the sight of her energy mixing and blending with that of everyone in the backyard was a sight she never thought she'd see.

She'd found a family to belong to. One who loved together and fought together. One that always stood together.

She was a part of them.

Turning in Gabe's arms, she opened her eyes and gazed up at him. Her heartbeat matched his and she smiled. "I never said thank you for saving me."

His pretty blue eyes sparkled. "You have a lot to thank me for," he said. "I killed a demon lord for you."

She grinned. His family had been surprised that Gabe had taken out Focalor with one strike of her butterfly sword, but she wasn't. After all, he was Gabriel, namesake of the Angel of Death, and he'd wielded a blade forged in hellfire with pure love for her in his heart.

Love was the strongest magic of all, she'd always known it. And now he believed it too.

Latin Translations

Gloria Patri, et Filio, et Spiritui Sancto.
"Glory be to the Father, and to the Son, and to the Holy Spirit."

Deus.
"O God."

O Deus, Ego queso thee, succurro mihi per vestri propitius inspiration quod fidelis vires in quicumque Ego operor. Amen.
"O God, I beseech thee, help me with your gracious inspiration and faithful strength in all that I do. Amen."

Jackie Barbosa takes you
BEHIND THE RED DOOR!

On sale now!

London, England—July, 1816

The blank paper, unblemished by so much as an ink blot, mocked him. The page as empty, it seemed, as his soul. Except that where the page was white, his soul was black. Or so his father, the mighty Duke of Hardwyck, was ever fond of reminding him.

Nathaniel St. Clair, sixth Marquess of Grenville, grimaced as he lifted the glass to his lips and took another deep swallow of whiskey. At least there was great amusement to be found in living down to the old man's expectations.

In fact, given his appalling lack of productivity this morning, Nathaniel could see no reason not to begin his pursuit of profligacy a trifle earlier than usual today. A visit to Brooks' for an afternoon at hazard, followed by a long night of fucking at The Red Door, appealed a great deal more than waiting for the arrival of the proper English words to capture the lyrical frivolity of Ovid's Latin.

What stopped him from following through on the impulse was not the sudden sting of conscience or a spontaneous flow of poetic verse, but the unexpected sound of tapping feet and voices in the hall outside his private study.

"I say, miss, I told you the marquess is not to be disturbed. You cannot mean to go in there." This squeaky protest came from one of the footmen, though Nathaniel would have been hard-pressed to remember the fellow's name even if he could have seen his face. The Hardwycks went through footmen the way other aristocratic families went through ready cash.

"I most certainly can," came the reply, calm and crisp and delivered in velvet tones Nathaniel would have recognized from the other side of a wall of granite.

The voice belonged to the Honorable Miss Eleanor Palmer, whose long, slender limbs and small, round breasts could claim no rival, either in his imagination or in reality. The only respectable lady Nathaniel had ever desired, she was also the one he'd always known he could never have.

For what would a proper, sensible Unmarried like Miss Palmer want with an inveterate wastrel like him? He came to his feet. His heart gave an oddly hopeful, arrhythmic lurch as the doorknob turned.

He was about to find out.

Heedless of the footman who jabbered incessant objections at her heels, Eleanor marched into the surprisingly bright, airy study. She slapped the note from her former fiancé, the Earl of Holyfield, on the desk in front of the Marquess of Grenville and glared up at him. "What, may I ask, is the meaning of this?"

She cursed the bone-softening, knee-weakening heat that spread outward from her belly as she met his cornflower-blue gaze. No other man of her acquaintance had ever had this curious effect on her. It was most provoking. Straightening her spine, she did her best to adopt her most regal and imperious expression. She was here to dispel any notion that she might be remotely interested in accepting Grenville's suit, not to melt at his feet into an ignominious puddle of feminine longing.

What could Holyfield have been thinking even to entertain such an idea, much less commit it to paper in this letter to her father? Of all the unsuitable possible husbands for a bookish, reserved lady such as herself, the high-living, wild-loving Marquess of Grenville was surely the most unsuitable of all.

The marquess leaned down and plucked the letter from the desk. His long, elegant fingers bore several blue-black ink stains.

She ought to have known better than to come here. Perhaps she could forgive herself for having forgotten how tall and imposing a figure he cut, for few men had more than a few inches on her unusual height, but she could not excuse her failure to recall how preternaturally handsome he was. And surely it was unnatural for a man as dissolute and disreputable as Grenville to appear the very picture of robust masculine health. From the glossy sheen of his chestnut-brown hair, to the crystal clarity of his eyes, to the tightly corded musculature scarcely concealed by the close fit of his perfectly tailored coat, he exuded youthful vigor. In fact, with that lock of hair falling across his forehead as he scanned the missive, he more resembled a newly formed and wholly innocent Adam than the devil he was reputed to be.

His mouth quirked up on one side, Grenville looked from her to the letter to the footman, who stood behind her babbling incoherent apologies.

"Oh, do leave off fussing, er . . ." The marquess paused, his dark, straight eyebrows drawing together. "What's your name again, old chap?"

Eleanor could not suppress a smile at the words *old chap*. The doughy-faced youth could no more be characterized as old than a freshly baked loaf of bread.

The footman cleared his throat. "Beardsley, my lord."

Grenville nodded briskly. "You are dismissed then, Beardsley."

"As you wish, my lord." Beardsley sounded as though he'd swallowed a particularly sharp fish bone.

Her stomach dropped as Grenville's half-smile was replaced with a full grin. "You needn't fear I'll mention this lapse to my father. It shall be our little secret." Though he spoke to the footman, his gaze focused on Eleanor.

"Oh, thank you, my lord." The servant's heels clicked against the polished wood floor as he retreated. "And Beardsley?"

The sound of footsteps ceased. "Yes, my lord?"

Silence stretched out for several long, aching seconds as Grenville's gaze traveled from her face and over the length of her body with a searing intensity that left her breathless. And wanting—something.

"Close the door behind you."

Nathaniel studied Miss Palmer's delicate features as the footman beat his hasty retreat. The door clicked shut. She ought to be frightened, or at least alarmed, at the prospect of being trapped alone in a room with the notoriously amoral Marquess of Grenville. She ought to follow Beardsley out of the room as fast as the long, slim legs concealed beneath the rose-and-cream-striped muslin of her day dress could carry her.

Instead, she stood her ground, meeting his regard with a steady gaze, her dark blue eyes sparkling with challenge and . . . was it excitement? The flush rising in her cheeks and the pulse fluttering visibly in her elegant throat suggested not fear, but interest. Perhaps even arousal.

How utterly unexpected.

"Surely, you do not expect me to remain here behind closed doors with you, my lord," she said at last.

He gave her a negligent grin and wiggled his eyebrows. "I

most certainly do." When she opened her mouth to protest, he added, "What else is a gentleman to do when a young lady accosts him in his private study without benefit of a chaperone but protect her reputation by means of ensuring her privacy?"

"I came only to tell you I would not look favorably upon your suit, in the event your friend Holyfield has given you cause to think otherwise." The words came out in a rush, forced and a little breathless. She looked over her shoulder at the door. "And now I shall be going."

She extended her hand, a clear request for him to return the letter. He looked down at it, still clutched in his hand, and reread the passage that had brought Miss Palmer to his lair.

Despite my need to break our betrothal, I continue to hold your daughter in the highest regard and would not wish my perfidy to adversely affect her ability to make an advantageous match. To that end, I observe that the Marquess of Grenville is once again in the pool of Eligibles, and, further, I believe he would make an excellent husband for Miss Palmer. I am aware you do not hold him in high esteem, but I am of the opinion that a lady of Miss Palmer's faultless character could do much to temper his tendencies toward vice. Moreover, it cannot escape your notice that, should she marry Grenville, your daughter would one day be a duchess, a goodly step above the mere countess I should have made her.

A small smile quirked Nathaniel's lips. He owed Alistair de Roche, who had absconded to Gretna Green just four days past with Nathaniel's former intended, a singular debt of gratitude. Lady Louisa Bennett had been his father's choice, after all, not Nathaniel's. If Holyfield hadn't done the ignoble thing and eloped with the girl despite their respective commitments to others, Nathaniel would have been sticking his head into the marital noose tomorrow morning.

Unfortunately, Holyfield's second act of magnanimity was destined to go to waste. No matter how well he thought Nathaniel and Miss Palmer might suit, her father, Viscount Palmer, would never consent to a match between his daughter and a man he referred to as Marquess of Devil.

But then, Nathaniel wasn't particularly interested in the sort of union that would require paternal consent. Marriage was not on his agenda. However, she'd claimed it wasn't on hers, either. And she had come here alone. His cock twitched, stiffening at the thought.

Ambling round to her side of the desk, he crossed one ankle over the other and leaned against the corner, a deliberately indolent pose. Her eyes widened at his proximity, and her chest rose and fell more rapidly than before. *Excellent.*

When he stretched out his hand to return the letter to her, she stepped backward with a small gasp, then reached out to snatch the paper from him. He pulled it back toward his chest.

"Before I give it to you, tell me: why did you come alone?"

Her eyes narrowed, but her dilated pupils suggested she was more excited than annoyed. "I didn't. My aunt is waiting for me in the coach."

He made a mock frown. "I don't believe the venerable ladies of Almack's would consider a companion left out of doors to be any sort of chaperone a'tall."

"Aunt Eppie gossips," she admitted with a resigned sigh. "So I told her I'd come to return a parasol to Jane, and I'd only be a moment."

Nathaniel nodded. Jane, his younger sister, and Miss Palmer had become particular friends when they'd met in the queen's presentation queue two years earlier.

"I simply wanted to be certain you would not attempt to court me now that we are both free." She held out a hand, her expression pleading. "May I have the letter now? If I don't return soon, Aunt Eppie will wonder what's become of me and come after me."

Ah, but the moment was too delicious, too perfect to allow it to slip through his fingers.

"You must know I wouldn't dream of courting you, Miss Palmer. To do so would imply that I have honorable intentions toward you, and we both know I am not an honorable man." A slow smile curved his lips, one he knew was both wicked and beguiling. He turned and placed the letter purposefully on the desk behind him. "Which is why, if you want the letter, you'll have to come and get it."

"You can't be serious!" Eleanor exclaimed when she found enough breath to speak.

His smile didn't falter. "Of course, I'm not. I'm far too shallow to be serious. But even so . . ." He shrugged, indicating he didn't intend to back down.

Drat him, anyway! If it was a game he wanted, then it was a game she would give him.

She darted forward and to his left, determined to go around him to gain access to the letter. He uncrossed his ankles and mirrored her movement, blocking her with astonishing ease. She managed to pull up short before colliding with him and lunge to his right. Again, he foiled her, but this time, she wasn't able to halt her forward progress and landed tight against his chest. His heat and hardness and tangy male scent permeated everywhere their bodies touched, until it seemed she could taste him with her skin.

And, oh, he was delicious.

She ought to get away, ought not to stand there pressed against him in this near embrace. But the letter was right there behind him and once she had it, she could leave, her mission accomplished. She stretched her arms around the solid breadth of his torso, but he foresaw this gambit as well and gently grasped her wrists before she could reach her objective.

"I win," he said, the words delivered so quietly, she felt their rumble in his chest before she heard them issue from his lips.

Her eyes widening, she glared up into his face, intending to deliver some stinging retort or other, though she hadn't the foggiest notion what it would be. The impulse died in the hot intensity of his gaze, an expression she had never before seen on a man's face—at least, not directed at her—but recognized anyway: desire.

The broad smile he'd worn earlier had become smaller and a little pained. "I demand a forfeit."

"A forfeit?"

"A small one in exchange for the letter. Say, a kiss."

Her heart jumped into her throat and pounded there like a butterfly beating against a pane of glass, desperate for escape. Only it wasn't escape she wanted. Insanely, she pressed closer to him and tilted her chin upward. "Then do your worst," she whispered, "and be done with it."

He chuckled. "Oh, no. For you, Miss Palmer, nothing but the best will do."

Then his palms were on her cheeks, smooth and dry, and his lips touched hers, firm and warm and full of promise . . . and demand.

The effect of the contact was both instant and alarming. Heavy heat descended to her belly as if she were being filled with molten metal. The blaze spread from there outward to her fingers and toes. She didn't mean to hum with approval, but the sound vibrated from somewhere deep inside over which she had no control. His hands slid from her face to the back of her bonneted head, and he slanted his lips more urgently across hers, coaxing her mouth open.

He sucked at her lower lip, rolling it between his teeth, and she reeled with the sheer, mind-numbing pleasure of the sensation. His tongue flicked once, twice into her mouth, then slid all the way inside so that she tasted the sharp, pungent flavor of the whiskey he'd drunk mixed with a sweet, almost buttery essence on her taste buds.

He spread his legs, and her hips naturally settled into the space between them. With one hand, he continued to hold her head steady while the other coasted down her back to her buttocks. He cupped one cheek in his palm and pushed her tight to his groin, rotating his hips as he did. A thick bulge pushed insistently against her belly, and the soft flesh between her thighs responded with an instinctive rush of warm moisture.

In the one small corner of her mind that remained rational, she wondered how Grenville could evoke so effortlessly the sort of response she'd wished a thousand times to feel at even a fraction of this intensity for her former fiancé. But Holyfield's brief, perfunctory kisses had never made her feel as though she might ignite into a pillar of flame or melt into a river of hot wax.

They had never done anything at all.

Grenville lifted his head and thrust her abruptly away, though with regret rather than anger, she thought. He breathed raggedly, his cheeks were flushed with color, and as he turned to retrieve the letter from the desk, she saw that his fingers trembled.

"Here," he said gruffly, thrusting the paper toward her. "Go, before I think better of it."

Eleanor ought to take the letter and flee, but the molten ore pulsing in her belly seemed to have grown cold and hard in her feet. So instead of snatching the parchment from his hand, she stood there and stared dumbly at him for several long moments. In the ensuing silence, two equally dizzying thoughts impinged upon her slowly sobering brain.

First and most frightening, she wasn't incapable of passion, wasn't cold as she'd always believed. No one cold could be made to burn.

Second, the Marquess of Grenville was not nearly so amoral as he liked people to believe. He didn't want to let her go—that fact was writ in the taut lines around his mouth and eyes, in the tense sinews of his neck—but he was going to anyway.

And more fool she for wishing, however fleetingly, that he would confirm his reputation and thereby ruin hers. Aunt Eppie was waiting, and surely it had been much longer than ten minutes.

Her fingers at last found the will to take the letter from his hand.

"Thank you."

She was ready to break for the door when she saw he had picked up a book from the desk and was idly caressing its spine. A pretty volume, it was bound in dark blue leather with ornate gilt lettering spelling out the title and author. Close as she stood to him, she read the words easily.

And gasped.

"How did you come by that?" she demanded.

He looked up, his eyes widening. "This? Er . . ." He looked away, as if fumbling for an answer. As well he should, for the book he held was Clarence Mathews's translation of Ovid's *Metamorphoses,* and Eleanor knew the book was not due to be released by the publisher until early next month.

She knew because she had been counting the days until she could purchase it. No one had ever captured the voice of the Latin poets as beautifully or as accurately in English as Clarence Mathews. A fledgling translator herself, though of Greek poets rather than Latin, Eleanor admired Mathews above all others and considered his work the gold standard to which her own work might one day be held.

Grenville cleared his throat. "It is an advance copy. Mathews and I are friends."

Eleanor straightened, both surprised and excited. "Truly?" She frowned. "I have heard he is a recluse. However did you come to be friends?"

Grenville laughed. "Since I am clearly anything *but* reclusive?" He shrugged. "We've known each other since we were boys. You might even say we were raised together."

"Oh. Do you see him often now, then?"

A shadow of a smile passed across the marquess's lips. "Nearly every day."

The idea was born so quickly, she didn't think at all before the words popped from her mouth. "Could you introduce me to him? I am most anxious to meet him."

Grenville raised an eyebrow. "But, as you say yourself, he is a recluse."

Eleanor's shoulders slackened. "I am sorry. I shouldn't have asked."

He studied her, his forehead furrowing in thought. "No, no, it's quite all right. You admire his work then?"

"Oh, very much! He is the greatest translator and poet of our age. Ever, really." She couldn't help gushing, though it hardly seemed appropriate to speak so flatteringly of another man after what she'd just shared with the one she was speaking to.

For some reason she couldn't fathom, Grenville appeared . . . well . . . *pleased* by her enthusiasm. "He would be gratified to know that, I'm sure. And, as it happens, I believe he is seeking a proofreader for his next manuscript. Perhaps I could offer him your services?"

Eleanor couldn't believe her good fortune. She clapped her hands together. "Oh, yes, please, that would be splendid!"

251

"Excellent. But I should warn you . . ."

His eyes had taken on a devilish, predatory glint. An answering heat rose in Eleanor's breast and belly. She should put an end to her ridiculous fascination with the marquess this instant and walk away. The opportunity to read Clarence Mathews's work in advance was hardly worth the very real possibility that she might do something that would lead to the outcome she'd come here determined to avoid: marriage to the notoriously depraved Marquess of Grenville. The devil himself.

But she couldn't bring herself to leave, and she wasn't sure upon which man to blame her lack of willpower.

"You should warn me of what?" Her voice quavered, thin and reedy in her ears.

"You'll have to come here to get the pages. Alone. And I won't be responsible for what happens while you're here, should you be moved by what you've read to throw yourself at me."

"And why would that happen?"

He grinned again. "Mathews is translating *The Amores*. And I have every intention of using that to my advantage."

Lorie O'Clare's your guide to
PLEASURE ISLAND!

On sale now!

"I didn't realize I'd get to choose from so many men!" This was unbelievable.

I couldn't remember the last time the sun warmed my skin without making me sweat. Not too hot, and absolutely no chill in the air. And there were no bugs. None. The smell of the salt water mixed with aromas from nearby flowers and created a tangy scent in the air that was unforgettable. But staring at the view in front of me, I could appreciate that the perfect weather and lack of bugs had nothing to do with why they called this paradise.

And, oh, my God, was this paradise!

"You can choose several." Rose Bontiki, the owner of Paradise Island and referred to as "Guardian" in the handbook, grinned at my astonished expression. "Not many of our guests manage to get through more than two though."

I could see why. "When do I have to give you my decision?"

"I need to know now." Rose gestured to the row of men, standing shoulder to shoulder, and wearing nothing more than tiny skin-colored loincloths.

"So I have to tell you right now how many men I want as my companions during my entire stay here?" I remembered the manual was clear on this, but now that I stood here, I didn't know how I would be able to decide right away.

"Yes. Then, whichever one you choose will escort you to your room. Of course if you wish to have more than one they will both escort you. I should warn you though, your choice is final."

"Final."

"Yes." Rose's pale pink skirt blew around her slender calves as a warm breeze picked up from the ocean. "Once you take your choice or choices to your room, you will enter their names on your contract."

"Oh, yeah. I read that in the handbook." The handbook, more like a thick encyclopedia, explained all the rules for the island. Everything in it was broken down like an owner's manual. I patted the top of it, which stuck out of my over-sized purse. "I think I've got all of it memorized," I added, grinning and feeling like the student craving the teacher's attention.

"Good girl." Rose nodded her approval. She then gestured to the line of men standing at attention in front of us. "So which one do you want?"

I tapped my lip with my index finger, taking my time looking at the long line of men who stood so solemnly in front of us. This was a very important decision, and one I wished I didn't have to make in a matter of minutes. The man I chose now would be my best friend, fuck me, and do anything I wanted for the next two weeks while I was on the island. There was something odd about leasing a lover, although admittedly, a flare of excitement surged through me as well.

I glanced from one guy to the next, counting them first. Twenty-three guys all gave me impassive stares. Of course, they couldn't look anxious for me to pick them. Instead they simply stared straight ahead, almost as if none of them noticed me and Rose standing there staring at them. A memory of the guards at Buckingham Palace popped into my head. Choosing one who looked interested wouldn't work. Story of my life.

I looked at each one of them again, this time comparing height, and mentally determining how many of them were taller than me. Call me silly, but I like a guy who is taller than I am, although maybe it didn't matter how tall they were if we were lying down.

Hell, it mattered to me.

Ten of them appeared quite a bit taller then my five-foot-six inches.

I was narrowing it down—on a roll now.

Out of the ten finalists, I tried to determine eye color, but I stood too far away.

"Can I get closer to them?" I asked, glancing at Rose.

It amazed me such a young looking woman owned this small island and ran this resort. She hardly met the image I had created in my mind of the shrewd business person reputed as a self-made millionaire and owner of this reclusive island. When we spoke before on the phone she sounded much older.

Rose answered the toll-free number on the pamphlet I found in the backseat of a taxi I'd taken to see a show about a month ago. She explained that Paradise Island was anything but a joke. I made my reservations and gave her my credit card number on the spot.

And I'm not a spontaneous type of gal. I honestly couldn't believe I was doing this. But maybe a soul can take boredom for only so long.

"Not too close. I prefer minimal contact before the contracts are signed. It's on page twenty-three of your handbook."

The handbook was heavy inside my purse. On the small chartered plane that brought me here to Paradise Island, I'd read every word on every page. It was the lawyer in me—automatically checking for loopholes and legalities. I was amazed at the simplicity in the wording, and how exciting it made Paradise Island sound. One thing was quite clear by the time I'd read the handbook from beginning to end, Paradise Island wasn't about finding love. It was about escaping, fulfilling fantasies with no complications. Of course now that I was here, with the sunshine warm on my bare shoulders, and breathtaking views in every direction, Perfect Island would be an even more appropriate name.

Interesting that according to the logistics carefully laid out in the handbook—paradise didn't equate love. I wasn't sure that I agreed. But, I didn't have a problem agreeing with the fact that I wasn't here to fall in love. That isn't something you can pay for—no matter how much money you have.

I remembered something and did pull the handbook out, adjusting my purse strap over my shoulder as I lifted the thick paperback book.

"Just a minute, I know it's right here somewhere." Flipping the pages with my thumb, I refused to glance at Rose and see any strain in her pretty young face. The rather large amount I charged to reserve my room here on the island had already cleared my bank. If I needed a minute, I would take it. "Okay, here it is." I glanced at the chart that explained how much everything cost. "There is an extra charge for more than one."

I ran my fingernail under the line in the handbook where it stated, $10,000 per week included a private room and bath and three meals a day in the dining room. Meals could be served in the room with advance notice. As well, the first escort was included in the package deal, but there was a $2,500 per day charge applied to the credit card on file for each additional escort.

"Of course." Rose smiled easily, and not one wrinkle appeared on her face. Standing next to her for too long would make a girl feel more than inadequate. Anytime I grinned, crow's feet appeared on either side of my eyes. I hated it.

At the rates she charged her guests Rose could afford to stay young and gorgeous for the rest of her life. I wasn't in paradise to get a complex about my looks though.

I returned my attention to the ten men I'd singled out so far. For two weeks—a package deal for twenty grand—the man I chose would be my companion, at my beck and call, to do anything I asked. Anything. No one would rush me with this decision.

Rose glanced at her watch after another minute passed although she didn't say anything. I narrowed it down to five, eliminating the men with facial hair and with no hair on their chests. Again, my personal preferences. I wanted perfection to join me in paradise, and at this price, I would settle for nothing less.

But that still left five to choose from. Damn. No wonder Rose was a self-made millionaire. Who could choose from the selection of men who stood before me, all of them made of stuff a lady would fantasize about?

Of course it would be nice if I could see them without the loincloths. You know, get the chance to look under the hood before I bought the car—or lease it as the case may be. But that was on page one and page twelve. The men always remained dressed in public. Rose had her reputation to consider.

Finally, after another few minutes, I narrowed it down to two. It was the best I could do. One white man, well more like brown with the perfect tan he had. And the other a dark black man. Both all muscle and drop-dead gorgeous.

"I'll take those two." I pointed to my choices.

Rose smiled. Her tone was gentle and soothing, like she never cared how long it took for me to make my selections. "Perfect choices. Tomas and Nicolas are two of my favorites."

Did Rose get to enjoy all of these men? Like I would ask her that.

"Tomas?" Rose held her hand out and Tomas, the white guy, stepped forward. "And Nicolas," she said, beckoning to the black guy.

They approached her quietly, both barefoot and walking with controlled, steady paces that made them look more like predators than studs just pulled off an auction block.

Both stopped when they stood on either side of her. Rose smiled at them and then looked at me like I was her best friend. "This is Natalie Green. She just arrived here on the island and is my special guest for the next two weeks. Please escort her to room three. I'll stop by shortly to make sure your accommodations are to your liking."

And so that I could sign the contract. The handbook made it very clear. All business matters were tended to promptly as soon as the guest arrived. Then for the rest of my time here, I wouldn't be bothered with anything pertaining to money. Made sense. They would run my credit card for the additional sum of $35,000 within minutes of my settling in. I had no doubts.

One thing about being alone in life, I didn't have to explain my actions, especially when they turned insane. But I had the money. It would serve me nicely in my old age, or give me the memories and adventure of a lifetime, which would also serve me nicely in old age.

Either way, I'd cashed in a few bonds, transferred money, and used my debit card. The transaction was complete before I even touched foot on this tropical island. Of course now, with my additional man, they would charge it again. No regrets. No looking back. My life wasn't exactly anything close to exciting. In fact, there were days when I wondered if I quit existing how long it would take before anyone noticed.

Don't get me wrong. I'm not suicidal. Not even close.

Working in my father's law firm for the past ten years, when all my father and grandfather wanted was for me to marry into an acceptable family, didn't exactly fulfill me. They never let me work on any of the good cases, but instead insisted that I present myself at all the charitable functions that they claimed were on behalf of the law firm. Which meant, until I became someone else's trophy to place on the mantle, my father and grandfather didn't have a problem making me their trophy to display. Being placed on display with nothing else to do is boring as hell.

Spending this kind of money to escape my life, to exist as someone else for just a couple weeks without anyone back home knowing what I was doing, sounded better than perfect to me.

And I hadn't been the only person on the plane. There were other people on this planet just like me, willing to pay a small fortune to indulge in a life that they could never have any other way. Not that I said a word to any of them. No one spoke at all on that plane. One couple and two men walked past me when they boarded the charter plane. But it was obvious on their faces—that dismal, over-worked, humdrum expression slowly faded the closer we got to the island. By the time we landed, I was so enthralled by the captivating surroundings and the young man who escorted me to Rose to choose my companion, that I didn't pay any attention to where the other guests went.

Although I didn't see anyone else from the plane as my two men walked silently alongside me up the wide marble steps toward the huge mansion on top of the hill, I knew there were other guests around somewhere. I didn't mind the privacy. I couldn't help mentally calculating how much money this island might bring in monthly. I also pondered what laws the island would fall under, since it wasn't part of the United States, and appeared to be privately owned.

God. I closed my eyes briefly and gave myself a mental

shake. Here I was in paradise, walking with my two men, who were damned near naked, to my private room to enjoy any pleasure I could imagine, and maybe even a few I couldn't. It was just like me to get lost mulling over the legalities of something. No wonder I was stuck on permanently boring and humdrum.

"Are we allowed to talk to each other?" I looked at Tomas, the white guy.

"Sure." He smiled warmly at me.

Nicolas chuckled on the other side of me and I gave him my attention. "We can talk, or do anything else you'd like to do," he said in a deep baritone.

I could listen to Nicolas talk all day. He had that deep sultry black man's voice that would curl any woman's toes as she melted like warm butter at his feet.

"I guess talking will work until we get to our room," I decided.

"What would you like to talk about?" Nicolas asked.

"Well." I thought for a minute, or tried to make it look like I was thinking. My mind was suddenly blanker than the pale blue cloudless sky above us. "Do you two like working here?"

"We don't work." Tomas gently wrapped his fingers around my arm, just above my elbow.

"Good answer," I conceded. If he acknowledged any of this as work, it would fall under the line of prostitution. The handbook must have been looked over by a fleet of lawyers before being published. Nothing in it could be construed as illegal. "I guess I should ask if you like it here."

"Trust me, this is paradise. Your room is this way."

The stairs ended and the men led me along a path surrounded by beautiful gardens on either side.

"You're right about that." I breathed in the thick perfume coming from the variety of flowers. Maybe touching on a lighter subject would force the men to sway from their scripted answers. "I'm not an expert, but aren't those orchids?"

"Among other things, the island is known for its gardens." Nicolas's hand was so warm when he pressed it between my shoulder blades. "Those are oncidium orchids," he informed me, pointing at bright yellow flowers that grew in a thick patch to our left. "And the lavender ones over here are dendrobium orchids."

"You know a lot more about flowers than I do," I offered, laughing easily at my ignorance.

The men chuckled but they weren't laughing at me. Years of analyzing people taught me when someone was relaxed or not. And Tomas and Nicholas were perfectly at ease as they escorted me along the wide sidewalk with the vibrant flowers and ivy bordering either side.

"Feel free to ask anything," Tomas said. "I know more about some things than others."

It was on the tip of my tongue to ask what he knew more about. Gorgeous was putting it mildly with him. His dark, sandy blond hair waved naturally around his face and curled at his neck. There was a roguish look about him. The way he held himself, walked with such confidence wearing next to nothing, was enough to know that very little would embarrass him. I'd always wished that I could move through life with such self-assurance that every emotion I had wasn't obvious on my face.

"What do you know most about?" I had to ask.

Tomas grinned and my heart kicked in to overdrive.

"Sex, my dear," he said without hesitating.